Their Last Resort

OTHER TITLES BY R.S. GREY

Available Stand-Alone Titles

*The Trouble with Quarterbacks**
*Three Strikes and You're Mine**
*To Have and To Hate**
With This Heart

Available Titles within a Series

Heart Series

*The Duet**
*The Design**

Allure Series

*The Allure of Dean Harper**
*The Allure of Julian Lefray**

Summer Games Series

The Summer Games: Out of Bounds
*The Summer Games: Settling the Score**

*Romantic comedies

Their Last Resort

R.S. GREY

 Montlake

Published by Montlake, Seattle

www.apub.com

Amazon, the Amazon logo, and Montlake are trademarks of Amazon.com, Inc., or its affiliates.

ISBN-13: 9781662517631 (paperback)
ISBN-13: 9781662517624 (digital)

Cover design by Hang Le
Cover photography by Regina Wamba of ReginaWamba.com
Cover image: © DOMSTOCK / Shutterstock

Printed in the United States of America

Their Last Resort

Chapter One
PAIGE

I love my job. I love my job. *I love my job.*

I just have to keep repeating the mantra.

There is a lot to like about working at this resort. Siesta Playa is known for its crystal clear water, white-sand beaches, luxury accommodations, and . . . grotesquely spoiled tourists, who all ascribe to the belief that their year's worth of credit card points entitles them to nothing short of royal treatment.

I'm staring at one now while she rambles on and on about how I'm ruining her vacation and, naturally by extension, her life. She's standing on the other side of the short desk, spitting venom. Her fury is so fierce, the little veins in her forehead look like they might burst. Her mood is in stark contrast to her bright Hawaiian dress and kitschy conch earrings. The glasses she's sporting on her head carry a little slogan, one glittery word positioned over each eye: ISLAND TIME!

Now I see why her husband is cowering behind her on wobbly knees, searching for a spine that she has long since quashed.

Sir, blink three times if you need help.

"Mrs. Daugherty, I'm *so very* sorry."

For the record, this is my fourth apology, but it gets ignored like the first three.

"You're sorry? What am I supposed to do with a *sorry*? I flew all the way here from *Miami*, y'know."

That's about a two-hour trip, runway to runway. With the way she emphasizes this point, you'd think she'd just backpacked here from a Tibetan mountaintop.

"We're so glad you came all this way, and I understand why you're upset."

No, we're not—no, I don't.

"I apologize again, on behalf of the entire resort team."

Actually, we all collectively want to banish you from the premises.

"And, of course, we're happy to offer you and your husband excursion vouchers—or would you two enjoy a private beach dinner instead? Courtesy of the resort, of course."

Giving in like this—rolling over and taking it—is resort policy. Just give the high-maintenance sociopaths what they want in order to defuse the situation before the other guests (the ones whose parents loved them) notice. I hate it.

In quick succession, she pounds her pointer finger down on the desk like it's a woodpecker made out of Vienna sausages. "I can eat dinner on the beach anywhere. I want to see some damn whales! Like I was *promised!*"

One of the excursions offered here at Siesta Playa is a guided marine-life tour where guests have the opportunity to see dolphins, reef sharks, sea turtles, and *potentially* whales. During the high season, from January through early April, humpback whales swim through the Turks Island Passage and give birth at Salt Cay. But seeing as how it's mid-August . . . the whales are otherwise occupied elsewhere, doing whale things. A fact made abundantly clear to any of our guests who might have their sights set on seeing a majestic humpback this time of year, including Mrs. Daugherty.

"I. Want. Whales," she demands again, enunciating each word like a grown-up version of Veruca Salt.

Her husband, temporarily abandoning his attempt to shrink into oblivion, speaks up with a wobbly voice. "Beatrice, I think if maybe we just—"

She makes no move to address him. Her focus stays pinned solely on me. "No, Mark. Don't. This is ridiculous! You know what?" Her fingers are aimed at me, mere inches from my face, wagging back and forth. "I want to speak to your manager. *Now.*"

I knew this request was coming. This righteous appeal to mythical authority is the last gasp of all frustrated complainers. I'd bet anything that on her deathbed she'll cry out for Jesus—not for comfort or mercy but because she'd like to complain to his dad about the poor service she got on earth.

I'm forced to radio for someone, except the person that shows up is the absolute *last* someone I want to see right now.

There's no need for me to turn around to confirm my suspicions when he walks up behind me. He might as well be accompanied by a theme song filled with deep, ominous organs. *Dun dun dunnnn.*

He's a regular in Mordor.

The devil's dinner guest.

Voldemort's pen pal.

Cole Clark is neither my manager nor my friend; he's a thorn in my side. His mere presence spikes my blood with adrenaline. My hands form tiny fists at my sides.

"Hello. How can I help you?" he asks over my shoulder.

I straighten up, trying to add inches to my height. I hate his stupid bones and the fact they allow him to tower over me.

"Who are you?" She's already losing some of the condescension in her tone. Women tend to do that around Cole. Soften, swoon, go a little weak in the knees. I've never understood why.

"I'm Cole Clark, the assistant director of operations at Siesta Playa."

3

"Yes, he's just the *assistant* director," I stress. "You'll want to compla—I mean, speak with Todd Weaver. He's the real head honcho around here."

Mrs. Daugherty doesn't bother to listen to or look at me. She's forgotten I exist. She's staring up at Cole with love in her eyes now. Those bulging forehead veins have receded, draining their high-cholesterol contents back into the recesses of her now fluttering heart. If she could, she'd push her meek husband headlong into an active volcano. That's how much she wants Cole. *Blegh.*

Realizing that my role here (in the daily theater play that is customer service) is done (thank god), I'm about to take a step to the side and make a speedy getaway, but then Cole's hand clamps down on my shoulder, ensuring I stay put exactly where I am. His grip says, *Not so fast.* My heel stepping back onto the toe of his size-twelve oxfords replies, *Let go of me, you jerk.*

He does, immediately.

I have to stand there and listen to Mrs. Daugherty's complaints all over again. She's pointing at me. "This . . . this *girl* promised my husband and I that we would have an amazing time out on the water today, but I'm sad to report that just was *not* the case. Not in the *least.* This one right here—"

"Ms. Young," Cole supplies for her.

"Ms. *Young* took us out onto the water all afternoon, and we have nothing to show for it. A few measly stingrays? A friggin' dolphin? *Big whoop.* When my cousin, *the travel agent,* hears about this . . ."

Throughout her wild diatribe about her "cousin, the travel agent," the threats of a "scathing Tripadvisor review," and even a confused rant about how her daughter has "quite the following on TickClock," Cole keeps his cool.

Ten minutes later—and with a heaping pile of drink vouchers in hand—Mrs. Daugherty walks away, barking orders at her henpecked husband to hurry up. Her complaint with me is officially settled.

I should turn around and thank Cole, but if I'm honest, I would rather go sip mai tais with the Daughertys.

I wish he would disappear in a puff of smoke or a cloud of bats and leave me to it, but no, he can't resist.

"To be honest I'm surprised the whales were her only complaint," he starts, and already I'm bracing myself. "Knowing it was your excursion, I was expecting to see blood."

I turn around, mockingly slow, and give him a withering look that says, *You're dust. Nothing.*

Unfortunately, I know what he's referring to about the blood. As a member of Siesta Playa's entertainment and hospitality department, my job is to lead excursions and activities for adventure-loving guests. Interested in surfing, sailing, or hikes that culminate beneath majestic waterfalls? I'm your girl. And so what if, very occasionally (well, the actuaries at our insurance say it's 11.7 percent of the time), my zany excursions result in mild to moderate injuries? Ships are safest in the harbor, but that's not why ships are built! Dr. Missick—our resort's resident doctor—absolutely hates me because I've turned his cushy retirement job into a full-time urgent care center. Rock climbing abrasions, bruises and bites courtesy of trendy but ill-tempered yoga goats, and a burn every now and then from the weekly hot-coal walk are only the start. *However*, I would just like to point out that there are *just* as many buffet-related injuries at this resort. Just last week there was a kebab impalement and a chocolate-fountain scalding. My point is Dr. Missick's ever-growing patient load is not all my doing, which is why it infuriates me that Cole keeps a whiteboard in the break room titled "Days Since Last Guest Injury" as an easy way to needle me.

During Mrs. Daugherty's rambling, Cole was probably running a fine-tooth comb over her, searching for a wrap or a sling. It feels wonderful that, this time at least, I've only inflicted emotional trauma to a guest and he doesn't get the satisfaction of erasing the single-digit number from the whiteboard.

I cross my arms and tilt my chin up, meeting his gaze with all the confidence I can muster.

"Just to be clear, that wasn't my fault."

One of his dark brows arches playfully. "So I gathered."

"I zoned out for most of that. Did you tell her you'd make the whales contract employees in order to hold them accountable for their truancy?"

The side of his mouth very nearly curls. "I told her to stick to the bar. I said your excursions could sometimes be more trouble than they're worth."

I narrow my eyes, trying to pick him apart.

I'm sure there are nice, happy adjectives to describe Cole, but I refuse to consider any of them. His height is annoying. His deep-brown eyes are too dark. His tie is entirely too neat. I'm sun kissed and blonde, and he's a workaholic grump. Truly, would it kill him to let down his expertly styled hair every once in a while?

We're on a tropical island, and this guy is in *dress shoes*. His entire closet consists of button-downs and blazers. For a casual night off, he casts aside his suits for a pair of "casual" dark jeans. His wardrobe is probably worth my yearly salary. If I ever saw him in a T-shirt, I'd die of shock.

"How are you so tan?" I asked him once. "You never step foot outside."

He cast me a look chock full of mock suspicion. "Keeping close tabs on me?"

"I just know the lore. The second your skin comes in contact with the sun—" My hands mimicked an explosion. "Poof. Gone. It's the same for all creatures from, well . . ." I clicked my tongue as my finger motioned toward the depths of hell.

He looked at me then with halfhearted annoyance, a common occurrence in our relationship, and replied, "My grandparents are from Sicily."

"You have *grandparents*?!"

This was news to me. The theory that's caught the most traction in the break room is that Cole only exists here because of a *Meet Joe Black* situation—i.e., Cole is Death, taking the form of a young man to experience life on earth. It explains the sharp-as-hell cheekbones and the fact that he can do math with inhuman speed and accuracy.

Now, here we stand, doing it again, pitting our wits against each other.

Thank god I don't have to see Cole every day. My nerves couldn't handle it. We work vastly different jobs here, after all. Most of the time, I'm out exploring the island with guests and he's stuck indoors performing his number-crunching desk job. Word on the street is that he has his sights set on becoming the director of resort operations one day. It's probably outlined meticulously in his five-year plan. It's color coded and leather bound. He keeps it under his extrafirm pillow at night.

My five-year plan? *Simple.*

Enjoy life on the island.

That's all.

Okay, not *all.* I would also like to experience love, and if that L-word proves too elusive, I will also happily accept lust. I even have the perfect target in mind. He's Blaze, a new bartender in Siesta Playa's beach lounge. I think he's just the man I've been searching for—fun, easygoing, and outdoorsy. And I'm hoping beyond hope that he's coming to the beach bonfire tonight so I have a chance to hang out with him. Our last few encounters haven't exactly proved fruitful.

"Oh! You like smoothies too?" I asked when I walked past him in the main lobby the other day.

He frowned, completely confused.

I pointed to the smoothie in his hand, the one he was half finished with.

Still, he didn't get it. "Oh, this? I had a coupon."

I only planned for a discussion about blended fruit drinks, not coupons, so all my brain could come up with was "Cool, see ya." Then I shot him some cringey double finger guns.

The next time I saw him, I was out at one of the local bars with some of my coworkers. I sidled up to him and asked over the loud music, "So, Blaze, where are you from?"

"The resort."

I laughed and spoke up. "No, silly. *Where did you come from?!*"

"I came from the resort!" he shouted back.

So, okay, who cares if he's not overflowing with brain cells . . . I have enough for the two of us, right? Plus, I've seen him without his shirt on, and those abs will surely get us through any hiccups that might arise from stilted conversations. But it doesn't matter now. I'll never get to that bonfire if I don't finish up here with Cole.

"Are we done?" I ask, crossing my arms over my chest so I don't do something stupid like yank on his tie. I want to so bad.

Cole looks me up and down, no doubt finding my Teva sandals, workout shorts, and Siesta Playa tank top sorely lacking. If he had it his way, he'd force me into a pantsuit, add a little plaque over my breast pocket, and shellac my hair to my head in a tight bun. "Why are you in such a rush? Big plans?"

I shoot him a skeptical glare.

Does he know about the bonfire?

It's hard to tell . . . I try yet fail to decipher his expression. He's Fort Knox, this one. I don't want to spill the beans and get anyone in trouble, but I also sometimes (very rarely) feel a little bad for Cole. As we lock eyes, I contemplate letting him in on the secret—something I'll surely come to regret—but then he rolls his eyes.

"I already know about the bonfire."

Suddenly, I'm on the defensive. "It's not against the rules or anything. Théo isn't setting it up on resort property."

He frowns. "You act like you're worried I'll write you up."

I'm not totally certain he wouldn't . . .

I mean, he hasn't before (that I know of), but Cole is *very* "by the book." And I mean that literally—the book is actually kept in his desk drawer.

It's why most people keep a healthy distance from him. They're scared he's going to run and tell Daddy on us if we step out of line. There's more to it than just that, though. At Siesta Playa, there's a clear divide between management and the rest of us. There's the group of people who run the place: the CEO, director of operations, general manager, director of food and beverage, et cetera . . . I think I see those guys like once a year, *tops*. The rest of us have roles here that are far less glamorous: bartenders, surf instructors, boat captains, line cooks, lifeguards. We all live in staff housing on site. Picture a tiny room with a twin bed and not much else. But we make it work. Most of us are away from home and on our own, and we're an eclectic mix: recent college graduates, retirees, nomads, nature lovers. Or in Cole's case: stuffy boardroom types who get off on spreadsheets and ruining people's fun.

He belongs in neither of the two groups. An entity unto himself. He's too young to really fit in with the directors, and also he lives in staff housing like the rest of us. It's tricky, though, because he also doesn't quite fit in my world either. The very idea of him shooting the shit with Blaze or Théo or Oscar . . . it's inconceivable.

Still . . .

"I guess . . . if you wanted . . ." I'm forcing the words. They're thick and heavy on my tongue. It's like someone's holding a gun to my head.

He frowns like he's disappointed with me, and then he shakes his head. It's nothing new.

Before I can say anything else, he turns and walks away.

Chapter Two
PAIGE

It's no coincidence that I've found myself working at a place like Siesta Playa. My parents are both marine biologists actively working in the field, i.e., two absolute kooks who'd rather be swimming alongside sea turtles than having to deal with real live people. I'm surprised they even wanted a kid. Though lovely and supportive, they were ill prepared to offer me a structured childhood of any sort. My adolescent years were spent globe-trotting, hopping from school to school, friend group to friend group. They didn't see why a child should slow them down. Need two researchers to explore the Indian Ocean? Great! Paige knows how to swim; it should be fine.

Their adventure-loving ways clearly rubbed off on me because even in college, I never settled down for long. I studied abroad in Portugal and New Zealand and spent a year at sea after graduation before deciding that there was just something . . . missing.

A part of me worried I was only living that way of life because it's all I knew, not because it necessarily made me happy. In practice, it's harder than it sounds to be that casual and carefree. Logistically, it's a *nightmare* trying to figure out where exactly you'll be from one week to the next. Also, there's a real loneliness that accompanies that way of life. You end up feeling like a perpetual tourist, as if you don't really belong anywhere. Living only for the thrill of new adventures eventually starts to get old, and more than anything, I felt myself longing for lasting connections and a place I could get used to. Becoming a regular at a coffee shop—having someone call out to me, "Vanilla latte, extra shot?"—started to sound *way* more exotic than stuffing clothes into a backpack and taking off to parts unknown.

I wanted roots. I wanted routine. I wanted a home.

I decided if I was going to be in one place for a long time, I'd better pick somewhere amazing. So that's how I decided the island life was for me.

I've been in Turks and Caicos for a year, and I love it. There's still plenty of adventure. Every day, it's something different—between sunbathing on Long Bay Beach, exploring the caverns of the Conch Bar Caves, and snorkeling the Grand Turk Wall—I can see myself being here for a long, *long* time.

It helps that I like my job and coworkers. Unfortunately, my position pays absolute crap. Like some days it feels like *I'm* paying *them* to let me work here, but our food and housing are covered, and I otherwise make do. There's a real camaraderie among us, a *One for all and all for one* vibe, as evidenced by tonight's bonfire.

I've scrounged around my dorm to find an unopened bottle of wine and two cans of beer. Someone else will surely bring more alcohol and hopefully some good snacks. I'm crossing my fingers for marshmallows, because what's the point of sitting around a fire without them?

Théo and Oscar already have a nice setup going when I get down to the beach. As the unofficial party planners, they dug a firepit and brought a few chairs. Nothing else is required, really. The island does the rest of the heavy lifting. The sun's putting on a show as it drops down toward the horizon, gifting us a cotton candy sky, pink and orange and so beautiful I stop for a second to stare at it. I'll never get enough. The turquoise water is calm as the waves roll in, and the sand is soft. I slip off my sandals to traipse barefoot toward the guys.

Unlike me, Théo's from here, born and raised on the island. Oscar's a transplant from Australia. They both work on the golf course, which never fails to make me smile because of what a contradiction it is. All day at work they're stuck wearing pressed polos and khakis. Oscar hides his buzzed neon-blue hair beneath a Siesta Playa baseball cap so the guests are none the wiser. Théo's totally tatted from wrist to collarbone, but you'd never know it when he's wearing his long-sleeved uniform shirts. Tonight, though, we can just be ourselves. Oscar's wearing board shorts and a tank top. Théo's in cargo shorts and a vintage-looking band T-shirt.

I stop in front of them and dip down in a dramatic curtsy like they're two kings and I'm a mere peasant.

"I bestow upon you two lukewarm beers," I tease, handing each of them one as a thank-you for setting up the bonfire for the rest of us.

"Damn, I'll take it," Oscar says, cracking it open right away.

"How can I help?" I ask, surveying the cluster of chairs and pile of miscellaneous snacks and drinks.

"You can regale us with a story about your day," Théo replies with a smile. His teeth aren't perfectly straight, but his crooked smile only adds to his charm. "Heard you got an earful at the excursion desk."

"You could say that." I groan. "Have you dealt with the Daughertys much this week?"

"Just the husband. He's been at the golf course every day hiding out from his wife."

"Can't say I blame him."

"Someone said Cole came to your rescue, though . . . ," Oscar chimes in with a knowing smile.

"Hardly."

Théo laughs and points me toward the stack of chairs. "Want to set those up for us?"

"On it!"

I'm one of the first people here by design. I have a strategy for tonight that includes giving Blaze easy access to me. Spatially, that is. I don't want to be stuck squashed between two occupied beach chairs, so I purposefully lay out my towel on a nice patch of sand near the water with plenty of space on either side of me, and I wait.

The sun has fully set before more people arrive. I'm immensely relieved to see Camila and Lara stroll up. They're two sisters from Florida who started working here about the same time I did a year ago. They're slightly older than me, and a packaged duo, but they're always nice about letting me tag along with them when they go out to clubs and bars.

They're stunning, like stun-*ning*. They have long dark hair and sultry eyes. We could not be more polar opposite. My big blue eyes don't scream *sex*; they eagerly shout, *Hi there! Lookin' for a friend?*

They always modify their work uniforms to somehow make them less cheesy, and their after-work clothes are always edgy and cool, the types of outfits I wouldn't even *begin* to know how to put together. Like, is that a shirt or a dress? Shorts or Spanx? Also, ARE WE STILL WEARING HIGH-RISE JEANS OR NOT? *Someone help!*

I'm shocked they have anything to do with me, what with my hiking gear, workout clothes, and sports bras. What few dresses I own are hand-me-downs from them. When I first arrived here, they took one look at my closet and gasped in horror.

"Where are the clothes for when you go out?" Lara asked with thinly veiled disdain as she frantically leafed through my sensible moisture-wicking workout shirts.

I pointed to some jean shorts and then belatedly remembered that I also had a simple black tank top buried in my bag somewhere, yet to be unpacked. I held it up, proud. Lara signed the cross over her chest and shot up a silent prayer on my behalf.

Since then, Camila and Lara have decided that it's their sole mission in life to dress me up like I'm their own personal Barbie. It's, in their words, "a travesty" to let my body go to waste.

"Your legs! That waist! These breasts!"

I mostly let them play dress-up with me because it's fun and secretly I love that they're willing to help me out. They're sexy, and they make me feel like I can be sexy too. So I'm extra glad when they decide to lay their beach blanket out near me.

Tonight, to appease them and, *okay* . . . to step a little out of my comfort zone, I wore one of their old dresses to the bonfire. It's this tight lavender minidress with a thin tie that knots behind my neck. I felt a little silly when I first put it on—what with *so* much skin showing—so before I left my dorm, I threw on a denim jacket over it.

"*Off*," Lara says as soon as she sees me wearing the jacket over the dress. The order is accompanied by an impatient snap.

I laugh. "What? Why? I'll get chilly!"

Her eyebrows drop like she's not buying it. Her patience with me dwindles by the day. "We're in the tropics. It's never cold here, especially not in *August*."

Camila chimes in, taking up the cause on her sister's behalf. "You have a great rack, Paige, and it pains me, truly. It hurts my heart that you insist on hiding it away from everyone."

"But—"

"No."

"I—"

"*Nuh-uh*," Lara says, slicing her hand through the air like she's done negotiating.

They succeed in convincing me to slide off my jacket, and, as I expected, there's a moment of awkwardness where it seems like every person sitting around the bonfire is looking at me, blinking slowly, thinking the same thought. *Damn, hold up. Paige was a girl this whole time?!* Théo and Oscar aren't shy about whistling and teasing me, but I forgive them for it because I know they're just trying to make me laugh. Everyone else thankfully keeps their comments to themselves.

I know that I'm not homely. I look just like my mom, and I think my mom is drop-dead gorgeous. So why isn't Blaze proposing to me this very minute?

He's here now. I watched him walk up with his friends a second ago, just as I finished sliding off my jacket, but he hasn't looked this way.

Lara understands my predicament, and she wants to help. "Arch your back more. Yeah, like that."

Lara takes my shoulders in her hands and forcibly thrusts my chest forward. It looks like I have an extreme case of scoliosis, but it gets the job done. Blaze glances over, and his eyes widen in obvious appreciation at the sight of me (thank you, genetics), and then he gives me a little wave and a smile.

"Good, now look away. *Look away!*" Camila hisses frantically.

I look down at the sand, up at the night sky, to Camila, to Lara, then back to Blaze because I just can't help it. I'm flailing.

Lara laughs and shakes her head. "Girl, you're hopeless."

I sigh and shift so I'm facing away from him. Totally unbothered by his presence.

"Is he still looking over here?" I hiss out of the corner of my mouth, as if he could possibly hear me from way over here.

"No. He's talking to Cole now."

What?!

My heart lurches in my chest. I spasm, sputter, stall like I'm a manual car with a novice driver behind the wheel. Then I look up, desperately searching for Cole among the small crowd. My shoulders slump when I don't see him, and I feel silly. Of course he's not here. I didn't end up inviting him. Blaze is still talking to his friend, another bartender from the grotto poolside lounge. Not Cole. *Never Cole.*

I shoot Camila an angry glare, but it only makes her and Lara laugh more.

"Sorry, I just can't help it. God, it's so easy with you."

Lara agrees, flipping her long dark hair over her shoulder. "I know. You don't even have to say his full name to freak her out. Just *Co*—See? She already has goose bumps."

"I do not!" I swipe my hands over my arms to make all the little hairs lie flat again. "It's not just me. *Everyone has this reaction to him.*"

And because I'm worried they'll misconstrue what reaction I'm talking about exactly, I add, "*Everyone* hates him."

Lara shrugs. "Eh, not everyone. I heard Tamara talking in the break room the other day. Going *on* and *on* about how hot he is."

"Yeah, I was there too." Camila rolls her eyes. "She sounded obsessed. I didn't think I was going to be able to finish my lunch, listening to her droning on like that."

Tamara likes Cole? This is news to me. Why am I only finding out about this *now*? Surely, this is breaking news for everyone, not just me.

I lean toward them, suddenly needing answers. "Tamara? Is she that waitress from the Bistro? The one with the high-pitched voice?"

They nod in confirmation.

"Blonde? But more platinum than me?" I ask, just to triple-check I'm thinking of the right person.

"Yup." Lara nods.

Damn. From the few interactions I've had with Tamara, I know she's pretty and sweet. She's the kind of perky that guys usually lap up. Giggly and fun loving. I didn't think there was much going on behind the wide-eyed gaze, but maybe I'm wrong. Maybe Cole sees something I don't.

I need to be more like Tamara.

I try a giggle on for size, and Camila eyes me like I've lost my mind. "What are you doing? What was that?"

"A cough." I shake my head, dismissing her narrow-eyed suspicion. "Now. I need your help. How can I get Blaze's attention?"

"Are you sure you want Blaze?" Lara asks me with a healthy dose of skepticism.

"Who else would I want?"

They exchange a knowing look.

"*Who. Else. Would. I. Want?*" I demand.

Camila smirks.

Oh no. Absolutely not. We're not playing this game again, where they throw out subtle hints that maybe I detest Cole a little more than normal, that I talk about him, *complain* about him, to an unhealthy degree. So what if hating him is my third-favorite hobby, right behind disliking him and loathing him? It's important to have interests!

"So, just to be clear, you wouldn't care if Tamara dated Cole?" Lara wonders.

"He will never date her."

I say it like it's a fact. No, a *prophecy* I've read off some ancient scroll. *See here? It says Cole is going to die sad and alone.*

Lara shrugs and raises her eyebrows. "I don't know about that . . . Tamara seemed to think he was pretty into her."

"What proof did she give?!"

At this point I'm leaning so close to Lara I'm like a detective who's lost my cool in an interrogation. My fists are pounding on the metal table, and I'm snarling at the mouth. *Give me answers, damn it!*

She smiles as I clear my throat and sit back on my beach towel. Clearly, I got carried away.

I remind myself I don't care about Cole's dating life. I have more important things to focus on, like Blaze. Hunky Blaze with his bulging biceps and his perfectly imperfect smile. His brown hair is just long enough that he can tuck it slightly behind his ears. It's not my normal jam, but I'm kind of digging it.

Apparently, Lara and Camila aren't interested in helping me bag Blaze, so I'll have to take matters into my own hands. I'm hardly going to attract his attention by sitting over here on a beach towel, so I think I'll roast a marshmallow. *Yes.* A big fluffy white marshmallow that I have to seductively slide onto the end of a long stick, and if it looks slightly erotic (like I'm . . . oh, I don't know, giving a hand job), well, oopsies! I had no idea. I think I'll add another, slower this time. I really have to pump it into place.

Oh good!

He's looking now!

No one else is as close to the fire as I am because it's balmy and hot out tonight—the bonfire is more aesthetics than survival—but I prefer

17

it that way. I've got center stage. I imagine the flames dancing across my face in an alluring way, but clearly, it's still not enough. Blaze still isn't coming over here. So—and I'm not proud about this; *sorry, Mom*—I lean over to get my marshmallows closer to the flames while exhibiting *way* too much cleavage. I'm nearly toppling out of this lavender dress.

Then I smell something.

Oh right, burning hair.

"Ahhh!" I leap away from the fire, swatting at my head. It didn't really burn much, just a few strands, but it sufficiently put the kibosh on my little performance.

"You good, Paige?" Oscar adds with a barely restrained smile.

"Yes," I chirp, trying to brush off my embarrassment.

Now I've got nothing to show for all that effort aside from two blackened marshmallows and slightly less hair than I came here with. Blaze isn't even looking at me anymore. What a waste. I should have really gone for it. Maybe accidentally stuck a finger or two into the flames so Blaze could have played the hero and nursed me back to health.

I could have really played it up, had him carry me all the way back to the resort complex so we could wake up Dr. Missick. I would have been such a good little damsel, crushing my chest against his, nestling my head in the crook of his neck, whimpering on cue.

Yes, risk bodily harm to get the attention of a man. Feminism has got nothing on me!

Lara and Camila don't say a word as I reclaim my seat beside them on the beach towel. Lara passes me a beer, and I sit and drink, alone and hating myself for thinking of Cole and what he could possibly be up to at a time like this.

Chapter Three
COLE

I was raised by two robots. To this day, I'm not certain of the inner workings of my parents, whether they have real feelings or whether they're merely mimicking the facial expressions of the humans they live among. Whether they bleed blood or motor oil. Certain questions haunt me: Do my parents go for *real* yearly checkups at the doctor, or do they just sit in the parking lot for a designated amount of time before driving home for a tune-up in our garage? Do they need to eat to sustain life, or are they just doing it for my benefit? *Mmm . . . chicken.*

Susan and Patrick Clark raised me in the suburbs of Ohio—two accountants whose idea of a wild night consists of popping in a DiGiorno and working ahead on company audits. They live in a squat one-story in a suburb filled with squat one-stories. Their living room furniture all falls into a restricted spectrum of light gray with beige accents.

I'm smart. Like them, I'm good at math, so I went off to college and double majored in business and finance. I didn't even think much of it. Of course I would major in those subjects. It didn't strike me as anything all that important until the night of my college graduation, seven years ago. My parents took me to a world-renowned steak house where they both ordered salads with sides of soup, no bread.

My dad spoke up in a monotone voice and told me that he'd put in a good word at his company. If I wanted, I had a position there. Working with him.

I could get a house in their neighborhood, gray furniture of my own.

That night, I applied to graduate school for hospitality management. When looking for jobs, I only considered locations my parents would *never* go.

It's why I'm here in Turks and Caicos.

I understand it's not exactly the idyllic version of things. You're supposed to know your life's passion from infancy, right out of the womb. Bam—you want to be a doctor? Here, have this toy stethoscope. Apparently, I should have been playing bellman and concierge as a young child. Even still, I've found that I really enjoy this field. Coming from two robots, it's no surprise that I like searching out inefficiencies, numbers that don't add up, systems that can be tweaked and made perfect. I rose fast in the ranks because of my attention to detail, and now I have my sights set on a director position within the resort.

It's why I'm taking this early-morning meeting with Todd Weaver.

Todd Weaver has a paunch belly and a bad toupee. He's perpetually cleaning something out of his front teeth with the tip of his tongue, and never, not once, has he applied enough deodorant to mask the stench of his body odor. I want his job. I want him off this island. I never want to smell his particular brand of musk ever again.

"You're doing a damn fine job here, Cole. A damn fine job."

Yes, obviously. I already know that.

Todd sits behind his desk, leaned back so the buttons on his shirt are giving everything they've got. *Hold, brothers!*

Behind him, there's a panoramic view of the ocean. I love swimming out there in the morning before work. I enjoy running along the beach, too, hiking through the island trails, anything that gets me outside. Turks and Caicos has so much to offer, and I take full advantage.

Back in my suburb of Ohio, we had a man-made lake that shone sickly blue from the chemicals they pumped into it. Surrounding it was a pale concrete running path. No trees. Not a single one. It's like there was an ordinance against them.

I'm never leaving this island.

"I can trust you, can't I, Cole?"

Todd's been talking, and I accidentally tuned him out. This question has me shift my gaze off the beach, back to his sweaty face.

"Of course."

"You're my second-in-command, my wingman, if you will."

He winks, and I hope my expression skews more toward a smile than a grimace, but it's hard to tell without standing in front of a mirror. My people skills are admittedly lacking.

"I've been considering making some major changes around here. There's a few departments that I think have ballooned up out of control for no good reason."

"Oh? Which departments?" I ask, playing along.

He goes on to tell me that entertainment and hospitality was identified on a recent audit as having a "highly slashable" budget. He wants to restructure and trim the fat, banking on the fact that the resort's overwhelmingly positive guest reviews will remain on travel sites even after the team responsible for earning them has been gutted. Todd is a lot of things, but genius isn't one of them.

First up on his chopping block is the aging clown traumatizing hotel guests during what's meant to be a kid-friendly brunch (he's got a COPD cough and a penchant for making references to children's shows from the Reagan administration while bewildered kids frown at their uninspired balloon animals). He was a personal favorite of the previous CEO, but he's been working past his expiration date for some time.

Next is the rotating cadre of B-list musicians, one-hit wonders, and cover bands that serenade the crowds in the cocktail lounge on nights and weekends. Nothing a little Spotify playlist can't replace, he thinks.

I'm taking notes on my iPad, jotting down the gist of his speech right up until he says, "Paige Young."

My fingers still, my spine stiffens, and slowly, I look up. Todd has his feet propped up on his desk, his fingers digging through a bag of trail mix like a hungry little squirrel. He only wants the chocolate and the raisins.

"Paige? From excursions?" I ask, playing dumb.

He doesn't even look up from the bag. "Yes, her and a few others."

I clear my throat, trying to understand. The clown I get. He should have been shown the door about thirty years ago. But Paige?

I can't resist asking why.

Todd waves it off like the question isn't even worth his time. "Oh, I know she's pretty enough, but we have plenty of pretty women at Siesta Playa, some far more willing to show a little skin, if you catch my meaning."

I'm thrust into such a vivid daydream of wrapping my hands around his thick neck that I don't even realize he's waiting for a response.

"Guests like her," I say like I have no real skin in the game, like I'm just pointing out facts.

"Guests like *everyone*." He slides his feet off his desk and sits up, staring me down with conviction. "For now, this is just between you and me, got it? I can't just go around firing people. We'll have to be smooth about it. Cunning. Can you be cunning, Cole? *Hah*. Cunning Cole." He points at me. "I'm counting on you."

Right.

Counting me as an ally was Todd's first mistake.

Threatening Paige?

Absolutely not.

I force myself to sit in my seat until he's finished dismissing me. Then I stand and show myself out, trying my hardest to act as I normally would. If my departing words are a little strained or if my eyebrows are too furrowed, Todd isn't astute enough to notice.

I feel like I'm walking through a haze of smoke down the hallway, blinking slow, still in shock as I make it into my office.

Paige can't leave.

Paige . . . belongs here. With me.

She just doesn't know it yet.

I set down my iPad on my desk and rake my hands through my hair. I want to settle this the easy way: hire a hit man to take Todd out on his way home from work. Simple. Easy. Life in jail would be hard, but I'd manage.

Instead, I pull up a fresh Excel spreadsheet. A little zing of excitement trickles down my body. I do love a fresh spreadsheet.

Before I do anything, I save it to a restricted, password-protected folder. It's not that Todd would ever think to snoop around in my office, but I prefer to be as careful as possible, especially if I'm planning to go up against my boss.

It's the only path forward and something I would have done soon even if he hadn't threatened Paige. For a while now, I've suspected that Todd might *not* be one hundred percent squeaky clean. It's a hunch, a wild one. There have been whispers around the hotel. Rumors about Todd's worsening gambling addiction, the time he asked the accounting department if they could pay him in all cash instead of depositing his paycheck directly into his bank account like normal. I haven't put much stock into any of it, but I've tucked each rumor away in my arsenal, just in case.

I'd love nothing more than to pick up my phone right now and call our CEO, Scott Durliat. Unfortunately, if I rat out Todd at this point, I fear I'll wind up looking like nothing beyond an insubordinate tattle-tale. Everything I have on Todd is based on rumor, not fact. He's done nothing wrong that I can prove, *yet*. Furthermore, given how obvious I've been about my intentions and ambitions with this company, Scott could take it the wrong way, as if I'm merely gunning for Todd's job.

I know I need to act fast, but I don't want to rush and ruin this opportunity to save Paige from the chopping block.

There are several ways I could investigate Todd's dealings with the company, but most of them require access to accounts and files not at my disposal. I'm sure if I could gain access to Todd's office and log on to his computer, all his wrongdoings would be right there, dumbly saved in his internet's browser history. I know he's not smart enough to wipe that stuff. He once asked me the difference between *Cc* and *Bcc* in an email.

I drum my finger on my desk, trying to come up with a brilliant plan that doesn't involve any breaking and entering. It can't be all that difficult to outsmart Todd. I just have to be savvy about it. I have to use the tools at my disposal.

I could plant a bug in his office (surely they sell those on Amazon), but what would I do with twelve hours of audio consisting of Todd cycling through a series of burps and farts and grunts? How would that possibly be helpful?

Right. Let's see. If the gambling rumors are true, he could be strapped for cash. I could call his bank and try to gain access to his accounts, but that's illegal and highly suspect. I wouldn't know the answer to any of his security questions, anyway.

Think, Clark.

What *do* I have access to?

Inspiration strikes like a bolt of lightning. I grab my desk phone and hurriedly dial the extension for the accounting department before I've even fully formulated my plan.

Someone answers on the second ring. "This is Connie speaking."

Connie. I was hoping she'd pick up. Connie Phillips is a pipsqueak of a thing, no taller than five feet, with coke-bottle glasses and a wobbly voice. She's been with the company for ten years and she's a great accountant, but because she's so quiet, she's been largely overlooked for promotions. A few months ago, I tried to remedy that by awarding her with a substantial raise in line with the amount of years she's remained loyal to the company. Though the raise was long overdue, I still remember the tears welling up in her eyes when I shared the good news with her. I'd had no idea what to do and settled on a stilted *There, there* pat on her shoulder. Hopefully I'm still in her good graces, because I have a big ask.

"Connie, hey. This is Cole Clark. How are you? Good? Good. Could you do me a favor?" I don't pause to wait for a reply. I can't let her refuse me. This is all I've got. "I'm running numbers on my end, just going through some budgetary items, and I need you to provide me with last year's expense reports."

She stutters with her reply. "A-all of them? Sir, that's—"

"All of them. From every department." My tone implies there's no room for negotiating.

There's a pregnant pause where she's likely resigning herself to her fate.

"It'll take me a few days to get you copies . . . ," she says, already sounding weary about the task ahead of her.

"That's fine. Could you get it to me by Friday?"

"I . . . I'll try."

"Great." I'm about to hang up before I remember to add, "And Connie?"

"Yes?"

"I really appreciate it."

Chapter Four

PAIGE

I'm fully aware that the literal translation of our hotel name (Sleep Beach) does little to arouse fantasies of an exciting tropical vacation, but that doesn't seem to deter the gobs of pasty tourists from passing through our lobby day after day.

New characters erupt daily from the bowels of docked cruise ships. Batches of lanyarded convention goers arrive en masse. Each week brings a fresh horde of corporate tech bros or niche hobbyists. Last week there was the bridal and wedding expo where I watched grown women go to blows over the *possibility* of winning a free bridal gown from two seasons ago. Bathrooms were overflowing with crying bridesmaids that had been excommunicated and cut from weddings for such offenses as disagreeing with the bride or asking if they could *maybe, just possibly,* take a break for a late lunch since they'd been going nonstop since 8:00 a.m. "Where's your loyalty, Marie?! I told you to pack a protein bar!"

This week it's the Nifty after Sixty dating event. Next week it's my personal favorite: the doomsday preppers convention. I'm counting down the days. I'll be surprised if I can sleep before then.

It's Tuesday evening, a few days after the bonfire. I'm in one of Siesta Playa's ballrooms hosting a luau-themed bingo night for a room full of eager participants who range in age from 60 to 102. The number of medical devices and implants in this room would short-circuit a metal detector.

My only objective tonight is to ensure everyone is having fun. Oh, and also, Dr. Missick has insisted that I remind everyone that there are complimentary condoms in a bowl near the door that guests can (read: *must*) take at the end of the night.

I like to think I'm putting on a pretty great event. The energy in the room is lively and fun. We have a DJ onstage blasting hits from the '60s and '70s. A few waiters traipse through the crowd, passing around cocktails and denture-friendly light bites. I'm wearing a huge flower tucked behind my left ear and a flowy pink dress courtesy of Lara. Also, I've been given free rein on the microphone, which was a bad idea from the start.

". . . And so that's why we had to put down my childhood dog," I say, wrapping up a long-winded story.

Eyes blink up at me in stupor.

Right. I'm losing them.

I think fast and draw another ball so I can call out the corresponding number.

"B-5!"

"God fucking damn it!" Mr. Leroy shouts loudly enough for everyone to hear.

I don't miss a beat.

"*Wee-oh, wee-oh, wee-oh!*" I singsong like a siren, pointing Mr. Leroy over to the limbo station set up in front of the stage. There's a house rule: if people get out of hand with the cursing and foul language (which happens a lot with this group), they must limbo. I wave for the DJ to turn the music up as Mr. Leroy stands to accept his punishment. It's silly and dumb, but it's also really fun. And Mr. Leroy actually clears the pole, which is good because earlier I accidentally sent a guest to Dr. Missick after they accidentally threw their back out.

The crowd cheers for Mr. Leroy as I reach for another ball in the bingo cage.

Just when I hold it up, my gaze falls on the figure in the back of the ballroom.

I'm not sure how long Cole has been here watching me onstage, but seeing him is thrilling in the same way it is, say, when you get electrocuted. *Zap.*

I stutter over the number, and the crowd starts mumbling.

What'd she say?!

I didn't catch it.

Was it G-48 or B-48?!

"B-48!" I clarify, dropping the ball back with the other dead ones and then surreptitiously wiping a sweaty palm on my dress.

I'm desperate to look back up at Cole—to try to read his expression— but then someone near the back of the room shouts, "BINGO!"

They know the drill. The person's card will be checked by a staff member, and if they haven't cheated (at their age, these people have very little to lose), they get to pick something from a curated prize table, which includes such priceless items as a plastic Siesta Playa key chain, a large-print sudoku book, a needlepoint pattern of a whale and dolphin holding flippers, and a bag of Werther's Originals. They rave about the offerings.

"Okay, we'll take a short dance break while we check their card!" I tell everyone, waving for the DJ to turn up the music a bit. "Then we'll start the next round!"

I hop offstage with plans to head toward the bathroom, but instead my feet carry me straight to Cole because I'm a glutton for punishment and I haven't seen him in a few days. He watches me approach with a level of arrogance that makes me shiver. I'll never understand why he's so intimidating. He's not *that* much older than me, just a few years. It's the black suit, maybe. The shiny metal name tag: COLE CLARK, ASSISTANT DIRECTOR OF OPERATIONS.

Ooh la la.

We skip the polite greetings because neither one of us has bothered with them in months. I go straight for the kill.

"Come to play with your friends? I'm sure we can find you a bingo card. Be warned, though, the needlepoint patterns are going fast. I hope luck is on your side."

He almost smiles. "Just checking in on things."

He surveys the room as if to prove his point, and I'm treated to a view of his jawline. I focus my attention there before he looks back down at me and stares a beat too long at the big purple flower in my hair.

"I'm assuming you heard about the limbo incident earlier . . ."

It's probably why he's here, to slap me on the wrist and dole out the necessary punishment.

I swear he's fighting back a laugh as he pinches the bridge of his nose. I hold perfectly still, like maybe he'll give into the feeling if only he forgets that I'm here watching him. Laugh, damn it.

It doesn't work. He composes himself, drops his hand, and shakes his head. "Why can't you just take it easy on these people?"

"Because they like to have fun! *I* like to have fun. Look. See?" I start to dance in front of him, shimmying and being silly to see if I can succeed in breaking his character. He's like one of those stuffy British royal guards. *No smiling! No personality whatsoever or the king will hear about it!*

He sighs.

I continue, shimmying forward and back now instead of side to side.

It's a game.

How long can I force him to stand here and watch me make a fool of myself?

How long can he keep from laughing?! *I'm* laughing.

"Oh fine." I toss my hands up. "God, you're so annoying."

He ignores the jab. He knows there's no heat behind it. I've been calling him annoying for as long as I've known him.

Cole and I met my very first day on the job. In fact, he was the very first staff member I met at Siesta Playa. He gave me my uniform, showed me around the resort, and plopped me at my dorm room in staff housing like he was hoping he'd never have to deal with me again.

We were a disaster from the start. That day, my flight was late getting in. On top of that, the airline lost my luggage. I left a message with the hotel, but I guess word didn't make it to Cole. Apparently, he was standing there in the lobby for a good long while by the time I arrived, sweaty and flustered, blowing loose strands of hair off my face. I hate to admit this, truly I had plans to take it to my grave, but my first impression of Cole was that he was smoking hot—like *Do a double take, press a hand to your heart, blink three times, and try to figure out how to quickly conceal your reaction to him* hot. I made the mistake of trying to engage him in friendly conversation and managed to put my foot in my mouth almost immediately.

"So are you the concierge here?" I asked with a big friendly smile.

He took full offense to this question, frown and all. "I'm the assistant director of operations."

"That's . . . wow. That's pretty high up, right?"

He didn't answer me.

Small talk was apparently beneath him.

Right. Good to know.

I was about to apologize for the blunder, *and* about being late, but he was already in the process of taking my bags and turning sharply to walk off ahead of me. I assumed I was meant to keep up with him—he had my stuff, after all—but it was hard because one of my flip-flops happened to break just as I was hurrying out of the taxi out front. Surely Cole realized this, but I was left to sort of hobble along behind him as he kept his breakneck pace.

"Who wears flip-flops to the airport?" he muttered. I was sure the comment was meant to be under his breath, but I still heard him loud and clear. And at that moment, the tight hold I had over my bad mood burst like an overstuffed balloon. So far, I'd taken all the bullshit from that morning in stride: I'd put up with my delayed flight, the stress of being late to my first day of work, the fact that I was sweating through my clothes, the weird motion sickness from the jerky stops and starts in my hellacious taxi ride over here, my flip-flop deciding to break the *exact* moment I needed it the most.

I think I fired off something right back, like "Who wears a suit on a tropical island?"

His head slowly swiveled toward me and his eyes turned dark and dangerous.

And so, here we are, stuck in an endless loop of torment. I can't believe what Lara and Camila were hinting about at the bonfire. Cole is the *last* person I would ever envision dating, and I don't even need to ask his opinion. I know Cole would say I'm not exactly his type either. Even still, I know our banter and antics evince a deeper, foundational friendship. We're enemies because it's easy, our resting state, the natural order of things. We'll maintain the status quo only so long as we don't dig too deep or question our relationship too hard.

Now, I look at him. He has all the marks of a bully. I've always thought he had sort of an old money, East Coast feel about him: taunting cheekbones, shockingly black hair, dark eyes that seem to cut straight through me, and full lips that would feel so good pressed against mine, I know it. I blink and blurt out, "I didn't see you at the bonfire."

Of course he didn't go to the bonfire, not that I thought he would. It's not his scene. Getting soot on his dress slacks? Sand on his hands? He'd hate that. He wants to tame the elements, not join them.

"I wasn't technically invited," he points out.

"You could have come. No one would have cared."

He arches a brow, pressing the theory.

"It was just a small group," I add.

"I had other plans."

"Like what? Calling the mother ship and reporting your findings?" I continue in an alien accent, pretending I'm him: "Earth humans are more strange than previously theorized. Will need to extend my

31

research exploration trip before I can finalize my report on their habits. Beep boop."

The side of his mouth lifts in a smirk. "If you knew my parents, you'd realize how funny that actually is."

"Wait. Are they *actually* aliens?" I ask with wide eyes and mock solemnity.

He shrugs and looks away, looping back to my previous question when he answers, "I went out on Friday."

"Out? Like to the *bars*?"

This is almost more shocking than the fact that he might come from another planet.

His eyes lock with mine as he nods.

It's on the tip of my tongue to ask him who he went with. Tamara? Her friends? But I resist. If he spent Friday night sidling up to Tamara, flirting with her in a loud bar, their mouths inching closer to each other's—I do not want to know about it.

"Fun," I say with a cavalier indifference. It's like I couldn't care less about his comings and goings. *Go to twenty bars, for all I care! A hundred!* "I probably wouldn't have had much time to talk to you on Friday even if you had come to the bonfire."

"Oh yeah?"

He sees right through me.

Now he's amused. His smile hurts me.

"Yes, I was pretty *preoccupied* with Blaze."

I all but mime a blow job for emphasis.

This is a total lie. After the marshmallow incident I mostly hung out with Lara, Camila, Oscar, and Théo. We played a trivia game on Oscar's phone, and then I called it an early night. Blaze never came over to talk with me—not once—but I think he's just shy. I caught him looking at me before I left, like *really* checking me out, so there's still hope.

"Blaze the bartender?" Cole asks in a droll tone. Those three words hold a whole lot of meaning.

I laugh with heavy sarcasm. "Ha ha ha. *Yes.* Blaze the bartender. We can't all be assistant directors like *you.*"

I reach out as if to straighten his name tag for maximum teasing effect, but then I think better of it. We shouldn't touch. My fingers curl into themselves, and then I drop my hand back by my side.

He clucks his tongue and then tucks his hands into his suit-pants pockets. "Well, I hope that works out for you."

"It will," I say with absolute certainty.

"You should probably get back onstage." He nods his chin toward the front of the room. "Your adoring fans are waiting."

"Right, but you have to leave. You're not allowed to watch me make a mockery of myself."

His tilted head and the knowing glint in his eyes say, *Paige, I've seen you make a mockery of yourself a million times over.*

And it's true, he has.

Cole has seen the very worst of me.

Chapter Five

PAIGE

Six months ago, on a random Saturday night, I got really drunk at the Conch Bar. To my credit, it was ladies' night, and the bar was running a Jell-O shot promotion: two for the price of one. As someone who enjoys a good bargain and the taste of sugary alcohol, I simply could not turn down the opportunity life had presented me. Unfortunately, prior to this, the night was already headed south. There was a big group of us out on the town, all girls from the resort. We started with dinner that included copious amounts of wine. After that, we decided to go out and let our hair down, dancing, sharing stories of past sexcapades, and generally just acting like fools. The Conch Bar was our last stop of the night, and that first Jell-O shot was the beginning of the end for me. I was having so much fun until I wasn't.

I remember the tipping point. I was standing on the dance floor thinking, *They should really turn the strobe lights off in here.*

Of course there were no strobe lights.

Then the next thing I remembered, we were back at the resort, and I was being dragged down the pebble path through the dense forest that leads from a private circular drive down to staff housing near the beach. It was Camila and Lara who were lugging me down the path, but they were drunk, too, and we kept falling over and laughing. Everything was funny. The shapes of the trees. The color of the moon. The fact that my dress was riding up around my hips.

"My panties are showing! This is so bad!"

This was accompanied by peals of laughter. I couldn't stop if I tried.

I was lying on the ground, staring up, fully convinced that it would be fine if I just stayed there all night, asleep under the stars, right when a face suddenly cut into my view of the night sky.

Condescending frown, thick dark eyebrows furrowed in disapproval, full lips tugged into a flat line.

"COLE!"

My first gut instinct was sheer excitement that he was here. My archnemesis! My favorite person!

Then reality set in, and I repeated his name, this time with as much disdain as I could muster.

"*Cole.*" Lying on the ground—in no position to argue—I shook my head. "Nope. No. Someone else. *Anyone.* In fact, just leave me here and let the wild animals have me."

I squeezed my eyes shut like I was prepared to meet my demise. "Make it quick."

"What's wrong with her?" he asked my friends.

His tone wasn't chock full of concern like it might have been if he were a normal human with normal emotions.

Those assholes ratted me out in a heartbeat. "She's drunk."

"Can you two get back on your own?"

"Yeah, and we can get Paige back, too, if you help her stand up."

"It's fine, I've got it from here."

Lara and Camila didn't even put up a fight. They willingly left me there with Cole, which meant it was just him and me, alone on that dark path. We could have it out for real, *finally.* Guns drawn. Knives out.

I expected no mercy from him.

Instead, he heaved a deeply annoyed sigh and then bent down so we were more on the same level.

"You have to get up."

"Do I?"

Most likely realizing that he wasn't going to get anywhere with me, he took matters into his own hands, hooking his forearms underneath my armpits and lugging me to my feet. "Up and at 'em, champ."

I groaned as my world spun around and around. Vertigo on its max setting.

"Get me off this Tilt-A-Whirl," I complained with an audible gag.

He looped one arm around my back, under my armpit so he could take most of my weight.

"Can you walk?"

I didn't answer.

"If not, I'm going to carry you."

It almost felt like a threat.

"Dear god, no. Not that."

I would never recover from being in his arms, though walking alongside him like that wasn't much different. He had such a firm grip on me. Our hips, arms, chest, legs—everything touched, eliciting sparks, as we trudged slowly down the path. When I swayed on my feet, he held me tighter. When I was hit with a wave of nausea, he paused and told me to take a few calming breaths. I wouldn't even say we were going at a snail's pace. A snail shouted at us to get the hell out of his way as we took slow steps toward my dorm.

"Jell-O shots," I explained, even though he never asked.

"Mmm," he hummed without a hint of judgment.

"It could have happened to anyone."

"I have no doubt. I've been there."

"*You have?* When? Tell me everything."

He laughed then and adjusted his grip, which made his closed fist accidentally brush against my breast. I froze. He froze. Then we both slowly looked at each other.

Was it the moonlight, or did his eyes have a gentle kindness in them tonight?

I didn't make it very far with that line of thinking, because a second later, my stomach decided to steal the show.

I managed to get out a desperate "I'm going to be sick" mere milliseconds before bending at the waist and making good on that promise. At least I had the forethought to turn away from him.

Cole didn't abandon me like he could have. Tears streamed down my cheeks, and I begged him to go so he wouldn't see me at my worst, utterly defenseless, weak, and sick. I'd worked hard up until that point to make Cole like me, and if not like me, then at least respect me as an adversary. Now it was too late for that. It was so embarrassing to be a full-grown adult and drunk to the point of being sick. I have no doubt he wanted to chastise me for it, but instead, he held my hair back as I threw up again.

He told me it would be okay, that I would feel better soon.

His niceness made me cry harder.

Cole stayed with me on that path until I had the energy to walk again. I got the impression that he would have preferred to just lug me over his shoulder like a sack of potatoes and be done with the hellacious task of tending to me, though maybe it was in his best interest to make sure I was safe and well. What's a superhero without a villain? If I died, he'd lose his plot.

Outside my room, he took my key out of my purse and helped me unlock the door.

"Do not look at my shit," I said, like there was any dignity to salvage.

Thank god my room was relatively tidy. My bed was made, my pillows arranged just so. My bulletin board was covered with pictures of my parents and me that we'd taken during all our travels. Tiny Paige swimming with dolphins. Adolescent Paige suffering through the Drake Passage on the way to Antarctica. Teenager Paige waving from the side of a research vessel.

Cole didn't listen to me. He looked wherever he damn well pleased. I suppose he thought it was payment for his service. He helped me get here safely; he deserved some kind of reward.

"You were a cute kid," he said, leaning in to look at my pictures, pointing to a zoomed-in one of me going to town on a towering ice cream cone.

"And now?"

He looked back at me over his shoulder, eyes narrowed as if he was really thinking about it. My stomach squeezed tight.

"Never mind. *Don't* answer that," I said quickly. "I only just stopped crying. I don't have the energy for your barbs tonight."

He frowned like I'd wounded him, but I was already en route to my bed. It looked so good, so clean and welcoming. That fluffy white blanket was just waiting for me.

"I wouldn't," he warned, making me stop dead in my tracks.

Then he pointed at my clothes. I didn't even need to look down to realize why he thought it was a bad idea. Of course. I needed to shower and change immediately.

I didn't think I could muster the energy, though. The simple concept of having to prolong my collapse onto my bed sent me down to my knees. By this point I was crawling over to my dresser to get clothes. Showering? Not possible.

Cole stuck it out. "I'll help you. C'mon."

From my hands and knees, I protested. "*No.* Get Lara or Camila."

"They're as drunk as you are."

He was already ushering me toward my bathroom. There was no tub, just a walk-in shower with a translucent white curtain. He turned the water on and checked to make sure it was the perfect temperature. Then he told me to get in.

"I can't do that while you're here!"

He was exasperated with me by this point. Trying to get me to see reason, he asked, "What would you do if the situation was reversed? If *I* was the drunk one?"

Easy. I'd tend to him like my life depended on it. Sponge bathe him if I had to. Feed him like a baby bird.

"Leave you out there on that path to die" is what I told him.

He closed his eyes like he was holding back the urge to laugh. When he opened them again, he'd regained his composure and pointed to the shower. His eyes were the most magnificent shade of brown I'd ever seen. "Charming. Get in."

Then he walked out of the bathroom and pulled the door shut behind him, affording me as much privacy as he possibly could without leaving altogether.

I did as he instructed, trying to avoid looking down at my clothes as I undressed, knowing it would make me feel sick all over again. I was far from sober, but at least my stomach had settled down some in the last few minutes. Undressing proved . . . difficult. It was hard to figure out the thin straps of my dress, and the zipper was rooted in rocket science. I have no doubt that I would have been a comical sight had Cole not been safely on the other side of the door.

"How's it going in there?" he asked.

"Uhh . . . fine," I lied.

"I'll be right here if you need me."

I blew out air, like, *Pfft, yeah right.*

Only I did need him—almost immediately—because just as I was stepping into the shower, I slipped on a pool of water. In slow-motion horror, I simultaneously screamed, reached out desperately for something to catch myself with, and managed only to grab ahold of the curtain; then I yanked it free from the curtain rings—*ping ping ping ping ping*—on my way to the ground. I landed hard on my butt, a heap of drunk limbs barely concealed beneath a wet shower curtain. The shower spray rained down on my head just as Cole ran into the bathroom, horrified.

"*Shit!* Are you okay?"

I was okay. Unfortunately. The only thing bruised that night was my ego.

Cole averted his gaze and helped me stand up. While I huddled in the corner with a towel wrapped around me, he fixed my shower curtain the best he could and then demanded I try again. This time, he didn't leave the bathroom as I started to rinse off, but he turned around and faced the wall. It was deeply intimate. *Insanely* intimate. My hands shook the entire time I tried to squeeze out dollops of soap and shampoo.

I thought everything would change then. Our relationship as we knew it was officially kaput. But the next morning Cole did the nicest thing he's ever done for me: he pretended like it never happened. Not in the sense that he wasn't going to bring it up. He was.

"Rough night?" he asked the moment he saw me.

I just mean, he didn't coddle me over it. He went after me just as hard as always, the way I preferred it. Our little game was preserved, alive and well for a few more months . . .

Chapter Six
COLE

I lied to Paige at bingo night. I didn't go out on the town on Friday. I played *Call of Duty* with two scuba diving instructors until midnight, at which point I decided to punish myself by doing a slow walk by the bonfire. It was still going strong when I got there. I scanned the crowd, not that surprised to see the usual suspects. Paige sat on a towel with her friends, laughing, and she was so beautiful, the scene was so enchanting—it looked like it could have been a commercial for the brand of beer she was holding in her hand.

The thing about Paige is that, yes, she's obviously beautiful. There's not a soul alive who wouldn't notice that immediately upon meeting her. She has this vitality about her, like she's the physical embodiment of a sun goddess. Bright-blonde hair, warm tan skin, expressive blue eyes, and a smile that she shares equally with everyone (present company excluded). But her beauty isn't her personality or her persona. She doesn't stare in the mirror and admire herself because of the way she looks; she appreciates her body for what it can do for her: hiking, biking, singing, dancing, acting totally insane for the sake of entertaining hotel guests.

She intrigued me right from the start, if only because we're so different. I can't imagine taking her home to Ohio. I mean, I *have* imagined it plenty of times, and I know my parents would sit in shocked silence, staring at her like she was some rare exotic bird they had no idea how to tame. Picturing her perched in my parents' monochromatic living room is almost painfully funny. Paige would charm them, though, the same way she charms everyone.

I remember standing in the lobby waiting for her the first day she arrived at Siesta Playa. It wasn't shaking out to be the best morning. I was annoyed because one of the golf pros just quit on us, and we were expecting a VIP guest who'd specifically requested private lessons with *that* golf pro. It was a shit show, and we were working around the clock trying to find a replacement, and fast. I didn't have time to wait on new hires, but it's hotel policy. So there I was, checking my watch, clearing my throat, adjusting my tie, ticking seconds off in my head, when Paige stumbled out of the turnstile door and graced me with her presence for the very first time.

I don't remember our conversation from that day; I was so flustered by her.

I still am, unfortunately.

Growing up with ol' Sue and Pat didn't equip me with stellar people skills. I'm good with numbers, computers, inanimate objects. Sometimes I worry I have robot DNA, too, but then I look at Paige and I know for certain I'm flesh and blood, capable of feeling everything all at once whenever she walks into a room.

I see how effortlessly other people flirt and carry on, and I'm envious. It just doesn't come naturally to me. I want to be that way with Paige, but I know I'd make a mockery of myself. If I tried a pickup line on her, she'd burst out laughing and ask me if I'm feeling okay. Maybe at the beginning, before we tangled ourselves into this complicated mess, I could have been honest with her. I could have put myself out there and asked her on a date, plain and simple. Now, it just seems too late for simple. I can't get out of my own way. I have every intention of befriending her, of trying a smile on for size, but the biting banter is our autopilot. The barbs are all we know.

We're stuck.

It's the day after bingo night. Things are going well this week with the Nifty after Sixty crowd. The water-aerobics classes have been a big hit; last night, the late-night karaoke extended an hour later than usual to accommodate the line out the door ("Do you guys happen to have anything by the Who?"); and Dr. Missick has only had to send for an emergency medical helicopter once, and that was because of a fluke shrimp-cocktail choking incident. It could have happened to anyone at any age.

I've already been at work for hours. I've cleared my email inbox, checked in on reception, gone through the excursion schedule for the day, inspected the lobby and the lobby bathrooms to ensure they're clean and orderly.

The next item on my to-do list: check in on the lunch buffet. Walk through the tables; hold up stemware to the light to inspect it for fingerprints; make sure the French pastries are arranged in sharp lines, each croissant tilted exactly forty-five degrees left from center. I have exacting taste. I'm aware of that.

"Looks great," I tell Marcus, the head chef of our resort's main restaurant, the Bistro.

He nods in appreciation. He and I understand each other. I might be two decades younger than him, a novice for certain, but we share the same principles and values. We want the same thing. Unlike Todd. Todd spends most of his time holed up in his office, gambling online. He only ever bothers to observe the daily operations of the resort—*to do his job*—when Scott Durliat is on site. I once heard Marcus refer to Todd as "that obscene blob," and now I call him that in my head too.

After I leave the restaurant, I walk through the main lobby, en route to the grotto under the guise of checking inventory, when really I want to size up Blaze, get a feel for the guy Paige seems so interested in. I get sidetracked, though.

Near the excursion desk, Paige stands chatting with an older male guest in a cowboy hat. He's sloshing around a half-finished piña colada. From Paige's tight smile, I have no doubt he's already been chatting her ear off for long minutes, and I could save her . . . it would be the nice thing to do.

"Paige, aren't you supposed to be at your yoga class right now? Run along, you!"

Paige sees me, and her eyes widen with a plea. *Get me out of here!*

I give her a smile and two hearty thumbs up. "You're doing a great job," I mouth.

Her expression says she has murder on her mind.

During this exchange, I make the mistake of veering too close to them. Mr. Cowboy Hat sees me and jumps at the opportunity to get another employee on his hook.

"Ah, just the man I was hoping to see!" He stops me by grabbing ahold of my biceps and tugging me even closer. I don't have to comply. He's not that strong, but I have every reason to ingratiate myself to our guests. "I need to put in a good word for this little lady right here. Whatever you're paying her, *double it!* She really goes above and beyond. I tell you, the missus and I had our heart set on snorkeling, but the hotel's preplanned excursion was a little above our skill level. We're novices here, and Ms. Young, she didn't mind one bit. Told us to meet her back down at the beach an hour later, and she took us on a little trip of our own, just like that. Best experience of my vacation so far. Saw myself a barracuda!"

Paige has been watching me through this entire speech with a little gloating smile in place. Her blue eyes spark with mischief.

"You keep your hotel staffed with people like Ms. Young and we'll be coming back here year after year," he promises in a thunderous voice. "She's great, isn't she?"

I'm looking at Paige now, smiling for the guest's benefit.

"Absolutely. We really value staff members like Paige here at Siesta Playa."

The guy gives Paige a wink, and then he has to peel off quick when he sees his wife is beelining for the hotel gift shop. "Now, Bernice, I know you had your eye on that pot warmer, but I told you we've already bought enough souvenirs this trip . . ."

Now that we're alone, we could both back away slowly. Instead, Paige and I each take a step toward each other. Somewhere over our heads, a dangling race car light blinks red . . . red . . . *green*. She tilts her head back and looks at me like she wants to play.

"Say it again. Say I'm great."

"You're great," I repeat blandly.

"*C'mon*, where's the conviction? I want to *feel* it."

"You're one of a kind," I say, just as dry.

She snaps her fingers like she's just had a brilliant idea. "You know what? Maybe you should nominate me for employee of the month?!" She says it like she's a total genius for thinking of it.

My stomach plummets as reality sinks in.

If only she knew the truth of what's really happening behind the scenes. She's nowhere near getting awarded employee of the month. In fact, if Todd had it his way, she'd be packing her bags at this very moment. It makes me sick thinking about it. This problem with Todd consumes me day and night. Ever since our meeting earlier this week, I've been checking numbers, doing my due diligence, formulating a plan, a way that gets me, *us*, everything we want.

But the clock's ticking, and I'm still waiting on those damn expense reports. Worse, Todd fired the clown today. Which, honestly, big whoop, but now I know he's serious about what he told me. He's really going through with this shitty plan. Fine, whatever, he can get rid of a few employees—the ones who deserve the boot, anyway—but he's not firing Paige. *Over my dead body.*

"You're being quiet." Her eyes narrow. "Are you sick?"

"I don't get sick."

She thunks her forehead. "Of course not, duh. How could I forget that you're not susceptible to things like the common cold? No getting sick like the rest of us schmucks. Be honest, have you ever taken a day off in all the time you've worked here?"

Sure. "Once a year, I go to all my doctor's appointments on the same day."

She shakes her head like she can't believe it. "*Wild.* I have so many questions about the way you live. Are you a side sleeper?"

"Back."

"How do you take your coffee?" She slashes her hand through the air and steps closer. "Wait, I already know that. What's your favorite meal?" She starts talking faster, excited. "No! Wait, it's steak. I know that too. Damn it! I change my question! Where do you take girls on first dates?! *That's* what I want to know."

She's nearly panting with exertion by the time she finally pauses long enough for me to answer.

"You are so weird."

I say it like it's a compliment because it is.

She laces her fingers together in desperation. "Please tell me. The morgue!" she guesses. "The cemetery. A sad modern-art exhibit . . . a long-winded lecture on actuarial science . . ."

I'm already cutting past her to continue with my day. "Bye, Paige."

"A crumbling war memorial!" she calls out after me.

Because my back's to her, she doesn't see my smile.

Chapter Seven

PAIGE

On our days off, staff members at Siesta Playa are allowed to enjoy resort amenities so long as we follow two rules. The first is that we can play tennis or basketball on the sports courts, lie out on the private beaches, swim in any of the resort pools—all of the above—as long as we don't get in the way of any guests. If they want the tennis court, it's theirs. If they need the lounger I've claimed, oh well. The second rule is that we can't cost the resort money. No free food or drinks are allowed outside the staff cafeteria. It's why I'm guzzling water instead of some fruity cocktail adorned with a frilly umbrella straw. I can't afford a fifteen-dollar margarita on a regular Wednesday! Are you insane? *In this economy?*

There are three pools total at Siesta Playa. One is for adults only and, thus, pretty boring. Picture crusty old dudes with sunburns layered over fading upper-back tattoos. Another pool is geared toward children, replete with a ginormous play structure and eight water slides and, thus, a little *too* crazy. Then there's this one, the perfect Goldilocks compromise. It's large and centrally located and accepting of everyone. There's always fun dance music streaming through the speakers, and there's usually enough of a crowd that it provides a good backdrop for people watching. Lara and I have been here since the late morning. We scoped out the best lounge chairs and set up shop as close as we could get to the grotto. This was no coincidence, of course. Blaze is working today. I wore a bikini I borrowed from Lara. It's pink and made of mere scraps. It should be illegal. I have to stay in the water because I'm scared of walking the short distance from here to my lounge chair; there's no telling what will pop out.

The bikini seemed like a good idea this morning. Now, I just feel Naked and Afraid™.

I have a clear view of Blaze while he works behind the bar counter. He smiles easily at a customer, and I'm reminded of his easygoing nature. Guests and hotel staff *all* like him. *I* like him. While he might be chiseled steel on the outside, inside he's made of soft plush. More than that, I don't have to prepare myself for battle when we speak, *unlike with Cole*. Not to mention, he's *so* cute in his uniform. It's the same standard-issue short-sleeved black button-down tucked into black shorts that everyone else wears, too, but he's made it his own. For example: he has a little gold necklace hanging around his neck. A pen tucked behind his right ear. Okay, really that's it, just those two things, but I feel like he's so unique and different.

"Don't you think he's *so unique and different?*"

"Please stop."

Lara can't do it anymore. She's been here with me for hours. She wants to drown herself to get away from my incessant chatter about Blaze. But I'm sorry, it's called friendship. Suffer, bitch.

Lara's leaning over the side of the pool, occupying herself by scrolling on her phone while I keep a not-so-surreptitious eye on Blaze behind the bar.

"We've been pretty lucky so far this hurricane season," Lara muses out loud. She must be on her weather app. She checks it a lot. She's a constant worrier when it comes to tropical storms. If there's so much as a rain cloud in the sky, she's going to duck for cover. "But storm watchers are tracking—"

. . . gibberish . . . boring . . . don't care . . .

"Uh-huh."

"It could be really bad. Winds at *really* high speeds. A *ton* of rain."

"Oh no," I say with absolutely no inflection.

Then, as if someone just personally insulted me and my entire family, I explode with "Are you kidding me?!"

Some huge dude just plopped himself down on a barstool directly in front of me, blocking my view of Blaze. The guy has to be at least six foot five, built like a horse. His shoulders could span the width of the Grand Canyon. Is this a joke?

"Sit somewhere else, guy!"

Fortunately, (a) he can't hear me over the music, and (b) my view isn't blocked for long. Blaze moves to grab a bottle opener so he can pop the cap off a beer. Then he looks over and spots us. It's the first time he's looked this way all morning, and unfortunately, I'm still wearing the scowl I was aiming at the big guy. Ah! I quickly relax my features into a flirty smile. Then I wave.

He holds up his finger as if he wants us to wait; then he goes back to making drinks.

"Oh my god. *Oh my god.* He's going to come over here!"

I look down to confirm my breasts are still somewhat contained in the bikini top. I blanch at how much skin is showing. A lot. Holy hell. I shift material to the right, but then my nipple almost pops out, so yeah, we'll just leave it as it is.

A few minutes later, Blaze leaves his station carrying what look to be two innocuous water cups. I know because when guests order at the bar, their drinks come in fancy resort-branded cocktail glasses. These are boring clear plastic. When Blaze reaches us, he leans down and explains in a hushed conspiratorial tone, "Vodka sodas with a splash of lime."

"*Yes!*" Lara says, taking hers greedily. "You're the best."

I give him a big smile. "Awesome. Thanks, Blaze."

"No problem, Paula."

Wait.

Hold the phone.

Paula?

Lara snorts and nearly chokes on her drink.

Okay, so this isn't exactly great, but it's totally understandable! Blaze has only worked here for what? Two months? And we've only met a dozen or so times. It could happen to anyone. It's cute, actually. We'll be laughing about this moment next year when we're celebrating our one-year anniversary. *Remember when you didn't even know my name?! Ha ha ha.*

I'm about to clarify—sweetly, of course!—that my name is actually Paige, not Paula, but Blaze's attention cuts to something over our heads on the opposite side of the pool. His easygoing expression is wiped clean in an instant. The color starts to drain from his face.

Obviously, I turn to see what could possibly have him looking so worried.

It's Cole.

Of course.

He's standing on the pool's edge in a suit and tie. A menace in navy blue.

He's not scowling, not firing off uncouth threats. But all the same, he sends Blaze packing, running back to his spot at the grotto bar like his life depends on it.

Wonderful.

Cole doesn't look at me. He watches Blaze with his astute glare until he's working again, faster than ever.

Cole is far enough away that he wouldn't hear me unless I shouted, so I'm forced to use telepathy.

Good going, jerk.

His gaze finally flits to me, then down to my vodka soda.

What's in the cup, Paula?

I hate you.

During this heated standoff, a resort guest walks up to Cole to ask him a question, and Cole's entire demeanor changes, that smile, those eyes. He can be so charming if only he wants to be. With me, he *never* wants to be.

Lara lets out a slow, steadying breath. "*Jesus*, that man can wear a suit. God, look at his butt."

"I would rather permanently lose my vision."

"You're missing out. It's perfect."

"Perfect. *Pfft.* Hardly."

"Oh, look who's coming . . ."

Just as the hotel guest walks away, a pretty blonde with red-stained lips strolls up to Cole and touches his arm.

Bold, beautiful Tamara.

I haven't seen her in weeks. We work in different areas of the resort, after all, so that's to be expected. I sweat through hikes in the jungle; meanwhile, she earns big tips working in the Bistro, likely in no small part because of the way she looks. She's manicured and polished. Primping clearly comes easily to her. We're outside by the pool, the humidity in the air is at an all-time high, but her blonde hair looks sleek and shiny, completely untroubled by the natural elements.

It must be her off day too. She's wearing a bathing suit and a barely there cover-up that clings to her body. Her entire demeanor screams effortless confidence. When Cole turns his body to fully face her, something akin to jealousy wraps its talons around my throat.

Tamara smiles at Cole, striking up a conversation, and it seems so genuine and easy for her, I don't know how she does it.

Cole is not an easy man to get along with, and yet Tamara seems to have no trouble at all. She talks animatedly about something. Then there's a big laugh, and she leans forward to playfully touch his arm.

The moment comes when she should pull back, but she doesn't.

Her red nails *tighten* on his biceps.

I must make a sound because Lara asks, "You good?"

I hold my breath waiting for Cole to reach over and pry her hand off him, finger by finger. But he doesn't do it. He doesn't balk or push her away. He *lets* her touch him.

Having had enough, I look away from them and down my drink in one fast go. "Come on, I'm done swimming. Let's go play tennis."

I want to hit some balls really, *really* hard.

Chapter Eight

PAIGE

I'm carrying a deep, dark secret. It's bad. *Badder* than bad.

Two months ago, Cole and I kissed.

I know.

It's wild even to me, and I've had plenty of time to come to terms with it. This is the sole occasion where the shocked-exploding-head emoji is absolutely accurate.

The morning of THE KISS, I didn't wake up knowing I was going to kiss my enemy. We weren't like building up toward it or anything. Our relationship then is much the same as it is now, i.e., an *enemy*ship built on mutual loathing and deep admiration. Neither of us will ever, and I mean *ever*, cop to the second part. It would set in motion a sequence of events that would result in the death of every man, woman, and child here on earth. Or something equally bad, probably.

If I had known that day that I would be kissing Cole, I would have hiked my covers up over my head and just stayed in bed. No, *wait*. I would have taken the opportunity to borrow Poison Ivy's evil lipstick. I wonder if there's a dupe for it online . . .

The kiss just sort of happened, and here's how. Everything leading up to that point was absolutely normal. I worked a standard day at the resort: I led a group through the caverns of the Conch Bar Caves in the morning and then took a family out paddleboarding through Chalk Sound National Park in the afternoon. After dinner, I played tennis with Lara, Camila, and Théo. By the time I was ready to call it quits, they were still going strong, so I was solo on my walk along the pebble path back toward staff housing.

I love my walk home. It's a really nice feature of the resort. When the head honchos were designing the place, they tried their hardest to adapt the entire complex to integrate with nature rather than steal from it. Instead of bulldozing through the dense foliage that surrounds much of the shoreline, they wove the resort paths through it so that at any moment you could be greeted by lizards, or frogs, or huge colorful iguanas just chillin'.

Another pretty feature is that every few yards, the dense wall of tropical flowers and vines grows thin enough that you can see the stunning view of the ocean at night. That night, I was halfway back to my dorm when the vining flowers grew thin enough that I could make out someone sitting on the beach, alone in the dark.

I immediately recognized the back of Cole's head like I would recognize the back of my own hand. If pressed, I could probably individually identify every single strand of hair.

Curious, I stopped and turned so I could take a step closer toward the beach. He was down close to the water, sitting on the sand with his knees bent up so he could drape his arms casually around them, his hands clasped together in the middle. The waves rolled in, and he sat stock still, like he was deep in thought, contemplative, clearly needing to be alone.

For a moment, I stood there, frozen with indecision.

I'd never seen Cole sitting on the beach alone at night before. It felt like a rare opportunity I couldn't—*shouldn't*—pass up. On the other hand, it probably made much more sense to just keep walking and leave him in peace.

I started to do just that, but I only made it a few steps before I stopped short again. My mind was suddenly firmly made up.

I've wondered about this pivotal moment a hundred times.

I technically made the first move by leaving the pebble path, slipping off my shoes, and traipsing out onto the sand to join him.

He heard me coming, I'm sure. I wasn't being quiet. In fact, I hoped he knew I was coming so I didn't have to suffer the disappointment on his face when he looked up and saw that it was me. But he never turned back, and when he finally did acknowledge me, he didn't groan in protest, but he also didn't make any indication that he was happy to see me.

So I didn't pretend. Not like I would have with someone else. With Cole, it was always just saying the first thing that came to mind. The truth. Well . . . most of it.

"I know you don't want company, and I know you definitely don't want company that includes *me*, but here I am. Too late. Shove over."

He looked over at me, baffled. "There's plenty of sand. Why do I need to move?"

"Because I said so."

He shook his head and shifted a little to the right so that there was room for the two of us in front of the sprawling ocean. I took a seat beside him on the warm sand and held my breath, waiting for him to say something. *Anything!*

"Some stars, right?" I noted.

Nothing.

"The ocean's so pretty at night."

Nada.

"So as a kid, did you always see yourself working as a midlevel manager at a large-scale resort?"

He let out a short laugh and shook his head. Then he peered over at me out of the corner of his eyes and asked the last question I ever saw coming. "Do you ever wonder what the fuck we're doing here?"

"On this beach?" I inquired dumbly.

I thought that might have been his surreptitious way of asking why I was there bothering him.

He shook his head, nodding toward the ocean. "In this life."

I reared back. "Damn. What'd you take? Mushrooms or something?"

He pointed down to the sand near his feet, where a copy of *Calypso* by David Sedaris rested on a patch of compact sand. A scrap of paper hung out of the top of it, his makeshift bookmark.

"*Oh*, yeah, he'll do that to you. Make you think." I sighed. "It's okay, it'll go away soon, and you don't have to worry about me ratting you out to everyone. About you having a conscience, I mean."

He was quiet for a bit, and when he eventually spoke, it was like all the fight had been drained out of him. He was utterly empty. "Not tonight, Paige."

He stared back out at the ocean as my heart splintered in two. We'd never called a truce like that. Worry lanced through me, worry over something I felt like I didn't fully understand. I wanted him to be okay, for us to be okay, but I didn't know exactly how to help him. I didn't feel like I had the right words, and digging deep for something sincere held its own dangers. At any moment, I knew he could pull the plug on this conversation, so that I'd wind up being the one left feeling vulnerable and exposed.

Even with that worry in mind, I reached over to touch his arm, right above his elbow. He was still wearing his dress shirt from work, sans jacket and tie. He'd unbuttoned the top few buttons and rolled up the sleeves. His shirt kept our skin from touching. It felt important to keep that layer between us.

He was so sexy it hurt to look at him full on. Thank god it was so dark or maybe I wouldn't have been able to at all.

"I feel that way sometimes, Cole. Of course I do. Doesn't everyone?" I asked, leaning forward a bit, trying to get him to look at me.

"I don't know. Do they?"

He was asking the ocean, not me.

"Cole, Please. Don't be sad."

It felt like my own heart was breaking.

"I'm not."

He said it so sincerely that I believed him, but still, something was wrong, so I persisted. "Could have fooled me. C'mon, you're probably just missing home. Your old life. Some girl that's waiting for you back in—"

"Ohio."

I snapped. "Right. *Ohio.* The land of . . . hot dogs?"

"Buckeyes."

"Right, you miss your buckeyes, which are a type of *bean* . . . ?"

"Tree."

"Yes!" I said excitedly. "The majestic buckeye tree, of course! Listen, I don't know what's really wrong with you tonight, and I'm sure you wouldn't tell me even if I asked. But we all miss home sometimes. Even me, and I don't even *have* a home to miss! My parents strapped me to them right along with their backpacks and research equipment and carted me around the world, moving so often I wouldn't even be able to tell you where I'm from, not really. I've technically spent the most time in London, so am I British? And if I am, why do I have an American accent? *See?* You're not the only fucked-up one here, Cole Clark."

He almost laughed then; I could feel it. I wanted it. I was more desperate for it than ever.

"I'll cheer you up. Okay? This night is already weird. What's one more thing we'll have to forget in the morning? Let's go swimming."

He pulled away from me, and my hand slipped off his arm. *"What?"*

I was already standing up.

"Yes, c'mon. Take your clothes off."

I reached for the bottom of my Siesta Playa tank top so I could pull the thin material off over my head.

"I'm your boss," he reminded me with a stern tone.

"No, you're not. Not *technically.* Todd Weaver is my boss. *Scott Durliat* is my boss. You are . . . just some guy on the beach." I waved off his concern. "Okay? Now come on."

I reached for the waistband of my shorts to push them down and didn't let my trembling hands stop me. I'd gone skinny-dipping on so many beaches in my life it didn't even faze me to be in my underwear in front of Cole. I had on sensible panties and a cute bra. Big deal. *Gulp.*

Cole was watching me like he'd never seen someone undress in his company before. His eyes caught on every inch of me, the dangerous parts like my breasts filling out my bra and my panties sitting slightly askew, and the innocuous ones too. My little constellation of freckles that sits a few inches to the right of my belly button held a real mystery for him.

I couldn't take it for another second.

His eyes raking over me felt as tempting as a caress.

"You're really just going to sit there?" I asked as I started to walk backward toward the water.

He frowned his most surly frown, peeling his eyes off me to stare at the ocean. Then he warned, "Swimming at night is really dangerous."

"Okay, well, you stay up there safely on the sand, and if I need help, I'll call out for you, okay? Meanwhile I'll be LIVING MY LIFE, COLE CLARK. GET UP, TAKE YOUR PANTS OFF, AND GET IN THIS WATER OR SO HELP ME *GOD*!"

"Stop shouting, okay? I'm doing it."

He was. He was standing and starting to unbutton his shirt.

"Not fast enough! My toes are already in the surf. It feels divine. Heaven on earth. Why were we ever sad?"

I watched him work on those buttons, undoing each one in quick succession, and then, near the bottom, he grew impatient and just tugged the shirt up and over his head before dropping it on the sand. My heart beat so fast in my chest it was all I could feel—that heavy pounding continued as he unbuttoned his pants and slid them down. He stood in nothing but boxer briefs, and I stood in absolute shock. I was expecting withered biceps, a spare tire around the middle, a little coin purse *down below*. Instead, I saw arms that could easily hoist me up against a wall, powerful legs, a noticeable *bulge*.

His toned physique made sense once I thought about it. I'd seen him in the gym once before, disgustingly early, on my way home after a midnight mystery-séance excursion deep in the jungle. He was running on the treadmill like a bionic man, probably fueling himself on thoughts of how he was going to make my life hell later.

I couldn't fathom him being this hot, and he took note of my reaction to him.

"You're being weird," he said as he started walking toward me.

I still tossed my arms out in protest. "You're not being weird *enough*! It's like you see me in my underwear *all* the time!"

I held my breath as he got closer, closer . . . then he walked right past me, out into the water. "I'm trying not to look."

"Because you're a gentleman?" I called out after him, anxious for the truth.

Ignoring me, he dove cleanly into the crest of an incoming wave and started to swim out to sea.

I was the one who'd suggested skinny-dipping, and now I was being left in the dust. I had no choice but to follow him or keep standing near the shore mostly naked, looking like an idiot.

I'm a strong swimmer, but I still couldn't keep up with Cole. He sliced through the water like he trained in this ocean twice a day, every day. He made it out to an underwater sandbar and then stood up and turned around to watch me, swiping his wet hair back off his face like he was being filmed for an Armani ad. I couldn't get distracted, though. The waves were picking up out here, and my lungs were starting to burn. The sandbar was farther than it seemed.

I was almost there when he leaned down and hauled me up so I stood in waist-deep water.

"I was going to make it just fine," I huffed. In reality, I was glad for the rescue. I could barely catch my breath.

His hands were still on my arms, hotter than a thousand degrees, when he shrugged. "I thought I saw a shark coming for you."

"*Cole.*"

I shoved him playfully, not falling for it. I'm not scared of creatures that lurk in the deep. I know what lives in these waters: tuna, reef sharks, barracuda, boned fish, stingrays. They sound scary, but they just want to be left alone.

But just then, I *swear* I felt something slither against the bottom of my right calf, and I let out a bloodcurdling scream before jumping toward Cole.

He laughed as he caught me in his arms, steadying us so we didn't go tumbling back into the water. His grip tightened on my biceps reassuringly. "It's nothing. I'm sorry. I shouldn't have teased you."

"*Apologizing?* That's a first."

I laughed and went to pull back, to stand on my own two feet, but Cole didn't let me. Those hands grasped my arms like I would be in mortal peril if he were to let go.

Did he know what he was doing?

Had he forgotten who he was holding?

Me, of all people?

Slowly, I cocked my head back just enough to look up at him, and when our gazes locked, slow recognition set in, forming like a hot, heavy need in the pit of my belly. We were skin to skin, pressed together as tightly as two lovers. His chest expanded with each heavy breath, pushing against mine like a dare to come a little closer. I couldn't if I tried. We were already too close. A dangerous tangle of limbs.

I swallowed, and my gaze lowered to his lips, to that little salty tear resting on the edge of his mouth. I wanted to lick it away.

I shifted, turning my body only slightly, but enough that we were aligned now, chest to chest. More importantly, *hip to hip*. I felt him hardening, but I pretended not to, pretended this was all innocent fun, a PG exploration of each other's bodies. My hands slid higher over his pectorals, closer to his broad shoulders. It was exhilarating when it should have been terrifying. Relinquishing my arms, he grabbed around my waist, tightening his grip in fierce possession as a fissure of awareness spread like wildfire through my body.

We were equally to blame from that moment forward. Neither of us was stepping back, regaining sense. As my hand wrapped around the side of his neck, my thumb brushing against his pulse point, one of his hands traveled up along the side of my chest, toying with the frilly edge of my bra. We were falling into madness together.

It felt like we were circling an inevitable end, around and around and around. I grew impatient in those distended seconds, like the thing I wanted most was being dangled just over my head, out of reach.

Give it to me.

My fingers dug into his shoulder, and then, all at once, as though I had been given no warning at all, Cole bent down to kiss me. The sensation was too heady to grasp all at once, like suddenly everything burst to life inside me. Black and white swallowed by blinding color. I kissed him back with a frenzy I didn't recognize. I lifted up onto my toes as he pulled me into him. The moan that slipped past my lips sounded wanton and seductive, and I barely recognized this version of myself, this woman practically crawling up Cole like he was a palm tree. He must have sensed what I wanted—me, you, climb, yes—because he wasted no time hauling me up and winding my legs around his waist. Our bodies met just below the surface of the water. His rigid abs teased the inside of my thighs as we broke apart for no more than a millisecond, realigned our mouths, and started kissing again. This time, with tongues. Oh hell. I was lost. His hands were in my hair, tangled in the wet strands, as our lips pressed together harder, demanding more. It felt like a fever consuming me until I felt sick with need, *crazed* with it.

I was shredding his skin, tearing at him like there was something he still wasn't giving me.

I felt a spreading warmth, a hot jolt of desire when his hands left my hair so they could wrap around my upper thighs. He repositioned me around his hips, and I felt him—hard as steel—as he rubbed against me. All that delicious pressure still wasn't enough. I wanted more. I tried rolling my hips, chasing that feeling with everything I had, as his mouth slanted over mine, and we kissed like the government was about to decree that kissing was banned for life. *These two mouths shall never touch again.*

He was so fucking passionate.

I did *not* peg him to be like that. Cole is always so restrained, working his tidy little desk job, quiet and severe. But this version of Cole? This version was peeling me apart. Mr. Suit and Tie with his rough hands and sexy mouth. My bra strap slipped down my shoulder, and Cole helped it along, covering my wet skin with his warm palm, taking the weight of my breast in his hand like he owned it. My eyes pinched tight, and I leaned my head back, feeling the arousal thrumming between my legs. His thumb rolled over the tip of my breast, toying with me, and my legs clenched around him. He released a visceral groan, and then—like he couldn't hold off for one more second—he bent to take my breast in his mouth. His tongue lapped over me, and I gasped, losing control when he began to slowly *suck.*

Panic seized me so swiftly that I didn't think. I broke away and pushed him, *hard.* I scrambled back and caught myself, adjusting my bra strap, regaining my footing so I didn't fall back in the dark water.

We stood across from each other on the sandbar as the ocean waves lapped against us. We were breathing like we'd just held our breath underwater past the point of pain, gasping with desperation. My breath hitched as it mixed with a repressed sob. I shook my head, staring at him.

His eyes were still full of arousal, but it was dimming by the second, shifting, *dying.*

What did we just do?! I screamed in my head.

WHAT DID WE JUST DO?!

The question was so loud I almost covered my ears, like that would help dampen the alarm bells. I couldn't hear anything, not the rhythmic crashing of the waves on shore, not my name slipping from his lips.

I acted on pure impulse as I turned and fled back to the beach, swimming like I was being chased by a giant sea monster intent on swallowing me whole. I scrambled onto the sand and grabbed my clothes, tugging my shirt on and not even bothering with my shorts. I wanted to get away from Cole, away from my mistake, as fast as possible. I could only see things through the lens of my panic as I rushed away from that beach. What could have been consensual and fun felt dirty and wrong, like I'd thrown myself at Cole and he'd been forced to accept it. *I* was the one to invade his privacy on the beach when he was all alone. *I* forced us into the water. *I* jumped on him. And maybe now that I'm thinking back, I kissed him first. I can't remember it clearly.

I've replayed that night in my head over and over, trying to piece the puzzle together from different angles. Sometimes I can convince myself that Cole was equally as invested, just as turned on as I was. The moans weren't just slipping from my lips. Other times, I get so deeply embarrassed remembering it, it feels like someone is pressing a hot branding iron to my cheeks.

I considered calling in sick the next morning, to avoid the inevitable awkwardness, but I knew it would have to happen eventually. *Grab hold of the Band-Aid and rip that sucker off, Paige.*

I ran through all the possible excuses on my way to the main lobby: *Cole, oh my god. I was drunk last night. Sorry if I acted strangely!*

Cole, I think I sleepwalked last night!

Cole, I don't know how to explain this, but I fell prey to a Freaky Friday *situation. Yes, the early 2000s movie with Lindsay Lohan where two souls swap bodies, uh-huh. So if I did something—like kiss you hardcore while desperately clinging to you in the ocean—that wasn't actually me.*

Also, I was drunk.

I walked through the sliding doors toward the main lobby with shaking hands and a queasy stomach. Forgoing breakfast had been a bad idea, but the thought of forcing down even a single bite of scrambled eggs was inconceivable. Just inside, I froze and scanned the lobby, searching for broad shoulders and a familiar head of black hair. I looked past the tacky prints of sailboats, the sculpture of a swordfish that collected dust on the center table, the mom with a heavy Jersey accent telling off her kids while rubbing her temples— "Joseph Anthony! Antonia!

Giana! So help me, I'll lose my friggin' mind if yous guys don't stop jumping on those chairs!"

Cole was over by reception, dressed to the nines and put together like he'd just enjoyed a peaceful eight hours of sleep (propped upright in his coffin, of course). Never mind that I'd only managed thirty fitful minutes bookended by a lot of agitated tossing and turning. In the mirror that morning, my skin looked pale, and no amount of concealer could hide the dark circles under my eyes.

When he first saw me, I almost thought I saw worry play across his features, but as soon as I recognized it, it was gone. I doubted it had ever been there as he started to cross the room to get to me. I wondered if the truce he called for last night still held true in the light of day.

"Good morning, Ms. Young."

I immediately bristled. *Last names?* Who was he kidding?

"Morning, Mr. *Clark*."

He scanned the area of the lobby over my head and continued with a succinct announcement meant just for me. "To be clear, last night never happened."

My face fell before I could prevent it. If he looked down, he'd witness the hurt that sank its claws into me, twisting my stomach, shredding me to pieces.

What had I expected Cole to do this morning, after I bolted away from him? Gift me a smile? *Suggest a round two?*

Oh god.

Clarity gnawed its way to the forefront of my thoughts. I felt like a fool. *Worse.* Up until then, I hadn't hated Cole. Not at *all.* Deep down I knew I wanted his attention—his approval—more than anything. But "last night never happened" formed a thick sheath around my heart, so that anything Cole did or said from that moment forward only served to further my bad opinion of him.

He chose a blue tie today? That's so like him, to spoil my favorite color.

Another all-staff email? Surely, he's only doing it to annoy me.

I convinced myself my hard feelings at hearing his rejection only had to do with the fact that I hadn't been the one to turn him down first. *Yes*, that's it. I hated coming in second place.

So I played into that. I harnessed all those false feelings and shrugged indifferently as I replied with a nasty little "Oh thank god."

It felt good to pretend I felt nothing but relief at hearing his words.

"Never happened," I agreed quickly, eager to set things to rights with him. Well, as "right" as we could ever be. I imagine if we polled a group of board-certified psychiatrists, they would unanimously agree that Cole and I are dysfunctional at best, damaging on average, and at worst downright destructive. The product packaging for our relationship would warn that prolonged contact with Cole Clark or Paige Young may result in nausea, bleeding from the ears, and homicidal tendencies.

He reached up to adjust his tie, ensuring it lay directly flat in the center of his chest. Only then did he look down at me. My stomach did a little swoop and dip when our gazes met.

He gave me a quick audit, checking me over to make sure I was still in one piece after last night. Sure, yes, my limbs were intact. I wasn't down a finger. But my insides? Total goop.

Could he tell how badly I slept? Did he notice the unkempt top bun I'd had to do because I'd collapsed into bed with my hair still wet from the ocean last night?

His mouth flattened into a disapproving line. Then he gave me clear instructions. An alibi. "You went straight back to your dorm. I was never on the beach reading—"

"*Wallowing*," I corrected. "All alone in a sad pit of despair."

His eyes crinkled at the corners, not with anger or annoyance but with mischief. My relief was palpable. We could reset, just like last time. It wasn't too late. These hard feelings could go away, if only I forced them to.

He looked away, back to scanning the lobby. "Right. If someone asks, you can tell them you spent the evening like you usually do, brainstorming new ways to torment me."

"And *you* spent the night alphabetizing your ties by brand while imagining what it would be like to have a friend."

His mouth tightened. His brown eyes pierced me. "Is that what you think I need? A friend?"

"You're right. I can't imagine you with a friend. You need a hench-man. A three-headed dog to help warn people away." I tapped my chin as I hummed in thought. "What would you name it . . ."

He tilted his head, watching me with an expression that said, *By all means, continue.*

"Cole Jr."

He couldn't keep the amusement off his face. He wasn't laughing. No, no. That would be preposterous. But he was looking down at me like he thought I was absolutely fantastic. That, or deranged. It was hard to tell.

"You left your shoes on the beach when you ran off last night. I left them by your door. Figured you wouldn't be able to survive without your beat-up hiking sandals . . ."

He stared pointedly down at my feet, and I clicked my heels together like Dorothy.

I was wearing a *second* pair of beat-up sandals. For the record, I have this exact style in three colorways; I hate that he probably knows that.

"I'm surprised you didn't keep them for yourself as a little memento from the best night of your life."

His eyebrows shot up. *"Best night?"*

It looked as though he was considering the possibility for a moment before eventually casting it aside. He merely shrugged. "It was informative."

Informative, my ass. HIS MOUTH WAS ON MY . . .

I lifted my chin, threw back my shoulders, and donned my armor. "Informative, *yes.* Just for the record, you kiss . . . differently than I was expecting."

He frowned, eyeing me speculatively. "In what way?"

"I don't know . . . it's hard to explain."

I desperately wanted to look at his full, pouty lips, but that would surely give away my X-rated thoughts, so instead, I looked down at his hand and remembered how intoxicating it felt when he used it to haul me against him. He has quite the grip strength. Who knew?

Beneath my careful scrutiny, his hand flexed, and then he tucked it away into his suit-pants pocket as if it were giving away all his dark, sordid secrets. Those hands did a lot of his dirty work last night. I remember what it felt like when he slid down the strap of my bra, when his fingers bit into my skin, when he cupped my breast and toyed with my—

"Sorry I've ruined you for all other men," he quipped, tugging me back to the present.

I shot him a glare. "Ha ha. *Hardly.*"

His head tilted as he studied me. "Your cheeks are flushed." Realization dawned, and I could feel the energy shift between us as he regained the upper hand. "Are you thinking back on it right now? *At work?* How depraved . . ."

I pressed my hands to my face, *Home Alone* style, to conceal the evidence. "I walked briskly on my way here. That's why I'm flush. Last night? Pfft. I barely remember any of it."

"Liar."

Of course I was lying. I could recreate the entire night from beginning to end with painstaking detail. The moonlight reflected in Cole's brown eyes. The gentle pressure of his lips on mine. The slow teasing warmth that spread through my body, a promise of what was to come.

I shivered, and he saw it. The edge of his mouth moved, and I couldn't stand it—him circling the truth, so close to stealing the innermost part of me. I took a step closer, grabbed his tie, and yanked it so it was just slightly askew. God, it felt good. Juvenile, yes, but we were far beyond acting our age at this point.

"*Nothing happened,*" I reminded him, effectively ending the conversation like I was slamming together two sides of a heavy book just as I'd gotten to the good part. I was going to climb to the top shelf in the library, way up high near the ceiling where the cobwebs cover the spines of the books. I'd find a dark spot, and I'd shove our book there, hiding it away once again.

His shoulders stiffened, and he looked away with a firm set to his jaw. "Exactly."

Soon after The Thing That Never Happened, I had a hard time reconciling it. I didn't tell a single person about that night, and Cole must have kept his mouth shut, too, because word never spread through the resort, *thank god*. For the first few days I lived in a perpetual state of dread that Lara or Camila or someone else on staff was going to waltz up to me with a knowing smile and say something painfully accurate like "*Girl!* Oh my god! I heard you threw yourself at Cole!" But when the dust settled and I realized that I'd somehow gotten away with it, my feelings turned inward. They cocooned into me, all day, lying dormant and quiet, only to be reborn at night as I lay awake in my bed. I fantasized about every part of that night with Cole, but in different ways. Occasionally, I would replay it all from start to finish, imagining slightly different endings. Most of the time, my musings were mundane: our kissing would shift into heavy petting and so on. Sometimes, though, my imagination ran wild. The fantasy would end with Cole dragging me back to the shore so he could ravage me like some wicked pirate or, *or*, he'd not even bother taking me back to shore. Angry, possessed, in desperate need of me, he'd tug my panties aside, and we'd have rough sex right there on the sandbar.

I tormented myself with make-believe scenarios to the point where it started to become painfully obvious that I had a problem. A big six-foot-two, black-haired C-O-L-E problem.

Fortunately, Blaze started working at Siesta Playa two weeks later. A perfect distraction.

Chapter Nine
PAIGE

Yesterday, I had my chance with Blaze down by the pool, and Cole ruined it with that domineering-manager schtick. I'm sure he's been gloating about it ever since, walking around with a pep in his step. His evil deed for the month, done—*check*.

I just know he loves tromping around this place in those suits. He gets off on the power. If he had to wear cheesy Siesta Playa–branded merchandise like the rest of us, the spell would be broken. He'd shrink two feet, suddenly speak with a squeaky, high voice, and sprout a little rat tail.

That's my theory, at least, but it's yet to be peer-reviewed.

Today, I could leave well enough alone, but I have a fifteen-minute break before I have to lead an evening beach meditation, and I haven't seen Cole all day. Besides, I actually could use his help with something.

Past Siesta Playa's main lobby, down the hall from reception, in a quiet area of the resort meant solely for executive offices, I find Cole still hard at work. Everyone else is gone. Their doors are closed; their offices are dark. Todd probably clocked out at 3:59 p.m. and dashed straight for his car, tires squealing as he peeled out of the parking lot. Meanwhile, Cole's still standing at his desk. Yes, he has a standing desk, and I doubt it has anything to do with the harmful effects of living a sedentary lifestyle. He's simply too busy to sit. *Oh, there's a situation down in the spa? An argumentative guest in the lobby?* Why would he waste 0.01 precious seconds getting to his feet when he could already be out the door? If there's an opportunity for efficiency, Cole Clark is going to take it. I'm surprised he doesn't speed through the resort on a Segway or, at the very least, roller skates.

I'm not surprised he's still working. I imagine him there at his desk all night long. His version of sleep is standing with perfect posture, arms bent at exactly forty-five degrees, hands flexed like a Ken doll. He doesn't move or blink from the hours of 7:00 p.m. to 6:00 a.m. while his battery charges.

I peer through the cracked door of his office. He's standing in profile, hammering his fingers down on his keyboard with pistonlike precision. If he were forced to witness my hunt-and-peck typing strategy, he'd have an aneurysm.

"Knock, knock."

I tap my closed fist on the door and push it open a little wider.

He doesn't look up at me. In fact, he doesn't take his attention off his computer screen as he fires off a quick "No."

Just like that, he'd like me to see myself out immediately.

I don't have the energy to feign offense.

"As much as I would *love* to leave you alone, I have a matter of dire importance to discuss with you," I say, bypassing the invisible Do Not Enter line on the floor. I'm surprised he doesn't keep the place booby-trapped against me. Actually, I'm not certain he doesn't . . . at this very moment, a gallon-size paint can could be arcing down from its perch above the door to clock me in the back of the head. Just in case, I duck.

"Dire importance? *Who did you injure now?*" Quickly, he reaches for his phone to check the screen. His eyebrows furrow in confusion. "Dr. Missick hasn't called me."

"No one's hurt," I assure him with a casual eye roll before looking over my shoulder to make sure there's not a blowtorch primed to set my hair on fire.

He drops his phone back on his desk and resumes typing like he's in a competition to beat the world record.

"Well, I don't have time for any other dire circumstances, I'm afraid."

He leans over his desk and narrows his eyes, his gaze flitting across his computer screen like he's on a mission.

Is his job really that high stakes? He can't pause for even a *moment*? I find that a little hard to believe. I won't force him to give me the time of day. Instead, I'll coerce it out of him. All I have to do is peruse his office, glance over the framed diplomas, run my finger along the back of a chair that looks like it's never been used, take note of the mostly bare shelves.

It might seem weird, but I've never had a reason to be in Cole's office before. It's as sparse as I would have expected. There are no personal items whatsoever. No family photos, no childhood keepsakes. Not even a Glade PlugIn. The last I only make note of because in this confined space it's so easy to pick up the subtle notes of his cologne with its nicely spiced and wintery undertones. I've come to love that scent.

"If you break it, you buy it," he warns just as I start to pick up a heavy paperweight off a side table. It's an award for five years of excellence with the resort.

Right. I think better of it and decide to leave it alone. I couldn't hope to earn such a replacement trophy myself, and I doubt he'd be content to substitute in one I *could* earn: a *Year and a half of baseline competence* medal or a *More or less meets expectations* ribbon.

I turn on my heel to face him, surprised to find that he's not even looking at me. I narrow my eyes with suspicion. *How did he know what I was doing?*

"What are you working on?" I ask, stepping closer to him so I can peer over his shoulder at his desktop screen. My, my, my, that's a lot of information on those spreadsheets.

Like a teenage boy whose mom is about to walk in and find his hasty image search of "hot naked ladies," he scrambles to minimize his

Excel windows. The spreadsheets disappear before my eyes, revealing his desktop background. It's a screenshot of last year's record earnings report.

I wonder then if he has any dating profiles. I imagine his bio reads like a job posting:

Cole Clark, age 30

Seeking full-time romantic partner.

I enjoy pivot tables, closed loop communication, and achieving corporate synergy. I don't play games (unless rules are clearly defined).

Position Requirements:

5 years experience in polite small talk. Must be able to lift up to 2 pounds for occasional hand holding (waffle style preferred).

Benefits:

Requited love at fair market rate. To become vested after 4 years of service.

Is he on dating apps?

And why does the idea of him matching with some equally goal-oriented female cyborg twist my stomach into a tight knot? I can picture them now, nerding out over HTML codes and QuickBooks updates.

Or maybe that's not his type at all. Maybe he likes giggly girls who serve drinks at the Bistro. Yuck.

"I'd prefer to get this over with so I can get on with my night. What do you want?"

"Manners. Decorum. *A smile.*"

His scowl tells me I'm not getting a single one of the three, so I sigh. "You owe me."

His eyebrows arc up in disbelief. "*I* owe *you?*" He shakes his head. "I can't wait to hear where this is going . . ."

I step closer to him—attempting to go toe to toe—and appear as intimidating as possible. My blonde hair doesn't help with that. I should have worn a beanie.

"Yesterday at the pool, you scared Blaze away."

I cross my arms over my chest and cock my hip to the side. There; I'm no longer to be trifled with.

It's clear from the lack of contrition in his expression that Cole doesn't agree with my assessment of things. "He was on the clock, and last I checked, flirting with female staff doesn't constitute any of his daily tasks. He's not getting paid to ogle you in a bikini."

There's a distinct anger in Cole's tone. In fact, if he were someone else, *any* other man, I'd think he was jealous. However, with Cole, I know his anger lies solely in loss of productivity for the company. Equations are swirling in his head. *Maximum Drink Output – Bikini Observing = WARNING WARNING WARNING.*

"He wasn't *ogling* me," I press.

He all but snorts.

"His tongue was lolling out of the side of his mouth," he responds dryly. "If this were a cartoon, his heart would have danced out of his chest."

I hum like this is news to me. "Well, at least we're getting somewhere. You agree that Blaze is attracted to me . . ."

I dangle the sentence out until he's forced to give a slow, resigned nod.

I smile. "Good, now I need you to help me woo him over once and for all."

His expression clouds over with irritation. "That can't possibly fall to me. Go get Camila or Lara to give you advice about how to win over men, and leave me out of it."

His gaze shifts pointedly to the door in an invitation for me to leave.

I ignore him. "I've tried that, obviously. Camila and Lara have given me loads of advice and still . . . I've come up short with Blaze."

He remains unconvinced. "So why come to me?" he asks skeptically.

I know he trusts me as far as he can throw me. Which, strangely enough, might be pretty far, given the toned physique I can make out under his suit and tie. I saw him nearly naked on that beach two months ago. I know what lies beneath his prim and proper exterior. Maybe my theory about his suits holding all his power is wrong after all.

I clear my throat and refocus.

"Why *not* come to you? You're incapable of lying to me, Cole. In some people, honesty is a virtue, but for you it's just a weakness," I taunt, leveling a mind reader's gaze in his direction. "So tell me, where am I lacking?"

At first, he holds out. Long seconds pass as we endure a silent standoff.

Then, he props his elbow on his desk and crosses one of his ankles over the other, getting comfortable in his assessment of me. His throat constricts with a swallow as he gives me a drawn-out once-over. His perusal is so unnecessarily long it makes me want to squirm, especially as his gaze trails down my bare legs. When his brown eyes clash with mine again, they narrow shrewdly.

"Well, for starters, I think you're barking up the wrong tree. Blaze has the IQ of a gnat."

I bristle at his cruel tone.

"Well, he's who I want," I insist with a harsh finality. "And I'd be careful, *Mr. Money Man*. Disparaging the guy who brings in all that alcohol revenue for the resort isn't so wise."

He gives up leaning on his desk and instead tilts closer to me. The air shifts.

His breath is minty fresh, and I'm staring intently at his mouth as he begins. "Okay, you want Blaze? Here's what you're going to want to do."

I immediately wish I had a pen and paper to jot this down. He looks like he's about to dole out some seriously good advice.

"You'll need to buy a clicker." He air-clicks his thumb and makes a light popping sound effect with his tongue. "You can find one on Amazon. Oh, and grab a bag of M&M's—y'know, something small so he won't choke if he forgets to chew. Every time he displays some good behavior, like paying you any meaningful attention, you'll click the clicker and treat him. You'll have him eating out of your hand in no time."

I'm already giving him a *You're not funny* glare, my eyes narrowed into slits, but he continues, unperturbed. "Now, if he jumps up and starts pawing at you, you can try the choke chain. But remember, some guys aren't into that."

I'm already walking out of his office at this point, wishing I hadn't bothered in the first place.

"Have you tried one of those whistles?" he calls after me.

Cole, I decide, will be no help at all.

Chapter Ten

PAIGE

Sometimes you have to go after what you want. Love isn't going to just fall into your lap. I think whoever coined the phrase "Good things come to those who wait" probably just didn't want to have to pause Netflix and get up off their couch. Genius, when you think about it.

I don't have that luxury. It's time to make a move with Blaze once and for all.

I seek him out at work. The grotto isn't that busy since it's only 2:00 p.m.

He's behind the bar, slicing lime wedges and dropping them into a plastic container while he sways to the beat of the pop music playing over the speakers.

"*Blaze!* Just the man I was looking for!" I drum my pointer fingers on the counter.

He looks up, startled. "Uh . . ." Worry lines his forehead as he searches behind me. His eyes flit back up the path in both directions, like he's expecting someone else to appear. Cole, perhaps?

"It's just me," I say with a light laugh.

His demeanor visibly relaxes.

I made sure to wear my name tag today. It's pinned on my shirt, visible to anyone within a twenty-foot radius. Still, I straighten my spine and jut out my chest to make sure he sees it. *Paige.* Yes, that's my name. The effect my posture has on my breasts is a plus as well.

"So what's going on?"

"Just . . . slicing limes," he says with an easy smile. "Do you work today?"

"Yes, but I'm off at seven p.m., and I've been dying to try the new steak restaurant that opened last month. You know the one? Lara and Camila won't go with me . . . they aren't big meat eaters." This is a lie, of course. Today, they served hamburgers in the cafeteria for lunch. Camila ate a double with extra cheese. The juices oozed down her chin. Hopefully Blaze didn't notice.

He continues right on slicing limes, unbothered by my predicament. "Bummer."

"Yeah . . ."

Then he looks up, having put two and two together, albeit slightly slower than I would have preferred. "We could go?"

Ding ding ding!

"Okay! Tonight?"

He shrugs. "Why not?"

Mild enthusiasm aside, this could work.

"I'll meet you at eight? Umm . . . you know how to get there?"

This is a genuine question. Though well laid out and extremely intuitive, the resort grounds can be complicated for young children and . . . really anyone, okay? It's not just Blaze!

"I could draw a map," I suggest helpfully.

He laughs, but then he drops his knife to retrieve a pen and scrap piece of paper from behind the bar so that I'm forced to do it.

"So you know where the main lobby is, right?"

He looks stressed by the question.

"Okay, actually. We'll start from where we're standing right now."

Dear god, if Cole somehow catches wind of this, I'll die.

Camila and Lara are happy for me. Happy enough to insist I let them help me out as I get ready for my date.

"This eye shadow expired three years ago!" Lara says, holding up a brown shade she must have found at the bottom of my makeup bag.

"Makeup *expires*?!"

This is news to me.

Camila shakes her head and points to the bag she dropped on my bed when she first arrived. "Just use my stuff. It's in there. I brought it with me just in case."

Camila's behind me with a curling iron, concocting perfect beach waves before spraying my whole head with enough hair spray that I start to hack up a lung.

"Jesus," I say, waving my hand through the plume of particulates suffocating me.

"*What?* The island is humid. You want these curls to fall the second you step outside?"

I'm reminded over and over again that beauty is pain as they prepare me for my date. No simple outfit will do. They pour me into a red minidress that squeezes my boobs so tight I can't take a full breath.

When I complain, Lara levels me with a harsh glare. "Do you want to look insanely hot, or do you want oxygen? You can't have both."

"I'll take the oxygen," I answer swiftly, tugging my hair aside so that they can unzip the dress and find me something more practical to wear.

"Wrong."

Okay, then . . . apparently that was rhetorical.

On my way to my date, the absolutely best thing happens, and it's total happenstance! I'm just breezing past the executive offices in the main lobby (pacing, actually, back and forth)—when I accidentally bump into Cole leaving for the day. He has his suit jacket tossed over his forearm, a utilitarian leather satchel hanging over his shoulder.

When he sees me in my red dress, his eyebrows nearly touch his hairline.

He veers off the path and heads over. When he reaches me, his whistle is low and long, not quite a catcall, but effective in reddening my cheeks all the same.

"That's some dress. What's the occasion?"

"Oh, just a date," I remark like I'm exhausted about the prospect.

Another day, another date! God, I can't keep these men *off* me. I need a long stick.

He rubs his chin with his hand, looking away for a moment. Then when his gaze meets mine, it's sharp, almost spine tingling. "So the whistle worked," he notes. "Or was it the clicker?"

"I do enjoy your little witticisms, believe me, but if I stand here talking to you much longer, I'm going to be late."

"Where are you headed?"

"Smith's."

"That's over near staff housing," he remarks. I hate Cole's brain and his ability to cut through my bullshit so easily.

"Yes, well, I needed to check my mail," I lie.

Our mail gets sorted and stashed near reception.

"In those shoes?"

I look down, and down some more. My legs are miles long in these high heels I borrowed from Lara. They're a half size too small. In the morning, I'll be hobbling along, sporting blisters the size of Africa, but they're worth it just to watch Cole slowly swallow, his hungry gaze devouring my legs.

"These? They're *so* comfortable."

I try to shift my stance, to pop a hip and prove my point, but my ankle rolls, and I nearly go down. Cole reaches out to steady me, and I don't even push him away. I'm actually glad for the support.

"All right," he says with a long-suffering sigh. "Let's go. I'll walk you."

"If you insist." My tone is resigned, but my hand on his is desperately screaming *Do not let go of me.*

I should have practiced more in these high heels before I left my dorm.

"Why didn't Blaze come and collect you for your date? Surely he's dying to get his hands on you."

It occurs to me that Cole has his hands on me, securely, tightly, wonderfully. His arm is a tight band around my back. His hand squeezes my hip with just enough pressure that I don't have to worry about face-planting once we make it out onto the pebbled path and my ankles turn into spaghetti noodles.

"I think it's *so* much more fun to meet at the restaurant, don't you? That moment when you look up in a crowded dining room to find your date staring at you with unabashed *longing*." I pretend to shiver at the prospect of seeing Blaze like that.

"How sweet," Cole notes like the concept makes him viscerally ill.

"So what are *your* plans for the night?" I ask, staring up at him with my long mascaraed lashes. "Meeting Tamara somewhere? I saw you two flirting by the pool."

"We weren't flirting."

I hum like I'm barely interested in this conversation. "Really? Could have fooled me."

He frowns down at me, his gaze glued to my glossy lips. "I'm not hanging out with anyone. I have more work to do tonight."

"Oooh, sexy. *Tell me more.* Are you going to pop the cork on a bottle of wine while you *make love* to your spreadsheets?"

His gaze takes on a new challenging edge. He's had enough of my smart mouth. "You know who has good wine? *Smith's.* Maybe I'll go in and enjoy a glass while they prepare my dinner to go."

"You should!" I say, praying reverse psychology is a real thing. *"Definitely."*

Meanwhile, I think, *Listen here, you diabolical mastermind, if you so much as step foot inside Smith's, I'll . . .*

"Blaze!" I squeal with delight as I see him just up ahead, standing in front of the restaurant. I'm immensely relieved. A part of me regretted not checking in with him again this afternoon. I've been worried he'd find himself wandering aimlessly around the island, consulting my map in confusion as he reached a cliff's edge. *Well, it says to keep going forward . . .*

I step out of Cole's grasp and hurry toward Blaze, sending a silent thank-you to the inventors of concrete as my high-heeled feet touch solid ground again. Aware of our audience, I give Blaze a kiss on each cheek. It's something I've never done to anyone in my entire life, but it works out well.

"I *love* your dress." His eyes widen with appreciation as he steps back. *Thank you, Camila and Lara!* "Who's it by?"

"Oh . . . um . . ." I look down at it like that might jog my memory. Then I laugh. "I have no idea, to be honest." Do guys care about that sort of thing? I'm kicking myself for not reading the label. I could have impressed him with my fashion prowess.

"It suits you. It's the perfect silhouette for your body type."

"Thank you," I say, flustered by his genuine compliment.

Then Blaze sees Cole coming up behind me, and his entire demeanor changes. He blinks a half dozen times, like he's about to lose control of his bowels. "Oh, hello, sir."

I swear he's about to salute Cole. They're like the same age!

"Relax, you're not on the clock," I tease Blaze with a playful laugh.

He's still flustered, so I offer an explanation to help put him at ease. "I happened to bump into Cole on the way here. He's just going to order something to go while he enjoys a glass of wine at the bar. Don't mind him."

Blaze—probably aware that he has the opportunity to impress his superior—shakes his head. "No, no. You can sit with us while you wait for your food." He looks to me for backup. "Yes?"

I don't know why he bothers asking. He doesn't wait for my reply, which would have been a hard no. He's already leading the way toward the front door so he can hold it open for me and for Cole.

Much to my dismay, Cole follows right behind me. *So he's really going through with this?* Absurd. I can't wait to turn the tables on him one day. If I so much as see him eyeing a woman, I'll be sure to sabotage it the same way he's sabotaging this for me.

At the hostess stand, Blaze explains the situation to Sabrina. "We'll have one more dining with us. Hope that's okay."

Sabrina—who was slouching and looking at her phone before we walked in—now stands to attention once she sees Cole is in her midst.

"Mr. Clark, you guys, right this way."

I narrow my eyes and glare back at Cole as we begin to follow her. Is this how everyone treats him? Am *I* supposed to treat him this way? That ship has *sailed*.

We're being ushered to the best table in the house, the one with views of both the bustling kitchen and the sprawling ocean. Smith's is built up off the ground, high enough that you can see for miles, which is a fun little topic of conversation I could bring up with Blaze if only Cole weren't still here.

Once we reach the table, Cole pulls out my chair for me. Or he starts to before I yank it out of his grasp and finish the task myself. Blaze is talking to Sabrina, completely oblivious.

"*Do not sit down,*" I hiss under my breath. "Cole Clark, if you take that seat—"

He takes it and then rudely sets his leather bag on the fourth, unoccupied chair.

Great, now I'm on a date with Blaze, Cole, and that leather bag. It's like a cheesy '80s dating show. *Contestant Number One, what's your idea of a fun night out?*

Desperate for this charade to be over, I raise my hand and wave it wildly overhead until a waiter sees me. His eyes widen with worry, and he comes running over.

"Good evening, everyone," he says, winded. "Sorry about the wait. I'm Mason. I'll be taking care of you ton—"

"Mason, *pleasure*. I'll speed us along here a bit. He'd like to order food to go." I point to Cole; then I wave between Blaze and myself, even leaning toward him for emphasis. "*We* will be dining in, together."

Mason's smile turns placid. "Okay . . ."

Cole hands over his menu without even looking at it. "Hey, Mason, sorry to make it complicated. I'll take the fillet to go. Medium rare. Have them add on a side of the lobster mac and a Caesar salad. Also, while these two decide what they'd like to eat, would you bring us a bottle of the house cabernet?"

"What if I prefer white wine?" I interject.

Cole arches a brow at me. "Do you?"

"No . . ."

Blaze laughs awkwardly. "Cabernet is okay with me."

Mason nods and scrams, likely in a hurry to get away from me.

"So, Blaze, where are you from?" I ask, placing my elbow on the table at an angle that has my back turned to Cole, edging him out of the conversation altogether.

I've asked Blaze this question before, but hopefully tonight our wires don't cross.

"Los Angeles, and before that, New York."

"Big move. Are you happy here so far?"

"Yeah. I love it. I moved to Los Angeles for love, and it turns out that was a pretty dumb reason to haul my crap across the country. I got dumped a week after moving there."

"Yikes. That's hard. So why Turks and Caicos?"

He laughs. "It's actually funny. I thought I'd booked a flight to Turkey."

I blink really slowly, trying to process this.

He thought he . . .

"Wound up here by accident," he continues. "I didn't have enough money to get another flight." He shrugs and laughs it off. "So here I am. It worked out, though."

"I'm sorry." It's like my brain is fogged over, keeping me from understanding. "You wanted to go to Turkey, *the country?*"

"Yeah, I was supposed to go backpacking across Europe with a group of guys all summer."

Slowly, I ask, "And you wound up here by mistake, stayed . . . *and got a job?*"

Cole wisely keeps his mouth shut. I don't dare look at him.

Blaze laughs, but not hard *enough*, you know?

To him, it's something that could happen to anyone. Like, okay, I meant to go to Paris, France, but I ended up in Portland, Oregon, because they're both cities that happen to start with *P*. Whoops. *Guess I live here permanently now.*

The wine comes just in time.

Mason pours me a heaping glass, for which I'm incredibly grateful.

Blaze pushes back from the table. "Be right back. I need to use the little boy's room."

He leaves, and Cole and I don't say a word. I'm not sure we breathe. It's imperative that I don't look at him right now, or I'll break. I'm an *SNL* cast member midskit, trying to stay in character instead of losing it in a fit of giggles. I roll my lips between my teeth, press down, and keep a sharp focus on my wine. Cole clears his throat, only barely succeeding in stifling his laughter. My smile is fighting for its life, but I resist with everything I have.

"Turkey, huh?" he says, and I have to squeeze my eyes closed and think about sad things. A kitten stuck up in a tree, Bambi's dead mom, my credit card bill.

When I think I have my composure, I feign a superior tone and lay it on him. "What you see as a lost idiot stumbling through the world, *I* see as a free spirit adapting to new environments. How rare!"

"Imagine if he accidentally booked a flight to Syria. He'd be bartending for ISIS right now . . ."

A laugh bursts out of me before I can help it. Then I have to turn away and cover my mouth with my hand to keep him from seeing how much I'm struggling here.

Damn it, Cole.

Do not be funny right now. *Please.*

I sound suddenly weary when I finally manage to speak again. "You've made your point. Now leave."

"What point is that? I'm just here enjoying the company. Blaze is so . . ."

He swirls his wine in his glass with a slow taunt, and I nearly yank it out of his hand so I can dump it over his head. It's more than a little tempting. The sight of that dark-burgundy cabernet slowly dripping down his forehead would keep me satisfied for months to come.

"Don't," I warn.

". . . *endearing.*"

I shift so I'm fully facing him.

His gaze falls, and his jaw ticks. I look down and realize I'm nearly falling out of the top of this red dress. I'm a Victoria's Secret model on a casting call. I refuse to care. In fact, I play it up by leaning even more toward Cole as I respond to his needling in a sultry tone.

"*Blaze* isn't endearing. Blaze is just like his name, *a raging fire.* God, he looks at me and I just get so *hot.*" I let the word drip from my mouth, and as if it isn't erotic enough, I bite my lip and run my hand up my thigh like I just need to be touched there. *Now.* Cole's impenetrable force field splinters and cracks. His humor has burned away. Now he's *all* man. His heady gaze, his shallow breaths. He wants to eat me alive. I should stop, but I've never been good at heeding warnings. "Cole, a.k.a. *coal*, is just a fire that's gone out. Lukewarm ash . . ."

There's an invisible tug between us, a magnet drawing us together.

My gaze drops to his mouth, stained red from the wine. There's a little flutter of anticipation; like everything we do, all the teasing and taunting is just one big drawn-out foreplay session. It's maddening.

Cole looks like he's prepared to draw blood. Under the table, his hands must be biting into his thighs to keep from touching me. We're about to lose our heads. He'll swipe the contents of the table onto the floor and then hoist me up onto the tablecloth. Forget the fillet. He'll have me for dinner. I can imagine it. I've had his mouth on me before. I know how good it feels. How little I'd resist if he . . .

Then, *plop*. Cole's dinner gets dropped on the other side of the table.

"Here you go, man. I double-checked, and everything's in there, nice and warm."

Our moment is reduced to rubble.

Like we've been doing nothing beyond idle chitchat, Cole retrieves cash from his wallet and drops it on the table. I fold, then refold, my napkin in my lap, trying to regain my composure. Just before he stands, Cole pauses like he's mulling something over. I think he might draw us back to the conversation we were having . . . all that delicious tension hovering just on the periphery. Instead, he leans in close, his voice like a soft feather lightly touching my skin, and tells me, "Enjoy your date."

Then he walks out of the restaurant with his dinner.

Bereft doesn't cut it. I'm a hollowed-out shell as I watch him leave, wishing, for some inexplicable reason, that he was taking me with him.

Chapter Eleven

PAIGE

I don't have to wait long to see Cole again. He comes to find me the next morning as I'm manning the excursion desk in the main lobby. Of all my weekly tasks, the excursion desk is not the most exciting, but I don't mind it. I take pride in my position here, more so than anyone else on my team. Not to throw my friends and coworkers under the bus, but most of them are only here as a means to an end. I plan to be at Siesta Playa for the long haul. I've found my home here among people I truly care about, and hopefully one day, if I keep my head down and work hard, I'll get promoted. My friends, meanwhile, enjoy the perks of working in paradise, but they don't feel the need to go above and beyond for the sake of the resort. I understand where they're coming from—"*Why care about the corporate machine, it doesn't care about you*," yada yada—but it just so happens that I'm the one weirdo who actually really loves my job. Even this, manning an information desk, isn't so bad when I get to chat with guests and encourage them to try something new.

Splayed out in neat rows in front of me are informative pamphlets detailing every excursion we have to offer here at Siesta Playa: kayaking trips, meditation sessions, horseback rides—the list goes on. Guests can come to the desk and get up-to-date information, ask me questions, and reserve their spot for the week's activities.

I see Cole approaching out of the corner of my eye, and I make myself busy, straightening each individual pamphlet stack.

If this were a normal relationship, he'd keep it moving while throwing me a nod on his way to his office.

Since we're as far from normal as you can get without being officially labeled "deranged," he strolls right over and stops in front of the desk, too tall for his own good. I couldn't see around him if I tried.

I lay down one stack of pamphlets and grab another. I enjoy the sharp rap of papers as I force them to fall in line.

He drops something on the desk.

Coffee.

And not the burned motor oil they brew from dirt and pencil shavings down in the break room. He's ordered me something from the fancy resort coffee shop, the one I try to avoid so I don't get in the habit of spending eight dollars on a latte every morning.

"What's this?"

He nudges it toward me.

"Not poison, if that's what you're wondering. You have to pay extra for that sort of thing, and I'm short on cash."

I take a small sip to cover up my smile.

The taste of vanilla wraps around me like a warm hug.

Damn it. It's good.

"Thank you," I mutter with a hefty amount of reluctance.

Maybe he knows he owes me an apology after last night. Crashing my date? That's low even for us.

"So? How was the rest of your night? Did your spreadsheets fall in line?"

His dimple comes out to play. "They're getting there. What about you? How was your dinner?"

"My *date*? Great, thank you for asking. I'm so used to dealing with *difficult people*"—my gaze on him hopefully drives home my meaning—"I forgot how pleasant it can be to share polite conversation."

He narrows his eyes in assessment of my comment. "Is that right? Yeah, Blaze does seem polite."

I nod emphatically. "His little smiling face is probably pasted in the dictionary right underneath the word. Let's check."

His eyebrow quirks cynically. Maybe I'm laying it on too thick. "Tell me one thing you two talked about after I left."

Now, this proves difficult. I had quite the job of keeping our conversation rolling last night. I felt like I was working overtime trying to think of topics to discuss.

"We bonded over our love of steak," I swoon. "We split one, actually. It was *so* cute. The kitchen staff split it onto two plates for us, and they must have caught wind that we were on a date because they arranged our mashed potato piles into perfect hearts. I have a picture. Here, I'll show—"

He pushes away my phone. "So did Mr. Polite take you for dessert after?"

"He was too full."

Disappointing, I know. I put away my entire meal *and* had room for ice cream, but that's no surprise. I have a dinner column and a dessert column. They're totally separate, only I guess not for Blaze. I understand, though. He's very interested in keeping up his toned physique, and I can't blame him! I'm sure it helps him get good tips at the grotto. He didn't even touch his mashed potatoes. He scrunched his nose and made a comment about all the butter and salt. Meanwhile, my mouth was so full of the fluffy stuff I couldn't even respond beyond a hum of agreement.

"But after dinner, he walked me home . . ."

Well, he walked me to the outside of the restaurant, at which point he broke off to go meet some of his friends, but Cole doesn't need to know that.

"He and I, y'know . . ." I circle the pad of my finger on the desk like I'm scrawling Blaze's name in cursive in a journal.

Cole's throat bobs as he takes this in.

I puff out a breath like I'm still trying to recover.

"*After*, I couldn't wait to call and tell my parents all about him."

Well, I'd tried, at least.

They were out on a boat in the middle of the ocean when I called. The service was pretty spotty.

"You did what, hon?" my mom asked, shouting into the phone.

"I went on a date!"

"You *ate* a date?"

Yes, Mom, I'm placing an international call from halfway around the world to let you know that I just finished eating a piece of fruit from a date palm tree. I thought you ought to know.

I sighed and tried a different tactic. "I went out with a *man*!"

"Oh, that's exciting. Was it Cole?"

I panicked. "*No!* Not Cole!"

Yes, my parents know about Cole, and it was a total accident on my part. When I first moved here, my parents were slightly worried about me adjusting to life on the island, so I fibbed and told them I'd already made a ton of friends. I mentioned Lara and Camila, who were actually my friends already, but for some reason . . . I also told them about Cole. It felt like he *should* be included! Back then, our plans of mutually assured destruction were already taking up a lot of my time. If I put the same energy I use thinking about Cole toward, say, learning a second language, I'd be fluent *ten* times over.

"What was this other man's name, then?" my mom asked.

"Blaze."

"*Blake?*"

"BLAZE."

I shrug. "Yeah, anyway, they were *really* excited for me. They can't wait to meet him."

"Moving pretty fast, no?" Cole asks while reaching for a pen on the desk. He whirls it around casually like it's a helicopter blade.

"I guess it's true what they say: when you know, *you know*," I say with a confident smile.

"So then, it's settled. Blaze is the man for you."

Now he's squeezing the pen so hard, his knuckles are white.

"Yes."

The word is resolute and emphatic. A nail in a coffin.

Why does that send a frisson of panic through me?

He drops the pen, and it clatters to the desk. I frown, staring down at it as Cole starts to walk away. His name spills out of me before I can help it.

"Cole—"

I lean forward, suddenly desperate. A million possibilities could spring forth out of me.

. . . *maybe you aren't so bad.*

. . . *maybe I owe you an apology.*

. . . *maybe this thing between us has gone too far.*

. . . *maybe I'm sick of pretending I hate you.*

All the truths wage war with each other, lodging in my throat, so that all I manage is a weak "Thanks for the coffee."

Chapter Twelve
PAIGE

It's today! *Today!* It's happening!

The Nifty after Sixty crowd has vacated the hotel. They packed up their CPAP machines, dentures, knee braces, and hearing aids. They hobbled back onto the mainland just in time to have their rooms scrubbed clean and filled by a group of people so entertaining it feels like Christmas morning.

I don't even bother with a full breakfast. I grab some buttered toast from the cafeteria and scarf it down as I walk-run to the hotel's main lobby, practically elbowing people out of my way in an attempt to get there even faster. *Oof! Sorry! Sorry!* But between you and me, I'm not sorry. I would tackle and trample over people to get to the lobby. My shift doesn't start for two hours; I could be off in dreamland right now, but I purposely set my alarm early. In fact, I regret not camping out here all night.

The doomsday preppers convention is actually titled the Survival Preparedness convention, but these people aren't fooling anyone. Almost as soon as I come to a screeching halt in the lobby, I see a camo-clad enthusiast spare the use of his tactical laser-sighted "hatchet knife" and instead tear into his freeze-dried meal pack with his teeth.

"Hoo-rah!" he shouts, to no one person in particular, before eagerly sniffing the powdery contents. "Ooh, goody, corned beef hash."

For reference, it's 7:30 a.m. He's just been presented with a complimentary fruit cup and a mimosa. He's in no need of survival food.

"What did I miss? *What did I miss?!*" Camila asks, rushing through the side doors of the lobby. She's in a hurry this morning as well. She's in uniform, but her hair isn't done. She's still working through a cup of yogurt, and her eye makeup is smeared. Her shoe is only half on her right foot.

"Nothing!" I assure her with giddy anticipation. *"Nothing!"*

Now, the thing I love most about this convention is the pageantry of it all. You cannot say these men (and handful of women) don't put their heart and soul into this hobby. *Yes*, hobby. Don't get it twisted. The army fatigues, the eye black, the night vision goggles—none of it is serving a purpose here. What is that man going to do with his three-in-one Antarctic-approved parka on a tropical island in August? *Who cares?!* I love it!

Another important thing to mention is that most, if not *all*, of these "survival" items are brand new. The guy currently stuck in the turnstile entrance—*"Help! Someone help!"*—still has the tags hanging off his desert-op jacket.

I catch wind of a conversation taking place beside me. A man who looks like he's currently on the run from raiders in a zombie apocalypse has unzipped his oversize military-issue pack (because none of these people would be caught dead traveling with a normal suitcase) so he can show off his new gear to his friend. "Yup. These are my ice-assault socks. These ones? Rock-infiltrator socks. And of course, I've got my sand-raid socks."

Across the lobby, I hear, "Damn it! I forgot my sleeveless holster shirt."

Then, at the front desk, a man asks, "Now, do the rooms come with down pillows? Because I'm allergic to most synthetic alternatives."

I'm immersed in my viewing experience—a veritable fly on the wall—when Cole walks up and falls in line with Camila and me. Without a word, he joins us in surveying the scene. He's sipping coffee slowly. I'll bet it's his second or third cup. Not that it matters. Slightly more caffeine won't suddenly make these people make sense. I want to look up at him and crack a joke. I know he finds this as silly as I do. We'd never admit it, but we share the same sense of humor. I've been in group meetings and conference rooms where something funny happens—a tab is left open on Todd's computer with the search "hair plug Groupon"; Todd has a disastrous Freudian slip in which he introduces Alicia, the busty new accountant, to us all as our new *accountit*. I'll search frantically around the room for someone to share the moment with, and then I'll see Cole, with his head down, smiling to himself, completely in on the same joke I am.

"This week won't be easy," he starts. "Every year these people devise new ways to test my patience. Last year it was an underground government they ratified within the first forty-eight hours. By the time we got word of their insurrection, they'd already established a currency and trade routes to neighboring islands." As Cole continues, he sounds like a tempered war general giving a prebattle pep talk to his otherwise doomed warriors. "We'll be outnumbered . . . but we *will* survive."

I almost pump an imaginary sword in the air and pound my chest plate, responding with a mighty "*For the king!*"

"Camila? Where do you start today?" Cole asks, keeping his attention on the growing crowd.

"I have a deep-sea fishing charter that leaves in about an hour."

"Okay, make sure Oscar goes with you. After last year, I don't want to take any chances."

Oh right. I'd almost forgotten about that.

One of these guys insisted on catching fish with a harpoon rather than a fishing pole. The details are fuzzy. I'm not sure the boat captain knew about the harpoon beforehand, and things devolved quickly. A guest ended up in the water by mistake, screaming "Mayday! Mayday!" instead of listening to the boat captain's calm instructions to swim over and find the ladder to get back up into the boat. Or, at the very least, grab ahold of the life preserver they'd tossed in.

"Paige?"

Cole's looking down at me with careful assessment, as if he might be genuinely worried for my welfare.

"I'm taking a group out on a hike, and I already know how it's going to go . . ."

I did a hike with these guys last year. One guest came prepared to suck murky brown groundwater through an off-brand LifeStraw before wiping his mouth on his sleeve and raving about the 99.99 percent filtration abilities. The rest of the group was suitably awed, but given the opportunity to sample it for themselves, 99.99 percent stuck to their run-of-the-mill CamelBaks.

"But if you're worried about it," I continue, "I could take someone with me. Oscar's taken, but maybe Blaze?" I say it like the thought had only *just* occurred to me. *Oh right, that one guy, Blaze. He could work.*

Cole's mouth flattens into an unamused line. "Somehow I think you'll manage just fine without an accomplice."

Right. Good to know he values my well-being far less than Camila's. She gets a beefy Australian bodyguard. *I* have to fend for myself.

◆ ◆ ◆

The hike takes it all out of me. The guys aren't even listening to me talk about the trail's history. Like toddlers intent on putting anything and *everything* in their mouths, they immediately home in on the plants surrounding the path.

"What's edible here?" one of them eagerly asks.

"Oh . . . actually, I'm not an expert on that. Let's stick with the trail mix the resort provided us. If you're allergic to nuts, I also have some jerky."

Not two seconds after I finish this polite but assertive recommendation, one guy picks a few berries off a bush and eats them, claiming they're "completely harmless and chock full of fiber."

His tongue's already swollen to twice its normal size by the time I get him back to Dr. Missick.

There are two other preppers sitting in the doctor's waiting room when we arrive. One presses an ice pack against a pronounced goose egg on his forehead. The other clutches a barf bag, his face ashen, eyes glassy. I recognize him as the corned beef hash guy from the lobby that morning.

"Turns out, those things *do* expire," he tells his friend just as Dr. Missick opens the door with sweat trickling down his forehead. He sees me and groans. "Good god. *What now?*"

At dinner in the staff cafeteria, we all exchange war stories from the day. Cole's whiteboard in the break room has been claimed by a new countdown.

DAYS UNTIL THE PREPPERS LEAVE: 4.

"4" is written in red and circled a hundred times over.

That night, I linger in the lobby at the excursion desk as long as I can manage it, wanting every morsel of action I can get. My eyes eventually grow too heavy, though, and I know I'll need to rest up for tomorrow if I'm going to survive another day with these guys.

I'm taking a shortcut around the back of the resort when I see Cole outside, just past the double doors. Oof. He looks like he's been through the wringer a time or two. He's shucked off his suit jacket and rolled up his shirtsleeves. His hair is mussed, too, like he's been tugging at the roots all day in exasperation. He's not alone; he's talking to Beverly from HR and Annabelle, one of the singers from the resort lounge.

At first I think they might all be commiserating. If Cole were a smoker, he'd be draining a pack right now. No doubt his nerves are shot after today. I wonder how many fires he had to put out. How many staff members he had to placate. How many weapons he had to confiscate from disgruntled guests. *"Come on, now. This isn't a weapon, it's my hunting machete!"*

Only upon closer inspection, I realize that Annabelle is crying and shaking her head. Her shoulders are quaking, and Beverly is rubbing her back, trying to console her. I can't see Cole's expression, but it makes my stomach hurt, seeing them like that. I'm tempted to step closer, somehow insert myself in a situation that has nothing to do with me just so I can get some answers, but I wisely leave well enough alone, scurrying along before any of them see me.

I don't have to wait long for answers.

I'm working through a bowl of oatmeal in the cafeteria the next morning when Lara takes the seat across from me and hisses, "Annabelle got fired last night!"

My bite gets lodged in my throat, and I force it down with some effort. "What?"

"Yeah, she's gone. Like *gone*. Camila's dorm is right next to hers. She said she saw Annabelle leaving the resort this morning with all her stuff loaded on a cart. A security guard was with her, but Camila thinks he was just trying to help out. Not like escort her off resort premises or anything, but who knows?!"

My stomach squeezes tight. "How sad. I actually saw Cole talking to her last night. I knew something was wrong, but I didn't realize *that's* what was going on."

"Wait! You saw it happening?!"

I shake my head, unsure.

"It could have been something else . . . ," I mutter lamely.

She shakes her head, adamant. *"He's the one who did it."*

My body goes rigid as I meet her gaze. "How do you know?"

Lara checks over her shoulder like she's paranoid someone's listening in on our conversation. Once she confirms we're in the clear, she leans in and speaks fast. "There have been rumblings going around for a while about some layoffs. This is the third one in a week. First it was that old clown, which, okay, yeah, we all saw that one coming. Then a few days ago, one of the boat captains got fired. It was Dale, you know him? We assumed he deserved it, too, messed up or something, because he's sort of like that. He's late for his shifts *all* the time. But now with Annabelle getting fired too? What are the odds? I mean, everyone getting the axe is from *our* department. How do we know we're not next?!"

I refuse to believe it. "No, c'mon. Maybe it's a coincidence? We don't know for certain that all three of them didn't have it coming. You said it yourself, Dale wasn't the best employee . . . and not to be insensitive, but I've heard Annabelle sing and . . . you know what? Maybe the stage wasn't for her. When one door closes, another door opens, right? And the clown . . ."

I shiver just thinking about him.

My little speech does nothing to settle Lara's suspicions. She's as resolute as ever as she shakes her head. "I'm not buying it. Word on the street is that Cole and Todd are in cahoots. Annabelle told Tamara, who told Camila, that while Cole was firing her, he said something about how they want to reconfigure the resort staff and make this place 'more efficient.'"

Efficient?! Cole loves efficiency.

Crap.

"I swear to god, if I lose my job, I don't know what I'm going to do." She's already spiraling. "I have nothing saved. Nowhere to go. My life back home . . . it's just—" She shakes her head and pushes her tray of food away. She suddenly looks like she might be sick.

Before I've fully thought it through, I'm volunteering. "I'll talk to him, okay? I'll talk to Cole."

"Oh thank god. Just, will you please put in a good word for me?" She laces her fingers together with a plea. "Make sure he knows how important this job is to me."

"Of course, yes."

I agree to go through with it, but after I toss my barely eaten breakfast into the trash on the way out of the cafeteria, I wonder if I should have just kept my mouth shut and let her vent. Why did I feel the need to try to play the hero? Besides, I'm still not certain I believe Cole's a part of this. Deep down, I know he's not that cruel. He might not be great at showing it, but he really cares about the staff at Siesta Playa.

When one of the older groundskeepers, Vincent, hurt his back last year when he was painting on the property, Cole didn't fire him. He trained him to answer phones in reception while he healed up, and Vincent did great. He still picks up shifts in the lobby every now and then when he wants extra spending money. When Anita needed extra time off after having her baby, she told me Cole fixed it with HR so that she was given an additional six weeks of paid leave.

He's not heartless. I know it. This is just a big misunderstanding.

But . . . there's also this nagging feeling that Cole *would* put the needs of the company first, before any of us. I know he prides himself on running this place like a well-oiled machine. What if he *is* behind this?

I have to know. Now. I was going to wait and try to catch Cole later, but this will drive me crazy. I have thirty minutes to kill before I need to be down on the beach for surf lessons, and if I wait around until the end of the day to talk to Cole, I'll probably lose my nerve. So after I leave the cafeteria, I head straight to Cole's office, waving at reception as I pass them by. The two women give me a sheepish wave back, like they know something I don't. *What? Am I really the last person to hear about these rumors?!*

I grow queasy, and I'm tempted to turn back, but then I think of how desperate Lara was at breakfast. She and Camila have been so kind to me; this is the least I can do. No one understands Cole like I do. He and I can talk this through. I'm sure there's a simple explanation for the layoffs. There has to be.

After I'm done, I'll carry the good news back to Camila and Lara, and the others, and we won't have to spend the rest of the day worrying over something that's not that big of a deal. Probably just watercooler gossip that's gotten out of hand.

I walk down the executive hallway, experiencing déjà vu from the other night when I went to Cole's office to ask him for advice about Blaze. That seems like small potatoes now, frivolous and silly compared to what we're about to talk about. I brace myself as I pass office after office. Every door is shut except for Cole's. He's left his slightly ajar, just like last time. I'm about to knock and see myself in when two voices drift out into the hall.

Cole and Todd are inside talking.

"How did Annabelle take it?" Todd asks.

"Hard, but I think ultimately it was the right decision for the company. We offered her a severance package and the option to stay on in a different department, which she ultimately refused."

I go absolutely rigid with shock. My hand—the one that's poised, ready to knock—stays frozen in the air.

"Good," Todd says, sounding a little too giddy about it. "I knew I could count on you. Little by little, we'll continue trimming the fat. There's a storm headed our way that should help us. With any luck, we'll sustain some damage, which will help justify continued layoffs."

"That could work," Cole confirms.

I finally move, inching just a little closer and pressing myself against the wall. A terrible feeling settles over me as I continue eavesdropping. I feel like I'm listening in on two diabolical villains plotting to take over the world. Up until this point, I always had Todd in a league of his own. Gross, smarmy Todd with his perpetual bad breath and his beady little eyes. Now I realize I might have been wrong not to include Cole right along with him.

It's easy to miss. Cole, unlike Todd, carries himself so well. He's handsome and well dressed. I genuinely thought he cared about his employees, about . . .

"Who's next on the chopping block? Paige?" Todd suggests my name like I'm nothing, a speck.

My chest painfully constricts as I hold my breath.

"Yes. She'll be gone by next week," Cole promises without a single ounce of remorse. His tone is so clipped it snips something inside me.

Gone?

WHAT?

He could be talking about a perfect stranger, a nameless nobody.

The realization makes it feel as if I'm losing my footing and falling backward.

How could I have been so stupid? *So oblivious?*

This is their plan? They're going to fire me?

For a year, Cole and I have shared a playful rivalry, one I assumed was filled with shallow hostility and harmless banter. I thought we shared a perverse sense of loyalty to each other, even some kind of strange little friendship, but I was wrong. To Cole, apparently, the rivalry was the real deal all along.

We were never friends. I mean nothing to him. He wants me gone.

All of that is *crystal clear* now.

The realization comes as such a sharp betrayal I feel physically sick from it.

Leave it up to Cole to hurt me where it matters the most. He's really thought this one out. This is his grand finale: strip Paige of the thing she loves most! Torture the girl who's never had a real home until now!

It's brilliant. I have to hand it to him. If he succeeds in firing me, I'll no longer have a place here at Siesta Playa—no more work family, no more camaraderie. I'll be back at square one.

I shudder as the thought sinks in.

I've built a sanctuary for myself here, and with the snap of his fingers, Cole plans to take it all away.

An ugly twisted feeling starts to grow in my gut: pure hatred. How could he do this? How could he look me in the eyes day after day while plotting against me? Does he even have a plan for execution, or will he just come find me one day and explain in a simple, flat voice that I'm fired? *Pack your things and leave.* He'll dress it up in legalese. I'm sure he'll have an entire speech preapproved by HR that will include all the important talking points. Maybe he'll even offer me the same severance he gave to Annabelle. In my wildest dreams, during this exchange, I'd take the heel of my hand and shove it up against his face. With any luck, I'd succeed in breaking his nose. *You can take that severance and shove it up your—*

Cole walks over to the door to close it, but I don't move out of the way fast enough. Even against the wall, I'm not hidden well. He sees me and comes to a sudden stop as our eyes lock.

I've never felt emotion like this, like red-hot flames are licking me from the inside, crawling up my legs, my waist, consuming me. He must see how much I hate him. I'm not doing a damn thing to mask my feelings.

I expect him to mirror them. After all, I'm eavesdropping outside his door. Though anger doesn't seem to factor into the equation for Cole. It's panic that seizes his eyes first as they widen into round saucers. Then, his eyebrows furrow with worry. He's telling me something—screaming at me in silence—but I can't see past my own hurt right now.

Worried I'll make good on the fantasy of breaking his nose right here and now, I whip around and race down the hall, grateful that at least my tears don't come until I'm far enough away that he can't see them.

Go. To. Hell. Cole. Clark.

Chapter Thirteen
COLE

I've seen Paige sun kissed and happy on the beach, muddy and tired after a long hike, annoyed and on the brink of losing her patience with a difficult guest, drunk in the shower, bikini clad at the pool, and mesmerizingly beautiful on a sandbar under the stars. Never did I imagine seeing her like I did just now outside of my office.

The humor in her eyes, that light she always carries?

I sufficiently killed it.

When I caught her standing in the hallway outside my door, she didn't bother to try to hide her emotions. Every raw feeling bubbled to the surface. It was like watching a heart split in two before my very eyes.

Whatever it is we've been doing this last year—playing a game, flirting, falling for each other—that's done. She wanted me to see that loud and clear before she turned and fled down the hall.

My gut instinct is to race after her. I want to catch her, grab her hand, and pull her back against me. I can almost feel her body nestled against mine. That rage battling inside her. I can take it. I can withstand anything, so long as she eventually lets me say my piece and explain what she just overheard.

I almost do it. My feet carry me forward. My hand grips the door-knob. I'm swinging the door open, and then Todd asks me a question and I blink out of my trance.

I'm at work right now. My *boss* is standing behind me in my office, waiting for a response to an asinine question, and I have to stay here because Paige's future at Siesta Playa depends on me playing my part in all this to a T.

I can't chase after the girl.

Fuck.

Todd's oblivious to my pending meltdown. He sits in *my* chair with his feet propped up on *my* desk while his fingernail digs for food near his right incisor. He's stinking up my office to the point where, later, I'll have to call housekeeping and ask them to come Lysol every surface so at least it smells like antiseptic rather than his body odor.

I stand at the door, frozen. While my heart still races in my chest, my worry stays pinned on what to do about Paige—my bad day trudges on. Since 5:00 a.m., my phone has been vibrating with incoming calls and texts, all of which pertain to issues with the preppers. Each year, we hike up the price of the hotel rooms during their convention in an attempt to deter them once and for all, and each year, they still flock to the resort like flies on shit.

I scroll through incoming texts.

. . . unruly guest in the buffet, trying to load a canteen with lobster tails . . .

. . . guy trying to siphon gas from the grounds crew's truck . . .

. . . trying to steal and hoard antibiotics from Dr. Missick . . .

My morning continues like this, nose-diving from bad to worse as I respond to text messages and calls and try to tune out Todd's inces-sant chatter about who else he wants to fire. I think I'm sitting at rock bottom, but then I realize I'm only on a shitty plateau. Rock bottom comes when a weather alert pings like a ringing alarm, hitting me right in the solar plexus.

The storm Todd was referring to earlier, a run-of-the-mill tropical storm brewing in the Atlantic, has now been officially bumped up to a Category One hurricane.

"Goddamn it!"

The words explode out of me before I can help it.

I never lose my temper, never raise my voice. I just . . . don't.

But everyone has their breaking point. And apparently, I've found mine.

I quickly scroll through the details of the alert, trying to get the gist as I read it aloud to myself.

"Meteorologists suspect it will strengthen . . . potentially turning into a Category Two or Three before it makes landfall in less than forty-eight hours."

That would be early Wednesday morning. Fortunately, it doesn't look like we're in the hurricane's direct path. The Dominican Republic will bear the brunt of it, but we aren't in the clear. The proposed path puts us on the east side of the hurricane; rainfall estimates are already worrisome. There's only one course of action. I look up to see that Todd's on his phone as well, though when I look down to see if he's reading the weather alert like I was—no. He's placing an Uber Eats order. Oh, for fuck's sake.

"The tropical storm got bumped up to a hurricane . . ."

He keeps his focus down on his screen, trying to decide between waffle fries or curly fries before caving and adding both to his order. "What?"

I grit my teeth, surprised they can withstand the pressure.

I'm going to kill him. I will.

It's only through a herculean effort that I manage to keep my tone nonthreatening as I continue. "They're already expecting a lot of rainfall, and the hurricane will only strengthen. We should suspend check-ins and suggest that current resort guests search for earlier flights back to the mainland."

It's actually a win-win. We keep the guests safe, and we get the preppers out of here.

Todd laughs off my concern, and once he's finished placing his order—which, for the record, is either a second breakfast (he ate the first in my office; the fast-food wrappers are still on my desk) or a very early lunch—he tucks his phone away and gives me a pitying look. "How long have you lived on the island, Cole?"

"Five years," I say with a tired voice. I know where this is heading . . .

"Right. Well, I've lived here half my life. Practically an islander by birth," he says with a little self-righteous chuckle.

Visions of propelling him off a cliff keep me from losing it altogether as he continues. "Let me tell you something, Cole. This hotel has continued to operate through countless storms and even a few hurricanes while I've been in charge." He says *hurricanes* like he's a punk-ass teenager confronted by a perceived scaredy-cat, wiggling his fingers and adding a condescending tone. "I won't close down operations because you're worried about a little rainfall."

My jaw clenches so tight, I can barely force my next words out. "I'm not worried about a little rainfall, sir. I just think it's worth—"

His eyes darken with annoyance. He's not used to having to deal with my insubordination, but that's only because he's so far removed from the actual day-to-day operations of this place, he doesn't realize how often I totally ignore his orders and do what I want. Now here we are with an actual emergency on our hands, and he's fumbling the ball. "We aren't closing, and that's final. Have you forgotten who's in charge here?"

As he asks this, he's forced to retrieve a small handkerchief from his pocket so he can dab it across his sweaty forehead.

I ignore his taunt and, in a tired tone, confirm: "So we'll continue as normal? No evacuation orders? No gentle suggestion for guests to get back to the mainland?"

He scoffs and shakes his head as he stands. When he walks out of my office, he taps on his phone—presumably so he can refresh Uber Eats ad infinitum, just for the pleasure of watching that little animated car drawing closer with his food. I wait until he's down the hall, until I hear his office door close, and then I head straight for the maintenance and grounds crew office.

They operate out of a building just behind the main hotel. The group of guys, many of whom are *actually* native to this island, are clustered around a TV propped up on a desk, watching the news about the weather with bleak expressions.

"Not good," their manager says with a foreboding shake of his head.

They agree with me that it'd be prudent to take precautions. Behind Todd's back, I put in orders to prepare the resort for the hurricane. We have everything we need on site, like sandbags to contend with rising waters and plywood to reinforce weak points on resort buildings. Most of the main hotel complex is equipped with storm shutters, but not auxiliary buildings like staff housing. Todd will lose his mind if I start hammering windows shut, though, so I tell them to be strategic about it, to keep the guests calm and do what they can behind the scenes.

Next item on my ever-growing to-do list?

Find Paige.

Chapter Fourteen
PAIGE

I'm in a walk-in supply closet inside the main hotel. I don't have to be here. I'm technically on break until 11:00 a.m., when I have to be down on the beach for surf lessons, but I'm taking one for the team and restocking the shelves in here, cleaning up the space, getting my anger out in the healthiest way possible.

I've already been in here for over an hour, but it's not enough. I can't be in polite company right now. I'll scream. If I looked in a mirror, my eyes would probably be two red flames. My blonde hair will have turned into furious little snakes. I'm Medusa without the magical stone-making abilities.

So here I am, in a moderately dark, stuffy closet, organizing shelves and talking to myself while I do it. More specifically, I'm role-playing what I would say to Cole if he were the dumbass mop tilted haphazardly against the far corner. I even put a bucket on top of the handle and everything. If I squint, it kind of looks like him.

"And you know what else?" I say, pointing to Mop-Cole with so much conviction I could be a lawyer giving my closing arguments in a crowded courtroom. "I regret that time I told Théo and Oscar that you aren't 'that bad'! Yeah, I should have just let them keep tearing you apart. They were going on and on about what an asshole you are, and I felt bad for you. Can you IMAGINE THAT?! I felt *BAD* for *YOU*! The literal devil!"

"Everything okay in here, sweetie?"

I scream at the top of my lungs and whirl around to find a member of housekeeping poking her head in the closet.

I clap a hand against my chest. "Shit. You scared me."

She smiles. "Sorry about that. I just thought . . ." She lets her attention stray from me over to the mop, and her eyes narrow. I grow impatient.

I don't have time for this. I have a monologue I need to get through.

"What do you need?" I sigh.

She points to the bottom shelf behind me. "Toilet paper. Two dozen rolls."

I top off her cart in the hall and then watch her wheel away. The moment she turns the corner, I whip back around to face Mop-Cole with a lifetime's worth of anger.

"Another thing, you—you, *you JERK*!" It's not good enough. The word doesn't sting like I want it to, so I try again, with more conviction the second time. "You arrogant, no-good scum of the earth." *Now* we're getting somewhere. "I hate you. I really, truly hate you. I wouldn't talk to you again if you were the last man on earth. The last man in the entire fucking universe!"

"Tell me more."

Jesus! I shriek and turn around to find the man of the hour leaning in the doorway, as confident and smug as ever. It's like, for him, the game is on. All is well. There's no panic, no apology, no sign at all that he was just casually discussing my inevitable layoff with Todd.

I can't take it. Something in me snaps. Maybe my last shred of sanity. There it goes, drifting slowly to the ground, only to be crushed under the soles of my sandals.

I don't even think before I act. I look back down at the remaining row of toilet paper, and I start to load up. I've got a whole arsenal here, and an arm that's begging to be let loose. Without warning, I fire roll after roll of three-ply at him, satisfied when one roll pings off his elbow as he tries to deflect it, then his hip, his hand, and finally the side of his head. *Sweet, sweet victory.*

"Would you knock it off?" he asks, only mildly annoyed.

How dare he manage to keep his composure at a time like this? I want us on an even playing field. I want a proper drag-out fight, an even match at the very least.

I'm about to bend down for more rolls, but Cole's too quick. He comes into the closet and wraps his arms around my forearms, pinning them down at my sides.

My fury explodes. "Let me go. LET ME GO this instant or *I'll scream. I will.*"

"Stop thrashing around."

I try to stomp on his foot, but Cole's one step ahead of me. He keeps a tight hold on me as he kicks back with one foot, using it to slam the closet door closed. We're thrown into darkness.

My attempts to get away from him ratchet up tenfold.

"Paige," he growls. "Stop."

"I swear to god." I say it twice. *"I swear to god."*

I hear my voice breaking, the anger slowly being consumed by something heavier as he clutches me tight against his chest. Emotion squeezes my throat. Tears threaten the corners of my eyes, and I'm so sad. I'm so sad, and now so drained.

Left with no other option, I give up, all at once. I go limp in Cole's arms, and at first, he doesn't believe it. He keeps his hold on me just as tight as ever, like he's worried I'm trying to fake him out. He thinks I'll ramp it up any second now and start round two. In reality, I'm defeated. A sad little fish dwindling on the end of his line.

"You win."

I say it so quietly he doesn't hear it the first time.

"What?" he asks sadly.

I say it again, enunciating the words slowly, wearily. *"You. Win."*

Suddenly, he lets go of me and steps back so he can pull the string for the overhead light, the one I couldn't reach earlier. A shallow glow penetrates the space enough that, if I turn, he'll see my tears. Cole's done a lot of things to me—testing every boundary humanly possible—but he's never made me cry before today.

I hug myself and stay facing the supply shelves, wishing he would just leave already.

"Is that what you think I want? To upset you like this? *Paige.*"

"Oh sure, it's what you want. Gloating rights. The ability to send me packing once and for all. I'm sure you and Todd had a good laugh about it at my expense after I left. I can't even look at you. You're just like him."

His shadow steps closer, and I brace myself, eyes closed, but he doesn't touch me.

"I'm not firing you, Paige. *No one* is firing you."

God, he sounds like he means it with every fiber of his being. I don't hear any sarcasm, only conviction. But what does it matter? He could stare me right in the eyes and tell me whatever he wants. I won't believe him; I know he's a liar.

"The thing with Todd—" he continues.

The fact that he's going to try to do this, talk me out of hearing what I heard, is enough to reignite my anger. "Please, for the love of god, just *go away.*"

His phone buzzes in his pocket. It's something of dire importance, I suppose, because the second he silences it, it starts ringing again.

"This day," he growls under his breath. *"This fucking day."*

I heave a shuddery sigh and realize how close I am to crying harder. I'm balancing on a precipice, trying to keep my composure in front of him. Quiet tears slip down my cheeks, but so far, that's all. I'd like to keep it that way.

The door to the supply closet opens suddenly. Light from the hall pours in, but I don't turn around.

"Oh! I'm sorry—" It's the housekeeper who needed the toilet paper for her cart. She's back, apparently. "I just . . . I forgot to get some coffee refills a second ago, but I'll—"

The door slams closed again. I have no doubt Cole gave her a withering look that sent her running for the hills.

"Paige," he tries again.

But I don't look at him, and he goes silent. Maybe his lies are all used up. Maybe he realizes that I'm at my limit for today. Evil tendencies aside, even Cole must recognize that at a certain point enough is enough. I'm a dead horse.

His phone rings again, and with a curse, he turns for the door, whips it open, and walks out.

◆ ◆ ◆

The only thing on anyone's mind the rest of the afternoon and evening is the hurricane barreling our way—dubbed Hurricane Dominic by the people who get that privilege. Too bad they didn't name it Cole. A missed opportunity, if you ask me.

While the sky is still sunny and cloudless, the impending drop in atmospheric pressure has already started to make people loopy. I lead a sunset yoga class after more surf lessons, and the guests whisper among themselves the whole time.

"Should we leave?"

"The resort would let us know if it was really that bad, right?"

"I've been looking forward to this trip for the last six months. It's going to take a little more than hurricane winds to get me off this island."

It's actually nice that everyone's so preoccupied. No one pays any attention to my puffy face or bloodshot eyes. I'm nothing but background noise. The fact that my voice breaks every now and then as I lead the guests from one pose to another is completely overlooked.

Even the staff members are in a tizzy. Worry over the storm has surpassed the rumors about the layoffs. Annabelle is old news. Every group

I pass in the hall, in the break room, outside on the beach—they're all speculating on how bad it's going to get and what Todd's going to do about it.

I've skirted around these conversations easily enough. I've kept to myself, skipping lunch in favor of wallowing for thirty minutes alone in my dorm. I almost called in sick the remainder of the afternoon, but I didn't want to give Cole the satisfaction. Instead, I peeled myself off my bed, avoided looking in any mirrors or shiny objects, and forced myself back out into the ugly world.

As if everything isn't bad enough, all day I've been bracing myself for what to say to Camila and Lara once I bump into them. I know they were counting on me to gather intel from Cole about the layoffs, but I can't tell them the truth. I can't. It's too nasty and gnarly to bring back to the surface. My emotions are so raw, my feelings so hurt, I don't even think I could get the full story out without crumbling into a sobbing mess.

Fortunately, when they find me eating dinner alone outside the cafeteria, purposely away from the crowds, they assume I look so haggard and unkept because I'm upset about the weather.

Camila hurries over and wraps her arms around me. "No! Have you been crying? Don't be worried, Paige. We're really protected here, and I don't even think we're in the direct path or anything."

Camila squeezes me tighter, and I almost shatter into heavy sobs.

Lara shakes her head. "I've been checking the projections all day, and there's a slight chance it could veer—"

"Lara," Camila cuts her off sharply. *"Not now."*

She nods in my direction, as if to say, *Clearly she can't handle the truth.*

I can't. Baby me. Wrap me in a swaddle and rock me to sleep because this day has *got* to end.

"You want my dessert from dinner? I got a strawberry mousse. Here."

They end up tugging out the chairs on either side of me at the table and keeping me company while I pick at the mousse. It's easy to be with them because they're a self-sustaining duo. I'm really only a seat filler, and while that might sound overly critical, it's actually nice for someone like me, who enjoys the company without having to actively be in the spotlight. The two of them talk so fast, about so much, that oftentimes I feel like a spectator at a tennis match, my head on a constant swivel. Once they've exhausted all speculations about the storm, Camila brings up Blaze.

"How is that all going, by the way?" Camila asks me. "You told us that you had fun, but has Blaze reached out again? Tried to get something going for date number two?"

My date with Blaze feels like a million lifetimes ago. I've aged ten years since Friday. My faith in humanity, in men, has dwindled down to nothing.

Still, I shake my head. "No word yet. I haven't seen him since Friday, but I think everyone's been busy . . ."

"Yeah, this place has been *insane* the last few days."

It only now occurs to me that I should probably be anxiously awaiting contact from Blaze. A phone call or text would be nice, though difficult, considering he doesn't have my phone number. But he could get it from someone if he asked around. It's also not *that* hard to find people around here, between staff housing, the cafeteria, and the break room. To his credit, I've been out on excursions the last few days, and then I spent a good deal of today talking to a mop in a storage closet, so how was he going to find me?

Cole found me . . .

"If it's meant to be, it'll work out," I tack on, feeling very zen about the whole thing.

Now that I've cried out all my bodily fluids, a strange calm has settled over me. Nothing can faze me now, not even Cole's dumb face.

Which is good, considering what's to come . . .

Chapter Fifteen
PAIGE

My big plans for the night consist of rolling myself into a blanket until I resemble a human burrito and then turning in early. I'm going for a solid twelve, but I will accept a paltry eleven hours of sleep as well. My shift starts later than usual tomorrow, so I could really stretch this night of misery out if I wanted, but my plans get derailed by an ominous text message.

I've just polished off the mousse when my phone buzzes, right along with Camila's and Lara's.

"What the hell?"

Mandatory All-Staff Meeting

10 PM in the Turtle Cove Ballroom

"Oh, c'mon, are you kidding me?!" Lara groans.

"What could be so important?"

Hurricane Dominic, of course.

I consider skipping it. I mean, I'm getting fired anyway, so what more could they do to me? Unfortunately, it would only draw questions from Lara and Camila—I'm not someone to buck the rules, and a mandatory all-staff meeting is . . . mandatory. When it's time, I shuffle along behind Camila and Lara, a veritable zombie. There's no telling what this harsh hallway lighting is doing to my already splotchy complexion and puffy eyes. I keep my focus on the carpet and my head down so I can hide behind my sheath of hair as I join the chatty group of staff members already gathered in the packed ballroom.

Speculations are flying.

"I hear they're going to move us out of staff housing."

"Where would we go?"

"In the hotel, I guess. It's much safer, and it has generators. Y'know, if it gets that bad . . ."

In the ballroom, they've set out chairs in neat rows, but there won't be enough for everyone, which is fine by me.

Lara and Camila start to head toward the front, near the stage. I let the crowd surge around me before I break off and head toward the back, near a trash can. By the time they realize I'm not behind them, it's too late to do anything about it. They look back, worried, but I do a classic rendition of an apathetic shrug before I post up against the wall.

This is for the best. I can look down at my phone and avoid all human contact.

It works really well. I see everyone walking in out of the corner of my eye, and no one sees me. When Cole enters, and my stomach plummets, I swiftly turn my back to him and pray he doesn't look over. Is my hair that noticeable? My butt that noteworthy? Surely I just look like any other employee. I hold my breath, counting to ten in my head. Then, when I still don't feel confident, I sing "Happy Birthday" twice. By the time I peer back over my shoulder, Cole's made it up to the front of the room, far, far away from me. The chances of him spotting me in this huge crowd are slim to none.

I haven't seen him since he left the supply closet—during the quote, unquote assault with toilet paper. Not my finest moment, but I don't regret it. It clearly didn't have any long-lasting effects on him. Whereas we all look a bit lost, Cole looks assertive and confident as he speaks to a few members of the executive team crowded around him. He's leading the charge, whatever that may be.

I'm still scoping him out, looking for physical signs of distress, when Blaze walks in alongside Serge, one of the scuba diving instructors. Serge actually helped train me when I first started here, but I haven't seen him around much since then. He keeps to himself more than most of us, but a lot of that had to do with the fact that he had a serious boyfriend up until a few months ago—a chef at Smith's. But that ended pretty badly—with *everybody* in the resort knowing their business—and I felt really bad for him. Imagine if everyone knew the daily drama that is *The Paige and Cole Show*. Horrifying. Anyway, now here Serge is with Blaze, looking happier than ever. They laugh, and even though my body is chock full of bitterness from my shitty day, I'm still glad to see that Serge is doing well.

It occurs to me much, much later—like after they've taken their seats—that I should also be excited to see Blaze on account of us being a very serious, definitely dating couple. My heart should be pitter-pattering in my chest, a sure sign of young love. I check in to find that my heart is . . . maybe there. I'm not totally sure. If it's beating, it's doing so with lackluster ambivalence. *Hmmm.* Just to test a theory, I glance back at Cole near the front of the ballroom.

Ah, *there* it is.

It's racing now.

How concerning. The day after he kissed me, Cole joked that he'd ruined me for all other men. Maybe he did ruin me. Maybe, over the last year, he's operated like an overzealous army lieutenant during boot camp. Only instead of tearing me apart and putting me back together better, stronger, wiser, he decided to just do the first part and call it a day.

Instead of growing excited by the prospect of nice, happy Blaze, my body's been trained to want Cole, the human equivalent of Friday the 13th. The bane of my existence.

My vision tunnels as I realize this is much, much worse than I thought. My entire worldview has shifted in the last twelve hours— oh, and, *and* there's a hurricane hurtling toward me at breakneck speeds and I can't be bothered to care about it. I don't even listen when the executive team takes the stage. Todd gets up there with the microphone and just goes to town. Five, ten, fifteen minutes. The guy's trying out stand-up, I guess. Who cares. I'm too busy envisioning interesting and barbaric ways Cole could sustain an injury up there. Obviously, if this were a movie, the heavy chandelier would come crashing down on him from overhead. *Classic.* Then, of course, the stage he's standing on could collapse and he could get buried beneath the metal risers. That could be fun. I get creative with it, though, because why not? I've got time. There's a set of double doors right behind Cole, and I suspect, given the right circumstances, a large seafaring bird could swoop in and poop on his head. I wish I'd thought ahead and painstakingly trained a parrot over the last few months to bring about this evil plan. What would have started as a purely business relationship would have blossomed into a real friendship—me and the bird, a ragtag duo. But you know what they say: live and learn. Next time, I'll be more prepared.

I'm surprised when the meeting ends. Mostly because I was still in my own world. My brain managed to gloss over every minute detail that was said up onstage. If it's of dire importance, I don't know about it. For all I know they just told us that their plan of action is to have us build a fleet of rafts. Yup, we'll gather as many coconuts as we can carry and paddle to the mainland.

People stand and start shuffling out. Cole's already cutting down the central walkway as if trying to get to . . . *me*. His dark eyes meet mine across the crowded room, and I blanch. Oh crap. I can't just stay here like a sitting duck. For all I know he's trying to hunt me down so he can terminate me on the spot. Nuh-uh, not happening. He told Todd I had a week, right? I intend on staying until the bitter end, like the quintessential badass in action movies who takes eleven bullets to the chest but still somehow manages to pull himself up and keep fighting. (Plot writers: I'm sorry, *how?*)

At least I have the advantage of already being in the back of the room.

"Oh, excuse me. Yup, just gonna . . . yeah, slipping on through. *Oops.* Sorry. 'Scuse me!"

I slither right out of that ballroom like only a determined female can do when faced with a large crowd. Put me at the back of a concert, and I could be front row in no time, believe it.

Then I'm speed walking along the path like I actually expect Cole to follow me.

When a hand grabs my biceps, I scream.

"Relax, weirdo."

It's only Camila. She and Lara must have hurried out the ballroom right after me. We walk together back toward staff housing.

"I can't believe it," Lara says with a shake of her head. Her eyes are still wide with shock.

"Yes, I know. But more specifically, *what* can't you believe?"

I'm hoping they can give me the CliffsNotes version of the meeting so I'm not totally lost.

"Didn't you listen to any of that?"

I *pfft.* "All of it. Just . . . what were the craziest parts for *you?*"

Lara shakes her head. "Todd got up there first and told us this was nothing, that we had nothing to worry about. But after he left, Cole took over and sang an entirely different tune. I can't believe he talked through all those worst-case scenarios. If the hurricane causes as much flooding as they suspect it will, they'll move all of us out of our dorms and into the hotel. Since there's still so many guests on site, though, they'll have to maximize the empty rooms." She sees my shocked expression and frowns. "Didn't you hear them say that?"

"No, audio wasn't great in the back."

"Right. Well, it'll be groups of four in the double queen rooms and groups of two in each of the king rooms. But we don't get to pick! It'll all be randomly assigned roommates!"

Tragic.

"Surely it won't come to that, though. I mean, it's just a little hurricane, right?"

Cut to me getting swept up in a squall, carried away, never to be seen or heard from again.

Chapter Sixteen
PAIGE

From the moment I open my eyes the next morning, I hear the drumming of the downpour on my roof. When I open my door to check the conditions outside, I find a cobbled-together hurricane prep bag leaned up against my door, courtesy of the resort. Inside, there's a bright orange poncho, a flashlight, a bag of cashews, and a . . . Frisbee branded with the Siesta Playa logo. I know leftover swag when I see it.

Later in the break room, someone will ask me, "So did you get the Frisbee or the stress ball? I'll trade you."

Along with the kit, there's also a little note urging us to pack a go bag with essentials, in case we need them. Essentials, got it. It's tough deciding between my hunter green and navy blue sandals, but in the end, I make the right call and pack them both. I stuff in a few changes of clothes, underwear, bras, chargers, my computer, a few books, toiletries, and a file folder with my important documents. All said and done, it's not much.

After, I don my new bright orange poncho and head to work. The rain is relentless as I hustle along the path. I can hear the chaos of the lobby even before I enter. Ringing phones, demanding guests, apologies, assurances, arguments.

"What do you mean my fishing trip is canceled?!"

"Sir, the water is too choppy," a receptionist says with a compassionate frown. "It's a matter of safety."

The prepper guy waves a hand down his tactical vest and cargo pants. In the process, the half dozen carabiners hanging off his belt loops jinglejangle with survival accoutrement. "You think *I'm* worried about safety? I can protect myself. I'm carrying a Fällkniven F1 made of laminate steel. One of the all-time greats. Full tang with mixed-grade strength."

The receptionist offers him a little nod. Her eyes have nothing behind them. Physically, she's here. Mentally, she's rubbing coconut oil on Tom Hardy. It's self-preservation. I wonder how many people have already shouted at her today. I pity her. I *am* her.

There are a lot of orange ponchos in the lobby, a sea of Oompa-Loompas running to and fro, trying to help any way they can.

Lara is already at the excursion desk, so I join her.

She looks so relieved to see me I think she might tear up.

"*You!* Oh my god, thank you! Stay here for five minutes, okay?" She takes ahold of my arms and physically drags me behind the excursion desk, smack dab where she was. "I'll be back," she promises. "Just need to use the restroom for five minutes!"

Her departure feels both ominous and permanent. She's going to lock herself in a bathroom stall and scroll TikTok for the better part of an hour, I know it.

"You better not abandon me here!" I demand.

She doesn't even turn around. She just gives me one of those half-hearted waves over her shoulder as she picks up her pace to get away from me.

There's a TV mounted in the seating area of the lobby that's usually set to a nonpartisan nature show; today it's been swapped to news about the weather. A crowd of thirty watches intently while the junior meteorologist on screen thrusts himself into the elements, all in the name of good reporting. I mean, mister, we realize there's a hurricane; we don't need you to report from *inside* the damn thing. But there he stands, knee deep in the angry ocean, desperately trying to keep ahold of his microphone as harsh winds throttle him from all sides.

"The winds are really picking up!" he shouts at us. "The trees are *really* swaying! It's getting treacherous out here. For residents not planning to evacuate this morning, we encourage you to get a plan in place. Seek shelter and hunker down for the long haul."

A woman lets out a trembling gasp, like the weather is too much for her delicate sensibilities. Having had enough, she turns away from the TV and covers her face. Her husband consoles her with a tight hug and a tone of reassurance. "It's okay, Sue. If one of us dies, the other will probably get the trip comped."

Meanwhile, the preppers in the audience are absolutely *beside* themselves. They turn to one another with Cheshire grins. I'm surprised their eyes don't roll back in ecstasy. *This?* A real emergency where they can flex all their precious survival gear? They're about to pee themselves. *Rip the price tags off those LED headlamps and hand-crank radios, boys! It's go time!*

Immediately, I'm pelted with questions at the excursion desk, and it's not fun to flounder in front of the guests, so when I see Oscar running past, I call out to him in desperation. He looks relieved to have found me.

"Do you know what's going on?!"

"*Here,*" he says, forcefully shoving a printout at me. "This is the new schedule for our department. I'm supposed to be distributing them."

I look down at it, trying to find my name amid the chaos. "New schedule?"

"Yeah, all excursions are postponed until further notice. We're not under an official lockdown or anything." He leans in and drops his voice. "But they don't want the guests wandering too far, just in case . . ."

My voice carries a slight panic now. "What are we supposed to do with them?"

I swear the noise volume in the lobby explodes.

"Check the schedule and see where they want you." He gets distracted. "Hey, *Mitch*! Here, take this! It's your new schedule!"

I stare down at the paper. Someone (Cole, probably) has painstakingly divided the entire day into hour increments and by various locations. It looks like a music-festival set list. In the craft room, from 10:00 a.m. to 11:00 a.m., you can paint your own conch shell. From 11:00 a.m. to 12:00 p.m., kids can enjoy face painting and crafts in the Tiki Hut Kid Zone. In the Palms Meeting Room from 1:00 p.m. to 2:00 p.m., there's a magic show (suitable for all ages). The list goes on.

I finally find my name printed under an afternoon yoga class located in the hotel gym. After that I'm stationed in the Turtle Cove Ballroom to help with setup for an impromptu movie night.

It's bizarre having to keep the resort running at a time like this. We all want to be hunkered down in front of the TV, but there's really no more news. For now, we're not in the hurricane's direct path, and we should be fine.

I manage to feel moderately useful for the next hour, directing guests toward various activities while keeping a (mostly) positive attitude in the face of chaos. Then Cole walks into the lobby from outside, with Todd and a few department heads. They're properly outfitted in rain jackets and boots, though it doesn't seem to have helped them much. Cole whips his hood off, and his black hair is sopping wet, dripping water down his face. His expression is stern; the worry lines on his forehead haven't budged since last night. Did he even sleep?

I didn't see him again after I fled the ballroom. I thought I maybe heard someone knock on my dorm door, but I didn't answer it, of course. It was late, and I was already in bed midwallow, a bite of chocolate on its way to my mouth. If it was Lara and Camila, they would have called out to me through the door. And if it was Cole, well, I had nothing to say to him, so why bother? Still, I didn't like the nagging feeling that someone might have been out there. So a few minutes later, in a fit of annoyance, I threw off my blankets and opened the door, only to find absolutely no one. The path surrounding my door was completely empty save for a little hoppy green frog.

"Did you knock?" I asked him.

Ribbit.

Now, Cole brushes his wet hair back with his hand (becoming even *more* devastatingly handsome in the process, mind you), and then he speaks to the group with an authoritative edge. This morning's version of Cole is unlike anything I've ever seen. Soggy clothes aside, he's clearly leading the charge. Meanwhile, Todd's at the back of the group, trailing behind, trying to get something unstuck from the bottom of his rain boot. The group has stopped walking, but he hasn't noticed. He collides into a passing guest, and the woman shoots him a death glare.

"You mind?!"

Cole's giving directions to the group, pointing toward various parts of the resort.

Then he sees me, and he stalls midsentence.

I gulp and look away.

It's shit timing too. All morning, I've had a group of people clustered around the excursion desk demanding something. But not now. Most everyone who wanted to catch a flight off the island has left to wait at the airport, and everyone who's staying has settled down to an activity. There's an eerie calm in the lobby now. We're in the eye of the storm. Cole says something to the group, and then he breaks off to head toward me.

Oh brother.

Here we go.

Batten down the hatches! Gird your loins!

Why do I feel like I should be drawing a weapon? I have none, of course. There're no pockets on these shorts, so where would I fit a rifle or a long sword, anyway?

Just to cover my bases, I pat around the bottom of the desk. Nothing. No, *wait.* Gum. Gross.

He reaches me, and I ignore my quaking knees. Before he can get started saying whatever it is he's about to say that will undoubtedly be both witty and devastating, I cut him off at the pass. My heart simply cannot take it today. I should be back in my room convalescing after the events from yesterday, not standing here defenseless.

"Good morning, sir," I say with a tone I reserve solely for difficult guests. It's cheery and robotic. Coincidentally, exactly how I would like to keep my relationship with Cole moving forward. "If you're interested in booking a flight off the island, it's not too late. I can get you to Russia? Or perhaps Bangladesh? Algeria? We have a desk set up just over there with helpful staff who can assist you in calling the airlines. But if you'll promise to leave the premises within the hour, I'll personally fund your ticket myself.

"*If, however*, you're intent on weathering the storm with us, please take a pamphlet to learn about the exciting activities the hotel has organized for the day. Most guests will be occupying themselves with arts and crafts, but for you? I could organize a special trip straight to *he*—"

"Enough. You've made your point."

I'm a short-circuiting Stepford wife as I force a laugh. "I'm not sure what you mean, sir. Would you like a pamphlet? Or perhaps a beverage? They've finished serving breakfast, but we have the most excellent coffee station—"

"Paige."

I blink and it's me again, feisty and hardened. The lobotomy didn't take. "*What?*" I snap.

I'm forced to see him, then, really look at the man I've grown so accustomed to. From infancy, he never stood a chance of being easily palatable. His features are too pompous and severe. He has the nose of a haughty aristocrat. The cunning gaze of a ruthless titan of industry. He looks at you and you feel absolutely lacking in comparison. A nuisance.

But then, from certain angles, in the right lighting, there is a softness to him, I swear it. Take now, for instance. I know he's imploring me to do something. Trust him? Yeah, right. That ship has *sailed*.

"Did you pack a bag this morning?" he asks.

I scowl at him. "I don't see how that's any of your business. We are not friends. We hate each other. You no longer have access to any pertinent information about me. Now, if you'll excuse me"—I wave for him to step aside, like *Buh-bye. See ya*—"you're blocking the desk for all the guests who are patiently waiting in line."

Never mind that the lobby is a deserted ghost town.

I take matters into my own hands.

"You there, sir! Can I assist you?!"

I'm waving my hands, trying to get the attention of a teenage boy who's cutting through the lobby. He's dressed head to toe in black; his outfit is replete with menacing chains rattling around his thighs, a poky little metal choker around his neck, and heavy dark eyeliner. He has his headphones in, and when he sees me trying to initiate conversation, he flips me off with both hands and keeps walking.

"Okay, well, he's obviously already on his way to an activity. Strange, because I didn't see any satanic rituals on the schedule, but I could have missed it . . ."

Cole stands there, completely unperturbed. I'm only now realizing that when it comes to me, he has the patience of a saint.

"We're moving staff into the hotel tonight," he informs me with a defeated sigh. His hand runs through his hair. I see the fatigue in his expression.

"What? *Why?* It's not even supposed to get bad until tomorrow morning."

"Correct. And this way, everyone will already be here, safe and dry. I'm not spending all of tomorrow attempting rescues if shit hits the fan. It's a waste of resources. Any employees who want to leave resort grounds are free to do so without consequence up until nine p.m. tonight, at which point we need to know that everyone is accounted for inside the hotel."

I refuse to show my annoyance. He's already succeeded in seeing too much of me over the last few months. I'll have to get better about putting up a wall with him, tuning him out.

I look away and douse the fire in my tone as I continue. "Fine. Who am I rooming with?"

I already know he's going to say him. Of course he's going to put us together. He's a maniacal scientist, and I'm the rare specimen he's been hunting for the world over. *I've got her! I'VE FINALLY GOT HER!*

He doesn't even need to consult a clipboard. He has it memorized. "Desiree, a masseuse from the spa."

"Oh."

If I sound disappointed, it's only because I guessed wrong.

I mean, I wouldn't have put it past him to have orchestrated this entire thing—hurricane included—just to torture me. To put me with Desiree—who is a little older than me and nice enough—is *so* unlike him.

"And who are *you* with?"

Tamara's name springs to mind so fast it's troubling.

If he says Tamara, I'm going to hurl.

"Maddox."

One of the boat captains.

I hate that I'm relieved.

Word about the room assignments spreads through the resort quickly. I figured there would be murmurs of insurrection or, at the very least, voiced annoyances, but mostly people are relieved to be moving into the hotel. The building is newer and safer, not to mention much more elevated than staff housing. Water collects around our dorms even in minor storms, so as much as it pains me to say this, Cole is probably right to take precautions.

I'm even excited to room with Desiree. I don't know her well, and this will give us a chance to bond. Who knows, I might come away from all this with a new best friend.

It's actually lucky that I ended up with the room assignment that I did. Camila and Lara are together, but they're stuck in a two-queen suite with two other people.

"What the hell? One bathroom for four of us?!" Lara groans.

Camila shakes her head. "I'm claustrophobic just thinking about it."

I try not to rub it in that I'll be spared the worst of it. A king suite in a luxury hotel? That ain't half-bad. I'm already excited about all the little fancy soaps and shampoos I'll be able to pilfer. If Desiree wants them, too, we can always go halfsies. She gets the body wash, I'll take the lotion, and so on. I'm busy all day, so I don't manage to find the time to make it back to my dorm to grab my bag until after dinner. I check once more that I've taken everything I need for a few days, as well as anything I couldn't easily replace in the event that it's lost. It's not exactly sad, just strange. The entire day has felt like a weird fever dream. And the rain. THE RAIN. I know I live on a tropical island, but it's enough! We get it! As I leave my dorm, I have to tuck my duffel bag up under my poncho to keep it from getting completely soaked as I run back to the hotel.

At reception, there's a line to get our room keys. When I reach the front, a tired woman asks me, "Last name?"

"Young."

"Paige?"

I nod, and she passes over a silver key card with a discreet palm tree on it.

My vacation has officially begun! Pass me a cocktail, something served in a hollowed-out pineapple! Lather me up in sunscreen and plop me by a pool!

I've been assigned room 3124 on the third floor. I head up, glancing at the numbers as I pass them in the hall. 3075, 3076 . . . 3118, 3119. When I finally near my room, I see the door across the hall is propped open.

Cole is inside, placing a few folded shirts into the top drawer.

He doesn't see me, so I pretend I don't see him.

I scan my key card quickly and hurry inside my room, only to be confronted by a strange scent that I can't immediately place. But that's suddenly the least concerning thing about this room.

My roommate is already here. In fact, she's hard at work tugging the king-size mattress onto the floor. Maddox, Cole's supposed roommate, is draping the sheets from the bed over the lamps to dim them to a sultry glow.

"What is this?" I ask, concerned I walked onto the set of a porno. That's what it smells like, by the way . . . sex.

Desiree and Maddox aren't even fazed when they look up and find me surveying the scene. Never mind that Desiree is clad in revealing lingerie and Maddox is only wearing a pair of tight red boxer briefs. Is that . . . I lean in, eyes narrowing. Is that a little dog collar around his neck?

"It's our love den. We're all about to die, so there's no point in hiding our relationship anymore." Maddox nods in agreement, sidles up to Desiree, and pinches her playfully on the butt.

I blink several times as my overloaded brain unpacks the information.

"Okay, well, good for you, I think? But where am I supposed to sleep?"

Desiree takes my shoulders and ushers me out of the room. "You're going to have to find another room, sweetie. Byeee."

Fine. Who am I to stand in the way of . . . whatever the hell that was?

Out in the hall, I'm relieved to find Cole's door closed now. He's probably in there, pleased as punch. His roommate has abandoned him to set up shop across the hall, and now he's sitting pretty all by himself. Too bad Maddox and Desiree didn't tear *his* room apart instead of mine. I can only imagine the look on Cole's face if he were the one to walk in on that. I'd pay good money to see it. A week's wages, easy.

Out in the hall, I formulate a plan B rather quickly. It's genius, really. It takes some asking around, but I eventually learn that Blaze has been assigned room 5011. Perfect. He'll find me on his doorstep, all alone like a baby bird who's fallen out of her nest. Men love playing the hero, and what better way for him and me to really get this relationship going than to spend the night together? Watch out, Maddox and Desiree, we might be creating a little love den of our own.

Up on the fifth floor, I knock on room 5011 and then fix my hair, adjust my top, try on a smile, then decide it's too chipper. Instead, I opt for pleading innocence.

The door opens to two men's laughter.

Oh, what's the joke? I love jokes!

It's Blaze who answers the door, and he looks surprised to see me. "Paula?"

The edges of my vision start to get fuzzy and black.

Paula, he calls me. PAULA. We shared mashed potatoes and steak and an evening of conversation (albeit stilted), and he still thinks my name is Paula?!

"Paige," I say, somewhat rudely. "My name is *Paige*."

He laughs this off and thunks himself on the forehead. "Duh, yes. Paige. What's up?"

He sees my duffel bag resting at my feet and then takes a step closer to the hallway, closing the door tighter as if to say, *You weren't planning on coming in here, were you?*

"Who's at the door, sweetie?" a man calls from deeper inside the hotel room.

Sweetie is a common enough nickname among guy friends, right?

Sweetie, honey, you sexy thing, you—I think they call each other this stuff all the time.

It's cool that Blaze is so confident in his masculinity. No fragile male egos here! Harry Styles would be proud.

Blaze turns to reply. "It's Paige!"

Then there's shuffling, and the other guy approaches the door. Would you look at that? It's Serge! Shirtless!

He wraps his arm around Blaze's waist and gives me a big warm smile.

"Paige! It's been too long. I thought I saw you leaving the staff meeting the other night, but it was hard to tell. You looked like you were running—"

"That wasn't me. Anyway, are you two . . ."

I was going to say *a couple*, but Serge finishes with, "Gay?"

When I do nothing but blink dumbly, he takes pity on me and answers his own question. *"Very."*

"Congratulations" is the word that falls out of my mouth. And I really do mean it. I'm happy for Blaze and Serge. Now that I think about it, they're actually *perfect* for each other. But man, talk about a plot twist. I mean, sure, if I'd thought about it for even half a second, the signs would have all been there, in bold, lit up like the Las Vegas strip. Unfortunately, I've been a little preoccupied as of late . . . well, ever since Cole and I kissed, really. His rejection at the time hurt so deeply, I suppose I turned desperate. I'd pinned all my hopes and dreams on Blaze in an attempt to find a real, meaningful connection. And yes, if that connection happened to sidetrack me from my very real, very painful obsession with Cole . . . well, all the better.

I'm not sure how long I stand there, saying nothing, but it's long enough that Serge pushes past Blaze and rests a reassuring hand on my shoulder. "Are you okay, Paige?"

Nope. Not even a little.

"All good in the hood!"

Jesus, I gotta get out of here. I reach down, grab my duffel, and move on to my next—and final—option.

For the record, Camila and Lara are about to relent when I finish my very convincing argument for why they should let me be their fifth roomie for the night. I can tell. Lara's face is a mask of pity. Camila's bottom lip is jutting out a little. Of course they're going to take me in. They love me. They want to help me out, but one of their roommates puts the kibosh on the plan *real* quick. I barely have a toe nudged in the doorway before she walks up and takes matters into her own hands.

"No. No way. There's already three too many bodies in this room. I'm about to start killing people off. Find somewhere else to sleep."

I should be holding a speaker that's softly playing Green Day's "Boulevard of Broken Dreams" as I walk aimlessly around the resort for the next hour. I'm like Mary, adrift and alone. No Joseph by my side. Also, for the record, no immaculate conception to contend with.

Where, *oh where*, will I sleep tonight?!

Eventually, with so much reluctance I can barely finish the last few steps, I find myself outside Cole's room.

Am I really going to do this? Sleep with the gorgon? I don't see a way around it. I could stay on the couches in the lobby overnight, but I know management would hate that (and I'm not trying to get fired *early*). Not to mention, I need someplace to stow my crap. I can't just carry around this duffel bag everywhere I go.

From across the hall, the guttural, animalistic sounds of tantric lovemaking are clearly audible—Maddox and Desiree have hit an all-new crescendo—just as I raise my fist and knock.

Chapter Seventeen

COLE

I open the door to my hotel room just as Paige pushes her way past me like a whirling dervish.

All I see is the back of her blonde hair as she kicks off her shoes and drops her duffel bag on a chair. I'm still holding the door open in confusion as she starts unloading her clothes into the bottom drawer of the dresser like that's been the plan from the start.

Without looking up, she states plainly, "Let's establish some ground rules right now. No talking to me. That's obvious. No looking at me either. No touching my stuff. No . . ." She pauses her unpacking so she can consider other possibilities. Then she shakes her head. "Hmm, nothing else is coming to mind right now, but if I think of other things, I'll update the list then. But you should know that all of these afore-mentioned offenses will be punishable by death."

"Death, huh?"

No answer.

"What are you doing?" I say, lamely, trying to catch up.

Why is she in my room?

She looks up at the ceiling and speaks with a bone-tired tone. "It's a long story and I can't possibly get into all the details, but essentially,

Maddox shacked up with Desiree across the hall. Like they are *really* going at it. Once they're done with it, that room will need to be heavily sanitized, or potentially just taken out of the rotation altogether. Oh, also, Blaze is in love with someone else. You probably already knew that and were *reveling* in the fact that he and I would never end up together, but whatever. Moving on. The only friends who could take me in, Lara and Camila, have utterly abandoned me. I can either sleep in here or behind the back dumpsters outside, so . . ." It's like she's giving it another moment of thought before she shudders. "You narrowly won out. But *only* because I'm worried how high the floodwaters might rise. I don't want to wake up adrift at sea."

Well, that's a lot to unpack, and I'm only confident I caught maybe a third of it by the time she finally takes a breath. The important bits stick, though. "Of course you can stay here."

Though, to be clear, she's not waiting for my permission. She's making herself at home in the place already. This is *her* room now.

"But I can have a word with Desiree. Obviously, she's not allowed to take over that room and kick you out. It's unprofessional and inappropriate—"

She shakes her head, fully committing to the martyr bit with a weary tone. "Save it. Who am I to stand in the way of love? People should be happy. Not *us*, obviously. But other people. Better people." She finishes unpacking and slams the drawer closed. "Now, no more talking. That was rule number one."

I let the door close. "Talking?"

"Yes. If you've forgotten the rules already, I can jot down a list. In fact, I might have just come up with another—" She turns back to survey the room like she's intensely focused on solving a problem. I watch from the narrow foyer as she stands and walks over to the large window, flattens her back against it, and then starts taking steps, strategically lining the back of her heel up to the front of her toe. She does this over and over until she reaches me, pauses, and looks up with a challenging gaze. We're chest to chest. Her eyes are two tiny chisels trying to bore through me. It's the first time she's looked directly at me since she strolled into my room. It feels like someone's squeezing a tight fist around my stomach.

She doesn't look like she's going to cave anytime soon. We could be here all night, so I move aside for her, and she completes her task of measuring the length of the room with a satisfied hum.

"Thirty-one feet, give or take. I'll be generous and let you have the bigger portion. Fifteen feet for me, sixteen for you. I know maintenance is busy battening down the hatches, but I think you and I could jerry-rig a dividing wall easily enough. Where do you think we could find some plywood around here? And how good are you with a hammer?"

She's serious.

If I handed her a pack of nails and a two-by-four, she'd have a **KEEP OUT** sign erected within a half hour. By the end of the day, I'm sure she'd finish construction on her wall. I burst her bubble with a dry tone. "Every bit of plywood we have is going toward hurricane prep. Your wall will have to wait."

"Nonsense. Plywood's out, but we can get creative. How many shirts did you bring?" She opens the top drawer of the dresser. "Perfect! Look at this! We can string them on a line from wall to wall. Right over the bed and everything. That could work."

"Put my shirt down."

She holds my white T-shirt lower so that it falls exactly at her neckline. It's like she's a child at a fair poking her head through a silly backdrop. *Look, mom. Take my picture!* "Now, now, don't get testy. If you don't want me to use your stuff, I'm sure I can just borrow clothes from Maddox and Desiree. They aren't using them right now anyway. Also, for the record, I didn't realize you *owned* T-shirts. Not to mention, this one is decadently soft! *So* unlike you. I'd expect you to prefer fiber constructed of aluminum cans and old tires. Tough and durable."

She says the end part with a strong Soviet accent, heavy emphasis on the *r*.

Sometimes—okay, *all* the time—I look at Paige and think, *Goddamn it, you're the funniest person I've ever met. Simply existing near you makes my day that much better.* But the greatest travesty in all this is that I can't tell her. Not how funny she is, not how much I want to kiss her, even when she's being goofy, even when she waggles my T-shirt back and forth just to taunt me.

"I want my shirt back."

"*What are you going to do to get it?*" she asks, holding it up like she thinks it's out of my reach.

I snatch it, and it's like taking candy from a baby. Easier.

I tell her that, and she scowls.

"I can't believe I've forgotten myself. You've completely distracted me and made me break my own rule! No talking is no talking. Now, go to your side of the room and leave me alone."

The next thirty minutes go like this:

Outside, the rain picks up to a real downpour. Without the TV on, I can hear the storm strengthening, the wind howling. There's a palm tree just outside our room that keeps thrashing against our window. It would be an ominous backdrop if we were in any way paying attention to it.

We're not. There could be ten hurricanes, a dozen tornadoes, and an earthquake to boot and we would still be zeroed in on intently ignoring each other, nothing else.

I sit in a chair with my computer open on my lap. I'm working, answering emails, minding my own business.

Paige goes at it, rearranging the furniture in the suite. If it's not nailed down or ten thousand pounds (like the dresser and the bed), chances are it's found a new home. She learned that lesson the hard way. Watching her try with all her might to shift that dresser barely half an inch was highly entertaining, but I had to pretend like I wasn't watching. I made a sound—a blunted laugh that I had to swallow—and she looked up at me with a speculative gaze. I squinted down at my computer screen and moved my mouth really fast like I was reading the most important document I'd ever seen. Oh, look at this email, straight from the president, filled with the nuclear codes and the conclusive evidence that Jack from *Lost* was in purgatory the whole time.

I had a footrest at one point. That's gone. She came over and stood, looking down at it without saying a word. I eventually got the hint, picked up my feet so they hovered just above it, and like a little rat who'd been lusting after a piece of cheese, she swiped the ottoman away immediately. It's now stacked on top of an end table, alongside a floor lamp and a few spare pillows. Her rudimentary blockade means that if I want to go to her side of the room and peek out the window, I'll have to climb over the bed.

It also means that if she wants to access the bathroom, or the all-important thermostat, she'll also have to humble herself and shimmy across that comforter onto my side.

She shivers and rubs her hands up and down her forearms, trying to warm up. "Bit chilly in here, no? *Andbeforeyoureply*," she amends quickly, forming one long rambling word to get the sentiment out as fast as possible. "I was talking to myself."

She looks over at me, and without even having to stand from my comfy chair—(Oh yes, did I mention the best seating in the suite is on *my* side of the bed?)—I reach up and press the down arrow on the thermostat, cranking it cooler by one more degree. I just can't sleep well if it's too warm, you know?

Paige's teeth audibly chatter, and I almost feel bad, but then she whips the comforter off the bed and wraps herself up in it, sitting on the window ledge, looking out into the dark, menacing night.

I grab the TV remote, thinking I should at least check the weather to see if there are any updates.

"I guess he thinks he gets final say on what we watch," she says, now referring to me as if I'm not even in the room.

"Do you want me to see if I can do a split screen on the TV? That way you can watch your show and I can watch mine?"

With a groan of annoyance born from deep within her soul, she pushes her phone out of the rolls of the comforter so she can unlock it. "Hey, Siri, can you tell Cole that I'm not talking to him right now?"

In her doltish robotic voice, Siri answers, "I'm sorry, I can't help with that."

Paige lowers her face right near the microphone and, in an angry, catty tone, says, "Okay, well, what good are you, anyway?"

Siri replies, nonplussed. Cheery, even. "I didn't get that. Could you try again?"

"You know, it makes no sense for us to be in this room together and *not* talk about what you overheard the other day," I chime in. "Notice how I said 'what you heard' and not 'what you *think* you heard.' You got it right. I told Todd that I was going to fire you, but I'm not going to."

Paige looks up at me, and her expression is murderous. She's thinking of subjecting me to medieval torture tactics. Disembowelment, perhaps? What's the one with the horses? Oh yes, being drawn and quartered.

"Do you think I'm the absolute dumbest person on the planet? Like, there's ol' Paige, the most gullible idiot to ever pass through the lobby doors here at Siesta Playa. Here, take this commemorative plaque."

"You'd understand the truth better if you actually let me finish saying it."

"So *say it*. I'm all ears. I can't wait to see how you spin this into something that you think makes sense."

She wraps herself more tightly in her huge comforter and prods me to continue with an impatient glare. Never mind that she looks like she's cosplaying as the Michelin Man. I'm meant to take her seriously, so I do.

"We agree Todd sucks."

Her reply is icy. "That's the verdict the world has come to, yes."

"Great. Well, he's also my direct superior, and if I want to keep my job here at Siesta Playa, I have to play the game."

"You mean sell your soul to the devil."

"*No*, I mean placate Todd long enough to figure out how the hell I'm going to get him out of here once and for all."

Her expression hardens. "Impossible."

"No, actually. It's not. No one knows him better than I do. His comings and goings. His likes, dislikes. His *vices*."

She's intrigued, but she doesn't want to admit it. "What's that supposed to mean? What does any of this have to do with me?"

"He's not squeaky clean, and I know how to prove it."

"Oh, *okay*." Her eyes roll back in her head like she's heard this snake oil pitch one too many times. "You're a detective now too. Cool."

"I'm not a detective. I'm an auditor by nature. By blood, actually. It's what I do. I look at official financial accounts and I search for discrepancies. It's like a hobby."

"Okay, so you're a truffle-hunting pig, only you wear a suit and enjoy calculators. Still, I don't understand how—after working here for five years—you only *now* figured out that Todd is up to no good. Are you not a very good pig, or what? I mean, what are the odds that you figured it out at *this* precise moment? *Why now?*"

We're veering into dangerous depths, inch by inch, lowering ourselves so that, here in a second, we won't be able to easily swim our way back to shore again. Not back to where we've been, not to the safety of all our unspoken words and misread feelings, the cloaked banter and the disguised love. We're going to unmask the truth, and then what?

It doesn't matter. The unknown is our only path forward now that Paige thinks I'm going to fire her. She won't believe me until I tell her all of it. Every. Last. Detail.

"The correct question is *who*."

She furrows her brows.

"*Who* did Todd threaten recently that forced me to finally dig deep enough, care *enough* to figure shit out? I'd been somewhat lazy, I admit. The first few years on the job, I was learning. I knew Todd was horrible, but I didn't think he was *illegally* horrible. Then he started in with these layoffs. Some were warranted, fine. The clown, Annabelle . . . it's why I went through with them. But not you."

There's a hard set to my jaw, a determined edge. This is more information than she bargained for. She doesn't look like she's slowly recognizing and reconciling the truth. It's like she's rejecting it. A shake of her head, then another. She's up off the windowsill now, moving back and forth, not quite pacing but shifting her weight with agitated steps like she's a computer that's been forced to do too many commands at once. She needs a reboot.

"I don't believe you. *Why* would you do that?" Her eyes are so wide now, blinking in the sight of me like she's never seen me this clearly before. "Go through all that trouble for me?"

Lightning flashes outside—a colossal, deafening boom shakes the windows—and then the TV and lights cut out all at once, right along with the AC. We're plunged into darkness, and I wait for the backup generators to kick in. Any minute now would be great. I'm holding my breath, I realize, and I'm forced to exhale as we settle deeper into the dark.

"Shit."

"*Shit*," she says, nearly in tandem with me.

Chapter Eighteen
PAIGE

Just when we need them the most, the generator gods have failed us. We shouldn't be standing here in a darkness so intense I can't make out my own hand waving in front of my face. Doors slam out in the hall. Worried voices carry through our door. People are already starting to panic.

Cole and I don't say a word. It's like we reject this reality. We want another one. A brighter one.

If only we stay frozen, the lights might flicker back on.

Please, oh please, turn back on.

It's disorienting to say the least. My head is spinning, but then, of course it is. Hurricane and power outage aside, Cole just laid it all on me. I was ill prepared to hear that confession. I mean, it *was* a confession, right? The beginnings of one, at least . . .

He's trying to take Todd down for *me?*

My heart starts racing so fast I feel like I need to clutch my chest.

"Paige?"

I turn toward his voice. "I'm here."

"You're being quiet."

"I'm thinking."

"About the storm?"

Oddly, "No."

I'm unpacking his last few words. Everything he said before the lightning strike. His timing is truly impeccable. I wonder if there's a Hallmark card for declaring your feelings during a natural disaster.

"Are you okay?" he asks like I'm *this* close to losing it.

He's correct in his assessment.

"I think?" It's half statement, half question. Maybe *he* could tell me if I'm okay. Is *he* okay? Is anyone in this hotel right now truly *okay*?

Oh, so this is what existential dread feels like . . .

I listen to him start to try to feel his way around the room. His toe gets stubbed on something hard, and he lets out a sharp guttural groan. There's more fumbling after that, less gentle now that he's already in pain. No doubt he's trying to recall from memory how exactly I had everything stacked. There was the chair, end table, pillows, lamp. *Lamp!*

Too late.

He bumps it slightly, and it crashes down on my side of the room. The bulb shatters, and I jump back with an embarrassingly high-pitched squeal.

"Don't move!" he shouts.

I go stock still.

"There's going to be glass shards everywhere. You took your shoes off when you first came in. I don't want you cutting your feet."

I pinch my eyes closed as I berate myself for being so ridiculous. Why did I have to make this so hard on us? I essentially created a death trap obstacle course for him to navigate. "I'm sorry."

It's so faint, I'm surprised he hears it.

"You didn't knock it over," he assures me, trying to steal the blame when we both know it lies solely on my shoulders.

"I don't know why I tried to divide the room. I should have just locked myself in the bathroom and called it a night. At least I wouldn't have caused as much trouble in there. Although, who knows . . . I could have flooded the place, I guess."

He doesn't confirm or deny my stupidity. Instead, he stays on task. "I was trying to make it to the dresser. That's where my flashlight is."

Flashlight!

Duh.

I'm still holding my phone, and I quickly scroll through the screen prompts until I turn the flashlight feature on. I have officially redeemed myself, *slightly*.

Shallow light blankets the room now. I reluctantly look up at Cole, wincing as I brace for the worst. He should be scowling at me, angry beyond belief, his injured toe throbbing in tandem with his violent thoughts. But instead, his expression is soft and caring—his relief palpable. Suddenly there's a heavy lump in my throat, one I have a hard time swallowing past.

"Smart. I forgot about my phone."

He tugs his out of his pocket and turns on his flashlight too.

"Now that you have that light, check around you and make sure there's no glass. If you can, try to get up on the bed."

For once, I don't argue. With careful steps, I tiptoe toward the bed and scurry up onto it like there's a monster clawing at my heels.

"Now stay there," he says, holding his hand up like a stop sign.

With the light from our phones, he can easily find his way to the dresser. His flashlight clicks on, and now there's plenty of light to see the mess I've made around the room.

Good grief. It's like the hurricane's already passed through here and left its destruction.

"I need to get a broom and vacuum from the housekeeping closet."

His declaration is punctuated by a phone call. Ah, so it begins. *The frenzy.*

If the entire resort is without power right now, we're screwed. Guests are going to lose their minds. I mean, take their lights, fine. But their TVs?! How are they supposed to watch *Family Feud* now?!

Beyond that, there's the fact that it's late August. Outside, it's a humid ninety degrees. This hotel is well insulated against the elements, but it won't matter. If the backup generators don't kick on, it's going to get hot in here, and *fast*.

There's also the real fear of the hurricane to contend with. These guests are away from home, in an unfamiliar environment, rightfully worried about their safety. Poor Cole. He's about to be their punching bag.

"I'll do it!" I rush out as he frowns, still reading something on his phone. "I'll clean up in here. Just go. I'm sure they need you."

"The backup generators should have kicked on," he says to himself. His concern is etched in worry lines across his face.

"I know."

He drags his hand through his hair. I know he wants to let loose a string of expletives a mile long. I would. It's been one issue after another over the last forty-eight hours. Then I really helped things along by showing up at his door with my own basket of crazy. And he just sat there and took it while I rearranged this place. It's laughable how patient he is, but I see it taking its toll. The way he rubs his forehead. The way he squeezes his eyes shut tight, like he's steeling himself to open them again and face what awaits him. The stress would be too much for anyone.

He looks up at me with a fierce, determined gaze. I nearly gulp. "Listen, I need you to stay in here, okay? Downstairs is going to be a madhouse, and I don't want you anywhere near it. Just stay put."

Already, I'm creeping toward his side of the bed so I can swing my legs off. "I could help. I mean, I'm an employee here—"

"No." I freeze in place. His tone leaves zero room for input. "With everything else going on, I don't want to have to worry about you."

Ouch.

"I promise I won't mess anything up."

He's worried I'm a liability, like I'll go down and rearrange the furniture in the lobby too. Break all those lamps.

But then he shakes his head, his heavy gaze holding mine as realization dawns. He's not worried about the trouble I'll cause. He's worried about *me*. My well-being.

"Stay here until I get back," he implores.

And what can I do except to nod and agree?

This is the weirdest night of my life.

I can't even sit in my feelings about how Cole is acting toward me because he's gone and I'm still in this semidark hotel room, holding my phone and sitting on the bed, utterly useless—still wrapped in my comforter, mind you—while outside, the storm rages on.

I stay there for a minute, following Cole's orders, and then after the eerie quiet in the room sinks in to an uncomfortable degree, I put my shoes on, find my flashlight from the survival kit the resort provided, and head out into the hall, taking care to keep the door ajar so I don't get locked out.

Chaos has descended. Most everyone is standing in their doorway, holding a flashlight or their phone, trying to talk to their neighbors and figure out what's going on. It's a mixture of resort staff and guests, but no one has answers.

"Why aren't the generators working?"

"We were told the hotel had generators!"

I'm technically breaking my promise to Cole by leaving my room, but I can't just leave that glass on the ground. There's a housekeeping closet on every floor, and I'm relieved to find this one unlocked. There's a vacuum inside that should get the job done. I wheel it back to the room, ignoring any and all questions as I go, only to realize—once I get back inside the room and go to plug in the vacuum—that it requires electricity. Duh-doy. I wheel it back to the closet and swap it for a broom and dustpan. It'll make the job ten times more difficult, but at least it's something.

I'm actually glad for the task. I work slowly and meticulously, getting every last piece of the shattered light bulb thrown into the trash before I start to put the room back to rights. I didn't realize how much heavy lifting I'd done before. By the time I'm finished and all the furniture is back where it belongs, I'm sweating.

By now, the air feels stale and stagnant.

I check my phone.

There's a text from Camila asking if I'm okay. I tell her everything's fine before I ask for an update from their room. Are the four of them all stuffed in there sweating it out?

CAMILA: It's not great, but we're just sitting around and talking. Lara's telling ghost stories with a flashlight propped under her chin. Come join us. Where did you end up?

I can't tell her where I am.

Cole's room.

She wouldn't believe me.

Ha ha, no, really. Where are you? she'd say.

I don't feel like getting into it tonight, so I just tell her I found a spare room, and then I let her know that I'm turning my phone off for a while. Since it's the end of the day, my battery is nearly drained, and I don't want to waste it for no good reason. Especially if I don't know how long the power will be out.

I send my parents a text, too, just in case they happen to read the news and find out what's going on down here. I don't want them to have to worry.

Once my phone is turned off in my lap, I feel well and truly alone.

It's late. I could try to sleep, but I know that won't be possible.

I can no longer ignore the fact that it's hot as hell in here. Cole's attempt to ice me out earlier was in vain. I take off my socks and shoes and linger in my shorts for a while before dispensing with those too. Next to go is my bra. I don't want a single layer on my body that's not absolutely crucial. My T-shirt and underwear will have to be enough. Besides, I don't think Cole will be coming back in here anytime soon.

I hate that I can't check in with him. Even if my phone were on, I don't have his number. We've never exchanged them, which feels both appropriate *and* odd, given the circumstances. Sure, in the last year, I've spent more time with Cole than anyone else, but if he'd ever asked me to give him my phone number, I would have laughed in his face, and vice versa. Twenty-four-seven access to each other? Endless mayhem? Absolutely not.

I wish he'd just come back up to the room and give me a quick update, but of course, that's not at the top of his priorities right now. There's no telling what he's doing. If I know him, he's out in the downpour, assessing the generators himself.

I'm left up here to my own devices, and I'm bored. Also, a little worried.

This is embarrassing, and I would never admit it, not even under duress, but to help ease my suffering, I slide off the bed. First, I mosey down the side of it, running my finger along the sheet like I have no plan at all. I just want to see if there's an end of the bed, and yup, it's there. I'm putting on a show for cameras that don't exist. It's my way of making it seem like an accident that I've somehow ended up at the dresser. My hands move on their own. They open the top drawer— weird!—and pull out Cole's T-shirt, the soft one I picked up earlier. Then the T-shirt quite literally falls onto my face. Oh my god, *so* annoying! I have no choice but to press it there and inhale. Cole's scent is a morphine drip. I take the T-shirt back to the bed and hug it like a lovey.

If he comes in at this precise moment, I'll eat it. Anything to get rid of the evidence of how low I've stooped.

I lie there, listening to rain pelt the window, hot, annoyed, agitated. For so long, my thoughts whirl around and around on the same topic. Why would Cole try to protect me from Todd? Why does he care that much? Then at some point I fall asleep because I'm awoken a while later when the hotel room door closes with a heavy thud.

"Paige?"

I lift my head off the pillow and reply with a groggy, croaky, indecipherable "Yeah?"

Cole releases a steady exhale and walks deeper into the room. He still has his flashlight on, so I can see him there, sopping wet. His shoes squelch against the carpet before he toes them off. Then he sets the flashlight on the dresser and starts to unbutton his shirt. This is a dream. Either that or I've found myself in some weird, topsy-turvy world where it's normal for Cole to undress in front of me.

"How are the generators?" I ask as a way to remind him that I'm still here. He knows he's taking off his pants while I watch, right?

Should I avert my gaze?

Fat chance.

If I tried to close my eyes right now, they'd pry themselves open. *You're not ruining this moment for us, girl.*

He starts answering my question, something about how one of the backup generators *did* kick on. "The one that covers the kitchens, restaurants, and gym. That area of the resort has had power this whole time . . ."

I'm listening, but I'm also thinking, *Hello, Cole's abs.*

Hello, Cole's boxer briefs.

Hello, Cole's noticeable bulge.

". . . it's only this portion of the hotel that's been without power. The engineers are working on the issue . . ."

His voice fades out again as he turns toward the dresser and tugs open the top drawer.

His back is so sexy, broad, and muscular. I like the slope that extends from his neck to his shoulders, the defined taper down to his waist. I like that he's seemingly tan everywhere. Well . . . everywhere I can see.

I ogle his butt like it's my god-given right.

"They've assured us it'll be up and running again by morning."

"What time is it now?"

"A little after two a.m."

Then he turns slowly, giving me a dubious look.

"Where's my shirt? The one you had earlier?"

Oh, the shirt I'm cradling to my chest like a newborn baby?

"I was cold," I say, sitting up to hand it to him. *"Brr."*

He's not buying it.

"What did you do to it?" he asks as he leans over the bed to take it like he's worried I'll revoke the offer.

"*Nothing.* I thought it was mine. I have one that's really similar."

He stands there, silently interrogating me.

"I was feeling weird, *okay*?! It's been a weird day!"

His head tips gently to the side. "So you were hugging my shirt for comfort?"

"I was hugging your shirt for reasons I'm not willing to share."

He's too tired to deal with me. He takes the shirt and a new pair of boxer briefs into the bathroom with his flashlight, and then the water cuts on in the shower. And would you look at that? I'm depraved. Almost immediately, all sorts of X-rated images spring to mind. Cole discarding his last bit of clothing and stepping under the shower stream. Cole, lit by candlelight—(*Shut up.* It's *my* fantasy and I'd rather it be a candle than a flashlight. Sue me)—as he sudses himself up with shower gel, running his hands all over his body. He doesn't forget his biceps, his forearms, his chest and abs. He gets every single inch of himself. It's in his DNA, after all. He's so very thorough.

When the water turns off, I scurry onto my side of the bed and roll to face the window. I listen as he dries off with the towel. My imaginings are no less tame now than they were before, so that when he walks out of the bathroom once he's finished getting ready for bed, my cheeks go bright red as if I have a thought bubble hovering over me, televising every naughty detail.

My eyes are shut like I'm trying to convince him I'm asleep, which is frankly absurd. Cole and I are sharing a bed; it's not like I'm going to just conk out as if it's a regular occurrence.

I feel his weight on his side, the bed dipping down as he lies back and fluffs his pillow.

His flashlight clicks off, and we're back in total darkness.

I'M IN BED WITH COLE CLARK.

And he smells lovely from the shower, all clean and fresh.

I wish I could see him. I wish I could take him in from head to toe. Did he get all the water off with his towel, or is some sluicing down his abs? I could lick it off . . .

GO TO SLEEP.

Go to sleep!

Go. To. Sleep.

I can't, though. Cole shifts, and I *think* he's turned on his side toward me.

I'm shaking like a leaf.

I don't even have the benefit of blankets to hide beneath. It's too hot for that.

I'm still wearing my T-shirt and panties. Panties. *Ugh*, metaphorical facepalm. I didn't even realize that he saw me like this earlier. I was too preoccupied with him. Oh well, it's too late now. Besides, he's seen me in far less and I've lived.

Something warm and soft gets draped over my arm. Not a blanket . . . a T-shirt. *His* T-shirt from earlier. He's giving it back to me.

My nose stings like I might cry.

I tug it off my arm so I can clutch it against my chest. Then I wait for him to say something more, to tease me about it in a harsh way that will make me want to throw the T-shirt across the room and be done with it. But he stays silent, and it's louder than anything he could have said, any truth he might have revealed. I remember the conversation we had before the lightning strike, and into the dark hotel room, I let him know, "I believe you about Todd. I'm sorry I didn't trust you before."

Then I turn to face him. I can't see him; it's too dark.

I can't hear him breathing either. The storm is still going outside, a relentless downpour. Thunder rumbles right over us. *Is he sleeping?* I worry. *Am I alone in this?*

Then his hand reaches out to close the gap between us. His warm palm finds my biceps, then my forearm—and eventually his hand slides down until it takes mine. He drags my hand to the center of the bed, where he laces our fingers together, and he squeezes. His grip is so large. I've known that. I've felt it before, but somehow, right now, with nothing else to focus on, I'm memorizing its weight, the smooth skin versus the rough calluses, the long fingers . . .

We could scoot together and touch, kiss, *all of it*. I can practically feel the charge in the air; a cascade of goose bumps tingles up my legs and arms. The moment hangs in suspension, but I'm too shy to scoot closer and, maybe, so is he. Still, as he keeps ahold of my hand, I can feel this tight thing unfurling in my chest. It's not an epiphany; it feels more like coming into consciousness, holding a mirror up to something that's been there the whole time. There is no way around it, it seems.

I want Cole.

Chapter Nineteen

PAIGE

Awareness trickles in slowly the next morning. I make note of the soft pillow beneath my cheek. The sleepy heaviness still clinging to my limbs. It's relatively quiet now that the rain has stopped. The sun filtering through the window is what must have woken me up. We never did close the drapes last night; there was no need. Cole is still in bed. I know because he has me squeezed up against his chest the same way I was clutching his T-shirt last night. I'm his teddy bear.

His arm is a tight band around my waist. It's like I'm locked into a roller coaster, not going anywhere.

And then . . .

Then I realize that Cole's hand is flat against my stomach, the edge of his pinky finger innocently dipped beneath the waistband of my panties. My butt fits into the groove of his hips, and though I try not to notice, it's impossible not to feel how hard he is. I mean, he is absolutely *rigid* against my butt.

Long and thick.

Realizing this, I bite my lip and turn to press my face into my pillow because I'm so inappropriate! I should be hauled off to jail!

Stop thinking about it!

Cole's hand shifts and slides up. Ugh, I love the way it feels on my bare stomach just before he pulls it away and rolls onto his back.

He makes a noise, a morning groan that makes me feel like an absolute perv because even that's somehow sexy.

I gain just enough courage to peer over my shoulder to see him dig the heels of his hands into his eyes as he blinks away the last vestiges of sleep. After, he tilts his head to look at me.

Our eyes lock, then I betray us both by looking *down*.

He only then realizes the problem at hand.

The very *big* problem.

Another groan, and then he sits up.

He doesn't bother making an excuse about how it happens to all guys and that it doesn't mean anything. He's not even embarrassed, and why should he be?

If I were a dude and I was packing heat like that in my pants, good luck trying to force me into clothing. I'd be walking around nude from the waist down.

Cole, meanwhile, absolutely never let on this whole time!

The sneaky bastard.

"How did you sleep?" he asks.

"Oh . . . good."

A sudden urge to stretch washes over me, and I don't resist. I'm a lazy cat reaching my hands up toward the headboard, flexing and then curling my toes. It feels so good. Cole watches me while I do it, like I'm putting on a show for him. I mean . . . I wasn't, not technically. But I like the way it feels when his eyes are on me, hooded and dark.

"You?"

"Fine," he says brusquely. "I'm going to take a shower."

"Another so soon?"

He shoots me a glare, and I know, I just *know*, what he's going to do in there.

Tsk tsk tsk.

"Be quick, will you? I'd love one myself."

I'm surprised he doesn't shoot me the bird as he walks away.

I laugh as I push up to sit. I'd love to check the time, but the clock on the nightstand is blinking red. Blinking! That means there's power again! I reach for the TV and turn it on. Then I power up my phone and plug it in.

There are a million texts from my parents.

Call us as soon as you get this!

Are you okay?

News doesn't look good! Please answer your phone, Paige!

Guilt gnaws on me as I immediately dial their number.

"Paige!" my mom exclaims. "Thank god. Are you okay?"

"Yes, Mom. Totally. I'm sorry, I didn't mean to worry you guys like that. I had to turn my phone off last night because we lost power and I didn't have much battery. I didn't want to drain it, but the power seems to be back on now and I'm charging it up."

"Good. How was the storm?"

"I don't actually know. I just woke up and checked my phone. I haven't even looked outside."

I do it now, carrying my phone to the window, or at least as far as I can get to the window while my phone's plugged into the charger.

It appears to be a *good news, bad news* situation.

Good news is there's power.

Bad news is there's some serious flooding outside. I'm not sure of the extent, but the grounds are definitely underwater. It could be a few inches or a few feet. It's hard to tell from this vantage point. Debris is scattered too. Palm tree leaves, tree limbs, trash. I relay all this to my mom.

"There doesn't seem to be damage to any buildings, though," I continue, "but I can't see much from my hotel room."

"So they pulled you into the resort? Smart. I was worried you'd be out in your dorm."

"Nope. They thought ahead."

Cole thought ahead, probably.

Speaking of, the water in the shower isn't on anymore. He must have finished up there fast, knowing I needed to rinse off after him.

"Let me get going, Mom. I'm sure it'll be a busy day. I'll try you again this afternoon."

"Okay, keep me posted. I'm so glad it wasn't worse."

"Yeah, me too."

Cole comes out of the bathroom in a towel and nods to let me know I'm up.

Never mind that there's only a scrap of terry cloth covering his groin. I'm just supposed to mosey on past him and go shower without any fuss. Fine.

But I take my clothes with me.

In the bathroom, I take my time rinsing off because the water pressure is way better in here than it is out in my dorm, and I got pretty sticky with sweat last night. I wash my hair and do an all-out shave, not just the shins and lower part of my legs. I steal as much hotel product as I can manage, really going to town with the body wash and lotion. By the time I'm done and I've dried my hair (taking full advantage of this newfangled thing called electricity), Cole's gone down to retrieve me a coffee and some breakfast.

He leans against the dresser, sipping his coffee.

"Food?" I ask, hopeful, glancing over at the Styrofoam container on the table.

"*Warm* food."

I almost groan.

Apparently, the kitchen crews from various restaurants are working together to feed all the guests and staff. Resort guests have a limited breakfast buffet option. Meanwhile, staff get a set menu consisting of scrambled eggs, bacon, and toast.

"Thank you," I say, reveling in the sweet, *sweet* taste of coffee. I don't even care that it's not a specialty latte. Today, I'm happy with the black sludge.

He nods and watches me eat. I'm not sure why. Do I do it wrong? Am I shoveling it in too fast? Oh well, I'm too hungry to care.

"What'd you learn while you were down there?" I ask between bites.

For the record, I put on a Siesta Playa polo and khaki shorts after my shower. Cole is wearing work slacks and a hunter green sweater that looks absolutely divine against his olive skin and dark hair. Hair, by the way, that is back to its pristine condition. He's shaved his stubble and applied some deliciously scented aftershave. What would it be like to be *that* put together? And this, after going to bed at 2:00 a.m.!

"It's not great, but could be worse. You probably saw there's some major flooding. The grounds crew has surveyed everything, and it looks like most of the buildings have been spared, except for some staff housing."

I gulp, and he notices.

"Your dorm should be fine. We think it was only a dozen or so units down closer to the water, but we'll have to see. There's a large portion of the resort that's still without power, but that's to be expected considering how much of the island as a whole is without power. It looks like, from early reports, Turks and Caicos was mostly spared from the worst of it."

Thank god.

"What does all that mean for us? Staff?"

"We'll have you all remain in the hotel for the time being. No point in moving anyone until we get a better handle on the situation. It's easier to just keep things as they are."

"So . . . roomies for another day then? Interesting . . ."

He thinks I'm funny, *I know it*. There's a smile in that gaze. A little curl to those lips.

"I thought we did pretty good, don't you? No bloodshed. I mean, I didn't wake up handcuffed to the bed, so that's a plus."

His eyes narrow in amusement. "Where does your brain come up with this stuff?"

"I don't know. I read a lot as a kid."

He nods like this might explain things.

Then he pushes off the dresser and takes his coffee. "Lucky for you, I'll be gone most of the day. You'll have the room to yourself."

I frown. "I'll be gone, too, won't I? Aren't you going to put me to work?"

Turns out, I should have just accepted the day off.

◆ ◆ ◆

Originally, Cole wasn't going to have me go downstairs and clock in. For now, resort operations have temporarily ceased. Activities, excursions, the dog and pony show—yeah, it'll have to pause for the day as everything gets sorted out. Camila, Lara? They're holed up in their room watching a movie marathon. They texted me a picture of a bowl of popcorn with *Notting Hill* in the background. I mean, classic Julia Roberts? Say no more!

Meanwhile, where am I?

I'm playing triage nurse for Dr. Missick.

No scrubs or sensible clogs for me. I have a clipboard and piece of paper on which I write down every person who walks into Dr. Missick's waiting room, and from there, I have to decide where they rank in terms of least concerning injury to most concerning injury.

Why is this necessary, you might ask?

The preppers.

Yes, oh yes. While the rest of us were lying low for the last twenty-four hours, they've apparently been having a field day.

Why take it easy in the safety of a hotel room when you can throw yourself full force at danger and then come crying to the resort doctor (a.k.a. Mommy) when you accidentally hurt yourself?

I'm honestly shocked by how many injuries there are.

Let's go down the list, shall we?

There's the guy with a herniated disc from chopping up palm trees for hut building.

Oh, or how about the man who went out in the floodwaters to "hunt and gather" and wound up getting bitten by a snake?

More?

Okay. There's a case of bacterial gastroenteritis in the guy with the knockoff LifeStraw. ("It was the zero point zero one percent that must've got me.")

Currently, I'm sitting across from a guy as he explains that he went out into the storm last night because he wanted to test how windy it was, and while he was out there, he got whacked in the head with a heavy palm leaf. He's complaining that he can't hear out of his left ear at all.

"Could you speak up?!" he asks me as I go through the intake forms.

Instead, I speak softer and then act seriously concerned when he can't hear me. Oh dear, it's worse than we thought.

These guys just keep coming.

By the time I get my thirty-minute lunch break, we've run out of chairs.

I escape while I can. After all, Dr. Missick needs lunch too. My intention is to go directly to the cafeteria, but my feet lead me astray. I take a turn around the lobby; then I poke around the side hallways, acting casual about the fact that I'm doing a thorough search for Cole. I don't have anything I need to tell him. I guess I just . . . miss him. *Oh dear.* Maybe I should put my own name down on Dr. Missick's triage list.

Twenty-five-year-old female presenting with a case of lovesickness.

Proposed treatment plan? Unknown.

I don't even end up finding Cole, which leaves me feeling like a deflated balloon for exactly how long it takes me to get back to the clinic to find the waiting room filled with hotel guests, and then I'm too distracted to care.

Dr. Missick and I bond like two enemy soldiers on the battlefield. At the start of the day, we were adversaries. I was his last resort when I showed up this morning, offering my services. He very nearly turned me away altogether. "You know what? I'll manage fine on my own."

But as the day wears on and it becomes an "*us* versus *them*" situation, we learn to stick together.

Close to 4:00 p.m., he sends a patient out of his exam room and then calls me in. He's sitting on his stool, shoulders slightly slumped as he disposes of his nylon gloves in the nearly overflowing trash can nearby.

"How many more?" he asks, not bothering to hide the fatigue in his tone.

"Three, if you count the guy who rolled his ankle at the lunch buffet."

"Is it swollen?"

"No." I lower my voice as I continue. "And between you and me, I saw him walking on it just fine to go raid the snack basket a few minutes ago."

He nods, appreciating my candor. "Give him an ice pack and instructions to keep it elevated. If it's not better by the morning, we can send him off for an x-ray. Who's next?"

When I'm released from my post, I all but race back to the hotel room. I'm careening down the hall before I realize it and force myself to slow to a moseying walk. I hold my breath as I slide the key card over the door and then walk into the room, only to be disappointed when I find it's empty. But it figures. It's only a little past 5:00 p.m. Cole likely has to work late tonight.

It's actually better this way, considering my first objective is to immediately strip off my clothes. After spending all day in the clinic, I feel like I need a full spray down in one of those military-grade airlock chambers, but I settle for a quick rinse in the shower. After, in my comfy towel, while I hum a little tune to myself, I pick out lounge clothes: a pair of sleep shorts and an old T-shirt I got from the time my parents took me to Yellowstone National Park when I was a teenager. It's a little tight, and it exposes a teeny bit of my midriff, but it's too soft to part with.

I toss everything onto the bed, and *the* moment—I mean, truly, let's get an official in here to review the game footage—I drop my towel, the door to the hotel room opens.

I let out an involuntary shriek, and then I'm scrambling to pick the towel back up and cover all the important bits as fast as I can. Boobs are partly covered, vagina is . . . not so much.

"Hold on!"

It's too late. Cole's standing in the foyer as the door slams shut behind him. He looks like he's been frozen in place, a statue of shock. Michelangelo's *David*, only replace the weapon in his hand with two Styrofoam take-out containers.

The concept of turning around and averting his eyes doesn't even occur to him. My naked body has rendered him absolutely senseless.

"Cole!" I snap.

And finally he stammers, "Uh, yeah, um . . ."

He whips around toward the door; then a second later, his forehead drops against it.

"Say you're sorry," I demand dryly.

"And what if I'm not?"

Of course he's not. He just got the milk for free, no purchase necessary.

"How much did you see?"

"Most everything."

I can hear the smile in his voice.

"Erase it."

"It's already been cataloged." He double taps the side of his head with his finger. "I have a photographic memory for things I care about."

"COLE."

"Are you finished getting dressed yet?"

He makes like he's going to turn around again, and I emit some kind of squawk that forces him back around toward the door.

I wrench my T-shirt over my head and then sigh. "*There*. Done."

He turns and looks at me, and it's like his brown eyes are equipped with x-ray vision. The layers of clothing mean nothing to him.

I throw up my hands. "This isn't fair."

"Want me to take off my pants? Even the score?"

I let out a laugh and shake my head, pointing to the take-out containers.

"For you?"

He walks into the room and holds them up. "For *us*."

My greedy little mitts take the top container, and I bring it to my nose to inhale. "Thank god. I was too tired to stand in line for dinner, and I wanted to shower. I wasn't sure what I was going to do . . ."

"I figured. Tough day in the clinic?"

I groan in agony just thinking about it. "You could say that . . . Dr. Missick is a saint as far as I'm concerned."

He arches both brows. "You didn't use to think that."

I lift my chin. "I've had a change of heart."

And not just about Dr. Missick . . .

I open the lid on the container to reveal a cheeseburger (smash style) and a heaping pile of thin-cut french fries. *Hubba hubba.*

"Ketchup?"

He tosses me two packets, and I catch them deftly.

Then we sit across from each other at the small table in the hotel room, and we eat. It's civilized in a way we've never been before. When I run through my ketchup almost immediately (I need a dollop for every bite, obviously), Cole voluntarily gives me his spare pack without me even having to ask. It's a far cry from my date with Blaze, where he couldn't remember my name, *oh* and he was gay.

Not that this is a date.

I know that.

Cole knows that.

But if it *were* a date, it would be a really good one. The kind that feels spontaneous and unexpected, yet perfect. A picnic in the park versus a fancy dinner in a crowded restaurant; a stroll through a quiet bookstore versus shouted conversations in a smoky bar; a movie night where you make it fifteen minutes in and then lock eyes across the couch and turn absolutely *feral*.

"This is so good," Cole says, polishing off his burger in four bites.

He's almost done with his fries, too, but I don't want all of mine so I tilt my container toward him in invitation. He takes them with a grateful nod.

"So is this it?" I say, patting my full stomach. "Have we entered the friendship phase?"

"Friendship phase?"

"Yeah, you know, the type of relationship where we aren't constantly at each other's throats? We've moved beyond the enemy phase."

Cole assesses me while he finishes chewing. Whatever it is he's thinking about, it's making him irritated. I resist the urge to check for ketchup on my face. I won't buckle under his scrutiny, not anymore.

Finally, he reaches for more fries and shakes his head.

"Sounds kind of boring."

Oh, what's that I detect? An air of annoyance? Well, *excuuuuse* me. Remind me to never bring up friendship with Cole ever again.

"Friendship offer officially revoked."

He laughs. "So enemies again?"

"For life," I tease.

He clears our dinner as I go wash my hands. "What should we do now?" I call from the bathroom.

"I was going to head down and go for a run in the gym."

"But you just got back," I pout.

I dry my hands and walk back out into the suite to see that Cole's taken his sweater off so he can hang it back up in the closet. His undershirt is tight over his sculpted chest. His biceps flex in a way that zaps my brain cells.

"You don't need to go work out. Look at you! You're in tip-top shape. Your body-fat percentage is probably like point zero three."

His gaze slices to me. "Okay. So what should we do instead?"

I swear his eyebrow lifts slightly.

A flame ignites low in my belly, but I don't think he meant to turn me on with his innocuous question. I'm just a horndog.

"Argue about what TV show to watch?" I suggest helpfully.

I walk over to retrieve the remote off the dresser, and I wave it out for him to take. "Come on, you can go first. Pick something."

He walks over to take the remote from me, but when he reaches me, he pauses for a moment. Those heady x-ray eyes are back as he looks down, cocky in his inspection of my T-shirt and sleep shorts. I watch him swallow, and I fear for my resolve.

What would I do if he took another step closer?

If he bent down and fisted my shirt, tugging me toward him?

If he wanted to kiss me . . .

Knuckles pound on our door, distracting us.

I'm expecting housekeeping (Pavlovian response, probably, because who else knocks on your door when you're staying in a hotel?), but when I open it, Camila and Lara are standing out in the hall.

"She's alive!" Lara exclaims, throwing her hands up in celebration.

Camila wastes no time leaning in, trying to see past me. "Where is he?"

"*Who?*"

When she spots Cole still standing near the TV, her jaw drops open so wide I worry it might become permanently unhinged. Her gaze slowly shifts to me, filled with disbelief. "We heard you two were rooming together, but it just seemed like a dumb rumor. I mean, the odds . . ."

The two of them exchange a glance; then Lara looks to me.

"You said you found a spare room," she says like she's accusing me of lying.

I try to close the door a smidge, to make our conversation a little more private, but Camila won't let me. She props her foot out like it's a doorstop.

"I *did* find a spare room," I insist. "It just so *happened* to include Cole."

"So you're *willingly* here right now?" Lara asks, pointing inside the room. "This isn't like a hostage situation?"

"Damn it." Camila props her hands on her hips and shakes her head. "We should have come up with a safe word for this situation! With you two, this was bound to happen eventually . . ." She walks over to me and leans in really close, lowering her voice. "If he has you here under some kind of blackmail situation *or worse*, you just say the word and—"

Cole scoffs from his perch in front of the TV where he's scrolling through channels. "She's free to go whenever she wants."

Lara grins and reaches out for my hand, like problem solved. "Okay, good. C'mon. We heard there's some chocolate chip cookies downstairs. They're left over from lunch, but who cares? I'm in need of something sweet!"

"Oh . . ."

"Grab your shoes," Camila tells me.

But I don't move. In fact, I actively resist Lara's tugging. "I'm pretty full. I just ate a cheeseburger."

"Sooo?" Lara drawls, waving her pointer finger in a circle like she's waiting for me to get to the point. "You always say you have a dessert column and a dinner column. So . . . this should be no problem."

Okay. I didn't think I'd need to come up with another excuse here. I sigh, sounding exhausted. "I've had a long day."

Camila drops her chin and glares at me from beneath her eyebrows. *"Paige."*

"You don't have to stay," Cole says behind me, giving me the out.

And yeah, okay, but what if I *want* to stay? What if, for once, I did the thing that I truly *want* to do deep down, which is to hang out with Cole and actually admit that we enjoy each other's company?

"I think I'll just stay here . . . ," I say noncommittally. It's like, well, I'm already in the hotel room so it's not like I can just walk out, you know? I have to find my shoes, and it'll be a whole big thing.

But they don't buy it.

"Holy shit," Camila says, covering her mouth with her hands while she laughs with glee. "*It's happening!* It's finally happening!"

"What's happening?" I ask, feeling like I've been left out of the loop.

Lara doesn't answer me. She's looking at Camila like she doesn't know whether to laugh or cry. She's fluttering her hands in front of her face.

I turn back to Cole to see if he can make sense of any of this, but he just shakes his head and turns back to the TV.

"Right, well, see you later, weirdos. Enjoy your cookies."

Then I shut the door so I can willingly spend the rest of my night with Cole.

There's a sentence I never thought I'd say.

Chapter Twenty
PAIGE

The dust has barely settled on the closed door before buyer's remorse sets in about my decision. Not about hanging back with Cole—not at all. It's about turning down the cookies. I should have gotten more information. Like are they the thick, gooey ones or the thin, crunchy ones? What chocolate-chip-to-dough ratio are we talking about here?

I chew on my bottom lip.

Cole's still by the TV with the remote. He's given up finding anything worthwhile. Now, he watches me.

"Why do you look sad? You didn't have to stay with me."

"*No*," I rush out. "It's not that. I just kind of regret not going to get something sweet."

"You want something sweet?" He sets down the remote on the dresser and turns toward me. Already the cogs are spinning.

"Yeah. You?"

He tilts his head back and forth like he's letting the idea roll around his brain. "Yeah, I could do something sweet."

So it's decided then.

"Get your shoes," he tells me.

We head for the second-floor vending machines. I know that somewhere in the world there are newfangled vending machines that accept Venmo and retinal scans, but Siesta Playa has the old-timers that take coins and cash and complain about walking five miles to school, uphill. I have no cash on me because I never carry cash. I'm a card girl. Cole's only got a twenty, and the machines only accept one-dollar bills, so we make a pit stop down at reception, and Cole has them break it and give him change. All quarters. We need a bag to carry them all.

I'm already excited about what candy I'm going to buy, but when we arrive at the second-floor vending machine, we find it's been totally cleared out. Everything is out of stock save for a desiccated Honey Bun wedged between two rings.

"You've got to be kidding me."

"Everything? They got *everything*?!"

We both know who did it. One of the preppers got it in their head that we weren't going to provide them three meals a day, I bet. He's probably running some underground snack cartel out of his hotel room and charging people exorbitant prices. *"Listen, I don't make the rules. You want the M&M's or not?"*

"What do we do now?" I ask, turning to Cole.

We can't give up. My sweet tooth is aching.

"Downstairs, near the gym," Cole says with no further explanation. There's no need. I know he's thinking of where another vending machine is.

Lo and behold, that one's cleared out too.

"What the hell!" Cole erupts.

He's as mad as I am now. I don't even suggest giving up and going back to the room. Either we get candy or we die trying.

We both look at each other and say, at the same time, "Twelfth floor."

The twelfth floor has been undergoing renovations for the last few weeks because of water damage caused by a leak. No guests are allowed on the floor, but we are. We take the stairs up from the eleventh floor and push open the heavy door. Cole looks both ways, determining whether the coast is clear. Then we traipse right through the construction site. Considering it's after dinner, the crew's probably gone anyway.

Down at the end of the hall, we find a gloriously full vending machine beaming at us with all the light of ten thousand suns. Snack food glistens inside.

We make it rain on that machine.

I'm not sure if Cole planned on spending his entire twenty bucks on junk, but we do it. Hell, we probably could have cleaned out his entire wallet if this thing took larger bills.

It's a tedious process deciding exactly which snacks we need. You can't be hasty about this kind of thing.

"*Hold on*," Cole says, frantically reaching out for my hand before I can key in the code for a Butterfinger. "We already have a Hershey's and Reese's. We've filled our chocolate quota; now we need something fruity or sour and then something salty."

"Oh my god. Yes. Duh." I can't believe I was so close to leading us astray. What is this? Amateur hour?

"Okay, regular Skittles or sour Skittles?" I ask.

Cole looks at me, his eyes narrow subtly, and then he begins counting. "One . . . two . . . three—"

"Sour," we say together.

Zap. It's like Cupid's arrow just struck me square in the heart. I'm surprised I don't topple over.

The urge to make out with him right this instant is *strong*.

After I get our sour Skittles, I put my hands on my hips and turn to him again. My face is a mask of seriousness. I'm a researcher conducting a science experiment that could impact all humanity. "Cheddar and sour cream Ruffles *or* Cool Ranch Doritos?"

Cole scoffs like, *No way, man*, but he doesn't back down from the challenge. "All right. One . . . two . . . three—"

"Cheddar—" we begin in unison.

Oh my god, is this what it feels like to fall in love?

I swear he sways toward me like he's feeling it too. His nostrils flare. His eyes glaze over with a sultry heat.

We're going to kiss right here in front of this vending machine while getting slightly high off construction-site paint fumes. I can almost imagine it. As soon as our mouths make contact, I'll drop the candy and he'll grab my waist, hoisting me up against the glass, incensed and impatient. My lips will part, and his tongue will slip in so easily to find mine. I'll whimper like I'm aching for him because, in fact, I am.

We'll be complete animals.

It's so close to happening, and then a burly construction worker pushes past the crinkly plastic tarp I hadn't even noticed. "*Hey!* You two shouldn't be here."

I scream.

Are we *actually* in trouble? No.

Do we take off in a dead sprint like two delinquent teenagers anyway? Absolutely.

"Stairs! Stairs!" Cole commands, taking my hand and tugging me along when I start to fall behind. I didn't wear the right footwear for a quick getaway. My sandal strap keeps coming undone!

I can't control my laughter as Cole throws the stairwell door open and drags me in after him. We make it down to the eleventh-floor landing, and then, "The Skittles!"

They just slipped from my hands.

"Damn it, Young, we don't have time for this!" Cole says, as invested in the pseudoaction as I am.

That construction worker is up there scratching his balls, totally unbothered by us, but we don't care. We're fleeing for our lives. Cole runs back to pick up the Skittles, gets a firm grasp on my hand, and down we go, floor after floor, until we make it all the way back to our room.

Bonnie and Clyde have nothing on us as we slam the door closed and double bolt it. With relieved sighs, we flatten ourselves against the door and start to catch our breath. My heart's still racing when I slowly turn to face him. He turns to face me.

We don't say a word. We stare at each other, our eyes roaming with hungry abandon as we try to regain our composure.

Adrenaline's coursing through me like I've been hooked up to an IV filled with it. It's the same for Cole. I can see it in the way his pulse jumps in his neck. There's a spark in his brown eyes that seems to charge the moment with a dangerous edge. I realize now why couples are always making out at the end of action movies. Tom Hanks has just found Jesus's long-lost goblet, and now all he wants to do is suck face with the female archaeologist who helped him dig it up. I've always thought it was a little dumb, but now I *get* it. Sprinting from the authorities really gets your heart going. Everything is pulsing and alive, and I'm not sure Cole has ever looked hotter than he does right now.

I want to do something crazy: tangle my fingers in his hair, kiss up the side of his neck, wrap my legs around him and . . .

"Say something," he says with a gentle plea. Meanwhile, his attention is zeroed in on my lips like he wishes he could taste them.

I wet the bottom one, and it's like he can feel it too.

"I can't."

His eyebrows furrow in despair.

"Are you hurt?" he asks, his tone now filled with mock gravity. He's worried he missed a gunshot wound to the abdomen back there: I've been slowly bleeding out this whole time without him realizing. Our happy ending won't come after all. Roll credits.

He pushes off the door and turns to cage me in against it. I laugh as he pats me down like he's checking for wounds. His hands slide gently over the sides of my chest and stomach. It's playful and silly, but it's also extremely hot. The edge of his thumb accidentally brushes the underside of my breast. His hand finds a spot on the side of my rib cage that isn't ticklish, it's *sexy*. A moan nearly sneaks past my lips before I bite down, stifling it.

I'm not supposed to be majorly turned on, but soon, I'm panting for reasons that have nothing to do with our sprint back to our room.

His hands freeze on my waist, and he bends so his gaze can find mine. His expression turns knowing as he recognizes what he's doing to me. *How* does he know, exactly? Beats me. Maybe I'm drooling a little. Maybe my pheromones are wafting off me in great cloying plumes.

I'm too on display, with him looking at me like this.

"All good," I promise, pushing off the door.

The move brings me right up to his chest. I'm stuck unless he moves. In the small foyer, I can't scoot around him, not unless I want to brush up against him even more, which . . . doesn't feel like the best idea right now. Not while his gaze is as hungry as it is. Not while my common sense has officially left the building.

He doesn't move right away. There's a moment when he's crowding me, tall and foreboding. It's the way a high school bully would trap a cowering nobody against a set of lockers. The bell already rang; the hallway's deserted. He's playing chicken, testing me.

Let's finish what we started, he seems to say as he takes a tiny step forward.

I can do nothing but gulp.

I want to meet his challenge head on, throw myself at him, fuse myself to his body from this day forward as long as we both shall live. The last few days have felt markedly different for us. His confession about Todd, us sharing a bed last night . . . it could be the catalyst we need to *finally* get out of our own way. The trouble is we've been here before. That night on the beach felt like it could have changed things for us, but it didn't. We kissed, and then the next day, *poof*, nothing. So how can I be certain things won't go right back to normal the second this weird roommate situation wraps up?

A few days from now, we could be adversaries across the lobby.

Only this time, I know with absolute certainty that I won't be able to bear it.

Whether or not things have changed for Cole, they've changed for me. I've given him too many pieces of me, little by little. If things don't work this time, there won't be anything left. No more banter. No more friendship. I'll have to be done.

The thought hangs like a storm cloud over me, dousing whatever steamy moment we were building. I'm terrified he'll see it—*all of it*—before I've composed the full picture for myself.

I yank the Reese's out of Cole's hand and cut past him to get to the bed.

For now, I'm putting us on ice.

At least until I finish this chocolate.

Chapter
Twenty-One
PAIGE

I do a poor job of acting normal the rest of the night.

After I leave him hanging at the door, Cole catches the hint and backs off the buddy-buddy stuff. We sit on the bed and share our candy while we watch the second half of a zombie movie. I'm usually a wimp when it comes to thrillers, but not tonight. My eyes are on the screen, but nothing gets transmitted to my brain. Jump scare after jump scare, blood and guts galore—I don't even blink. Cole thinks I'm a total badass, when really I'm just distracted.

The movie ends, and Cole reaches for the remote and turns off the TV. It's dead silent when he looks over at me. I panic, thinking he's about to ask me what's going on, and I'm not ready. I'm not. I just need a little more time. A shower.

Sure, I took one earlier, but that run from the twelfth floor is my excuse for why I need another. And if I happen to stay in there awhile, it's because I'm being really thorough. You have to wash all the crannies, not just the nooks.

I've never taken more care with my postshower skin care routine. Sure, it's just toner and a moisturizer, two products I usually slap on while on my way to pee. Tonight, however, my skin is singing by the time I walk out of the bathroom and find Cole reading in bed.

I'm sorry, let me paint a better picture.

Ahem. Cole is lying back on the bed in nothing but his pajama pants. His legs are crossed at the ankles. One hand is resting behind his head on the pillow—elongating his toned stomach. His other hand cradles a paperback on top of his abs.

He doesn't pause his reading on my account. I think there's only so many times a person can try to strike up conversation and get shot down before they realize it's probably best to not bother at all. Hopefully he just thinks I'm in a quiet mood.

I skim around the edge of the bed and walk up along my side. Cole's T-shirt—the one I slept with last night—is folded neatly by my pillow. He put it there again. Before I can help myself, I reach out and feel the material between my thumb and pointer finger, rubbing the soft cotton. Maybe I'm a tactile person, because it actually calms me down a little.

I feel Cole's gaze on me, but by the time I glance up, he's reading his book again.

This is it, I think.

Now or never.

I gave myself the last few hours to come to terms with what I have to do: come clean once and for all.

I took the shower; I dawdled and delayed. Here I am with the perfect opportunity, and what do I do?

I hurry under my covers, tuck them up to my chin, then reach up and turn off my lamp. My half of the room goes dim.

Now.

No.

Now! Just say it and be done!

It'll change things forever.

That ship has sailed. You're hugging the guy's T-shirt. Just do it!

I go to turn over, but then Cole stands up to do his nighttime routine in the bathroom.

No problem, I'll wait up for him.

But then when he walks back out a few minutes later, he lies down, and his lamp cuts off.

Now the room is good and dark.

Good going . . . you waited too long, and now it's too late.

I listen to him getting comfortable.

"Night, Paige."

"Night," I reply lamely.

No. *NO!*

A few minutes pass—enough time for me to sufficiently berate myself for not being braver—and then I speak up.

"Psst . . . Cole? Are you awake?"

"What?"

He sounds groggy, like maybe he was asleep and I woke him up.

"No. Never mind. Go to sleep."

I roll over and face the window.

"Now you have to say it. Don't leave me hanging or I won't be able to sleep."

"It's okay, forget it."

He takes ahold of my arm in the dark and rolls me over, flat onto my back. *"What?"*

"You're not tired?"

"You've been acting weird and quiet for the last few hours. Please, for the love of god—"

"Okay . . . well, I have a question I've been wondering about for a while, actually."

"What's it about?"

"Us."

There's a long delay, and then he replies, "Am I going to have to pry it out of you, or are you going to get on with it?"

"I'll get on with it. Yeah . . . I can. Let me just—"

I sit up all the way, leaning my back against the headboard. I feel for his T-shirt and clutch it to me and speak like I'm inside a Catholic confessional, like nothing I say can be held against me. That's how those work, right? I'm not sure. Where's the pope when you need him?

"Paige," he prompts.

"Did you . . . have you . . ." It's like I've got a tenuous grasp on the English language, like that little boy in the viral video asking, "Have you ever had a dream that, that, that you, um, you, could, you could do, you, you, um, you want, you want, you, you could do anything?"

That's me.

"Do you sometimes think about the kiss we shared a few months ago?" I finally force it out. Then I press my face into his shirt, waiting for the inevitable heartbreaking comment that's about to come.

He doesn't answer within half a millisecond, so I immediately panic. "Yeah, me neither! *Good night!*"

I lie flat again, roll over, and squeeze my eyes closed, praying with every fiber of my being that a sinkhole suddenly erupts beneath us and we go down in a crumbling heap of rubble. Wouldn't that be wonderful? A nice big boulder, smack to the forehead.

Cole chuckles, and my eyes ping open.

"I can't believe you're even asking me that right now . . ."

I frown, confused. "Because I should already know the answer?"

He sighs. "Paige . . . *yes*, I think about it. I think about it all the time."

I hold perfectly still. "Why?"

I know why *I* think about it. It's my most frequented fantasy, the one I revisit every night, alone in my dorm. Never mind that I feel foolish doing it. I can't give it up, no matter how hard I try.

He scoots closer. "Because every moment of my day is spent the same way. Hour after hour. Minute after minute. I want you, always."

Holy hell.

That's . . . that's really something.

I repeat it all back to myself in my head, just to be sure I've got it right. There was no double entendre I was too stupid to pick up on the first time, right? No hidden meaning?

"But you never—"

"When would I—"

Oh my god.

I stare up at the dark ceiling as the numbness from the last few hours starts to lift, replaced by a delicious warmth.

"I think I've been blind," I tell him.

"And I've been too shy . . ."

It's too late for me to rein in my elation. I'm a confetti cannon, ready to fire. I turn over and hurriedly reply, "You don't have to be shy now. It's just me in the dark."

Me, the girl who's loved you in quiet for months and months.

A heavy pause sends a frisson of fear through me. Things aren't set in stone. My heart is still waiting on tenterhooks, hoping for the best. This could all go up in smoke.

Then I feel Cole shift on the bed, scooting even closer to me. I feel his heat before I feel him touch my arm. He drags his hand up until he reaches my neck, my face. Then he cups my cheek and turns my face so that I'm looking at him in the dark. What is he thinking? Where is he looking?

"Paige?"

His voice is the only thing I have to go by, and so I focus there. "Hmm?"

"No more war. Wave your white flag."

"I am. Can you see it?"

I take his hand from my cheek and put it on my wrist as I sway my hand back and forth. He laughs, and then he tugs free of my grip and comes over me, his heaviness like a blanket on top of me. His hips pin mine down as he falls forward, his hands on the pillow beside my head.

"Tell me the truth once and for all," he demands.

I can smell his minty breath. His mouth is so close to mine now.

"What do you want to know?"

"Am I alone in this?"

I shake my head, but he can't see it. It's not answer enough.

"Say it, please," he begs. "Say it and I'll believe you. Say it and we can be done." His mouth drops even closer. "No more pretending, I swear it."

When I go quiet, he leans down farther. His lips brush my temple, my cheek. I don't think he has a plan in mind except to tempt me out of my shell. Just when his mouth creeps toward mine and I think he'll kiss me—my excitement growing—he pulls away, and it's the fear of his departure that finally provokes me to speak the truth.

"I love you," I say as I grab for him, worried he'll leave. "God, more than that, *I like you.* I like you so much. This year, since I met you, it feels like you're the only one who gets me, like you're my very best friend but also . . . I feel so . . . so—"

"Scared?"

"Petrified."

He takes my hand then and brings it to his chest, pressing it hard against his heartbeat. He's showing me his fear too.

He's answering my worries.

"Paige, I . . ."

He stalls like the words are stuck in his throat. I'm not surprised he's having trouble expressing himself. Cole isn't the type to throw around casual endearments.

"*You* . . . ," I say, goading him with a smile.

"I love you." His words are a whisper. Even now, even in this, he's shy.

Then he lifts my hand to his lips, and he presses a kiss to my palm, my wrist, the crook of my elbow, my shoulder . . . on he goes to my neck, chin. Then his mouth finds mine, and it's like we've just cut our chains and freed ourselves. My arms loop around his neck as he falls down onto me, kissing me with a fierceness I've never felt. It's overwhelming, but that little voice of worry in my head doesn't get center stage. Lust wins out. The need to let him continue however he likes, to do with me whatever he wishes.

I would love to see him, but I can't be bothered to push him off me and turn on a lamp, so I feel him instead. I run my hands down his muscular back until I reach the dip at his hips. I press my body up against his, and he responds by pushing me down hard into the bed, rolling his hips, making me gasp.

When we started to kiss, I seemed too aware of everything. How I positioned my hands. How I moved my lips. Slowly, he coaxes me into just feeling the passion, letting go of all the insecurities swirling in my head. Soon it's only him. His touch. His kiss. His pleasure melding with mine.

He works my shirt up over my stomach, and his mouth falls there. He kisses my navel and travels up, pushing my shirt higher until cool air caresses my chest. Warmth replaces it as his hands cup my breasts, palming the taut flesh as he teases me. He lowers his mouth there, sweeping his tongue over each tip, making my back arch off the bed.

I'm adrift in pleasure when he suddenly pushes up and turns on the lamp. I blink, adjusting to the shallow light.

Then I see him there, his dark hair mussed up from my hands, his gaze wicked, his lips dark red.

He doesn't ask; he simply tugs my shirt off the rest of the way, up and over my head. Then it falls to the floor, an afterthought now.

He admires me without a word as I lie on the bed in nothing more than my panties. My cheeks are warm, and despite my efforts to remain still, I fidget under his intense gaze.

How did we get here?

How is he so calm?

Words don't tumble out of him the way I want them to. Beautiful, irresistible, *sexy beyond belief*—these are all good. I would accept any of them. Cole just seems . . . entranced. And while he might not say any of those words aloud, I feel them in his soft caress, the way his hands squeeze my waist, the way he wets his bottom lip and then blinks as if forcing himself back to the task at hand: giving me sweet, *sweet* pleasure.

"Do you think we'll continue?" I tease.

"Definitely."

"Then shouldn't you take your shirt off too?"

He does it so fast it's like he's been practicing for this moment all year. Every day, he times himself. *Faster, Cole, faster. Damn it.* The *Rocky* soundtrack plays in the background.

Now I'm the one who's gone mute as he sits shirtless above me. *Honestly, Cole. How dare you cover up every day in those suits?* Leaving *this* to the imagination? So cruel . . .

Since he took his sweet time exploring me, I do the same. I walk my fingers up his chest, over every subtle ridge and valley, taking detailed notes in my mind. Later, I'll be able to draw his body to scale, including elevations, like an expert cartographer. I make it all the way to his collarbone, and then I decide I haven't had enough so I start again. But before I can, Cole reaches out and snatches my wrist with the reflexes of a viper.

He doesn't give an explanation; it's not needed. Cole's impatience is heating the air between us. His hunger is feeding mine. While he keeps hold of my wrist with one hand, his other hand traces the top of my panties. Ever so slowly, like he's trying to catalog every last thread, he drags the pad of his finger along there. I'm flushed and needy. Every one of my nerve endings seems to have been brought to the surface. He eases off me a little. I twist my hips, and he slides his hand lower, over the soft satin material that covers me. His hand disappears between my legs, and then I feel him brush two fingers across the center of me. *Oh, Cole.*

I squeeze my eyes closed, partly in embarrassment, partly to keep from succumbing to his touch too quickly. I could. I mean, how long have I wanted this? How good does it feel to finally have Cole's hand where I want it, toying with me, teasing the material of my panties aside so that his fingers can touch me—skin to skin. I writhe underneath him, and he smiles. I don't even need to open my eyes to see it. I *know* it's there.

"I like when you whimper," he tells me with a cocky edge to his tone.

And then he rubs his fingers across the most sensitive part of me, and a small moan twists its way out of my throat.

I want more but I don't know how to ask for it, don't know how to even force an actual word out of my mouth with consonants and vowels. But then Cole doesn't need my help. He delivers all on his own as his finger presses slowly inside me. Then he draws it back out and adds a second.

My hand finds his wrist, and I squeeze with a plea.

Continue. Continue FOREVER!

He chuckles under his breath, and then he shifts, lowering himself to the side of me so his hand can stay where it is between my legs but his mouth can find mine.

He sinks his fingers in deeper, and I gasp for air just before he kisses me, stealing the last few shreds of common sense I had left.

It feels like too much to have so much of his attention focused on me, but it's like he wants me like this, completely at his mercy, rolling my hips up to meet his hand, fidgety, needy, totally on edge.

His mouth and his hand are savage now. His lips. His fingers. His teeth. It's all a blur. I feel so consumed. I'm hot, hotter, *hottest*—and then I come apart, crying his name like I'm almost in pain. Those little flashes of light behind my closed lids, the tendrils of pleasure lashing through me. Cole sees it all, the purest part of me, and when I'm done and I blink my eyes open and stare at him, I think I recognize love in his gaze. But then he kisses me again, tender and sweet, and when he pulls back, he assesses me with a lazy smile.

Now here is where we *would* continue. I mean, some could argue that we absolutely *have to* continue. He's supposed to crawl up over me and sink into me and we'd go at it all night long.

And for the record, I do argue for it.

When he stands up to go into the bathroom after my orgasm to end all orgasms, I sit up, confused.

"Wait, what about *you*?"

"What about me?"

"Don't you want to . . . y'know?"

"Not tonight."

"What?! Why *not* tonight?"

He doesn't answer, so I'm forced to scramble off the bed and follow him. He's at the sink washing his hands. Then he reaches for his toothbrush like it's any ol' night! Gotta keep the chompers pearly white!

I blink fast, trying to piece together what's happening. "Wait . . . are you a virgin?"

He's trying not to laugh now. "Paige . . . it's not that."

He finally looks at me in the mirror, and though he just had me splayed out underneath him on the bed, the sight of me naked in the doorway still stops him in his tracks.

For the record, I'm wholly unperturbed by my nakedness. I have a good body. You don't hike thirty-plus miles a week without having some kick-ass legs to show for it. And he's seen all of me now. Felt it, too, so what do I care about being naked? Besides, I have more serious issues to contend with, like why Cole isn't currently railing me on that bed.

"Do you have issues getting it up?"

He rolls his eyes and turns.

His li'l Cole is large and in charge, fully erect beneath his boxer briefs, thank you very much.

"It's dumb," he says, shaking his head and turning around to continue brushing his teeth.

"Say it."

"*Paige.*"

I throw my hands up in protest. "I was just honest with you! I thought you said we weren't going to pretend anymore. So tell me the truth."

In the mirror, his eyes lock with mine. "I want to be sure you feel okay about what we just did. I want you to sleep on it."

"SLEEP ON IT?!"

"I don't want you to change your mind."

CHANGE MY MIND?!

"That's absurd."

He doesn't reply.

He starts to brush his teeth.

Oh, I hate him. I hate him. He doesn't get to do that to me, to see me unravel like that and then shift immediately to his dental hygiene routine.

No.

I walk toward him, taking his shoulders gently in hand, and slowly turn him until he's facing me.

"*Paige*," he says around his toothbrush.

Ooh, I like the warning in his voice. There's a sharpness to it that I can't resist.

He wants me to turn an about-face and retreat, but I'm on a mission.

"What? I'm not doing anything."

I am, though. I'm kneeling down and positioning myself at his feet, wrapping my hands around his thighs. The cold tile bites into my knees, and maybe I'll be sporting bruises in the morning, maybe not. What do I care?

What should be a second warning never comes.

No, Cole's already lost to the feeling of my hand cupping his length through his boxer briefs. Oh yes. No issues here. Everything is working *just* fine in this department, let me assure you.

I peer up at him from beneath my lashes.

His toothbrush is gone, forgotten. He twists around, spits his toothpaste out in the sink, and then wipes his mouth with the back of his hand. He shouldn't be as sexy as he is, damn it.

Now, I slide my hand up higher along his thigh until I can slip it underneath the pesky cotton that's keeping us apart. I feel him first that way, hard as steel, soft and smooth. Blessedly thick. I work him up, pumping my hand a few times, just until his head lolls back and his eyes shut.

I can't keep the delicious smile off my face. I'm evil, truly.

I don't even need to take his boxer briefs off completely. No, I tug them down enough to free his hard length, and then I take him in my mouth. His hiss dissolves into a guttural groan.

When I take my lips off him, he looks down with dark, hooded eyes.

More? my cocked eyebrow says.

His hand cups my cheek before sliding back into my hair. He's so gentle about it at first, and then when I don't continue—because this is a game, after all—he pulls me closer, forcing me just enough to show me how much he wants this.

My hand closes around him harder, pumping up and down as I take the tip just past my lips and suck. Slowly, teasingly, I take him all the way into my mouth, working him as best I can. Victory tastes oh so sweet. Salty too.

I'm not overly adept at this, but the sounds he's making assures me that I've mostly got it right. Squeeze, pump, suck, continue. His hand fists tighter in my hair. I love it. I want it to go on forever, but my jaw is aching and he's sliding deeper down my throat. I feel like I need a huge gulp of air or my lungs are going to burst, and then he comes, hard. Pleasure racks through him in great heaving waves, and I take it like a champ, smiling even.

I know he's the one that just had an orgasm, so tell me why I feel like gloating as I push to my feet. Maybe it's the look in Cole's eyes. The absolute promise lurking in his gaze:

You're going to get it, Paige. Just remember while it's happening . . . you asked for it.

Chapter
Twenty-Two

PAIGE

When I wake up the next morning, the shower's going, Cole's half of the bed is empty, and my phone is vibrating on my nightstand. It's my mom, no doubt wanting an update on what's going on over here.

The brief report: Yeah, so hurricane destruction ended up not being so bad. I *did* give my indirect superior a blow job yesterday, though, so that's kind of shaking things up over here in Turks and Caicos. Stay tuned.

I answer with a sleepy hello.

"Bad timing?" my mom asks. "I figured you'd be up by now."

"No, it's fine. I'm up," I assure her.

"Dad's here with me too. Say hi."

"Hi, Dad!"

"Hi, Paigey! We've been worried sick about you the last few days. How are you holding up?"

I sit up and let my legs dangle off the side of the bed. "I'm good, promise." When I push off the bed and walk over to peer out the window, I find that most of the flooding around the resort's property has receded now. The grounds crew has been hard at work too. The debris and trash have been collected. If I didn't know better, it'd look like we just got a hard rain, nothing more. The plants and trees are green and vibrant, soaking up the hot sun.

I'm sure if I check my email, I'll find an updated work schedule. I can't imagine they'll stall resort operations for another day. Not if things are mostly back to normal.

"What about the resort?"

"It's totally fine, Mom. The flooding is pretty much gone now. I'm sure they'll have us—"

The bathroom door opens then, and Cole walks out, freshly showered, fully dressed for work.

"Hon? What were you saying?" my mom prompts.

Cole looks up to find me staring.

"Hi," he mouths while he finishes putting on his silver watch.

I smile and mouth back, "Hi."

"Did we lose her?" my dad asks.

"This connection is so spotty." My mom grumbles. *"Paige?"*

Cole starts walking toward me, and my breath stalls in my chest. When he reaches me, he bends down to kiss my cheek, and I close my eyes, savoring it.

"Paige?" my mom tries once more.

Then the call goes dead. I let the phone slip away from my ear as I promise myself I'll call them back later and answer any and all of their questions ad nauseam.

"Your parents?" Cole asks, nodding toward the phone.

"They've been worried."

He nods. "You should call them back."

"I will."

For now, I reach up to stroke a finger down the center of his shirt. No tie today, just a pristine white button-down with SIESTA PLAYA embroidered over the left breast pocket. Cole lets me trail my finger down all the way to his stomach, and then he grabs my hand and laces our fingers together.

"How are you feeling this morning?"

"About us?" I ask, chewing on the inside of my mouth.

He nods.

"Absolutely more sure than ever."

I'm proud of myself for speaking the truth for once without dancing around it.

"Good."

He bends down without warning and kisses me on the lips.

"*Wow*," I say when he peels back. "So we're just doing it now? Kissing in broad daylight?"

Cole smiles, and the sight of it, dimple and all, absolutely slays me.

"That's what couples do."

"What *else* do couples do?" I ask teasingly.

"They get ready for work so they're not both late."

I make a sound like a game show buzzer.

"Boring! What else?"

"They pack their bags because their resort vacation is officially over . . ."

My smile drops. "Say it ain't so."

He frowns too. "I got an email this morning that staff housing has been deemed all clear. Power has been restored to the entire resort, and the few employees whose dorms flooded have been relocated. There's no reason for staff to remain in the hotel."

"*Boo.*"

He squeezes my hand to let me know he doesn't like it either.

"Should we? Y'know . . ." My eyebrows waggle as I indicate the bed.

"I have to be down in the lobby in five minutes."

"So that leaves us what? Four minutes, thirty seconds?"

We didn't take things any further last night. After we cleaned up in the bathroom and put on our pajamas, Cole and I lay together in bed in the dark, talking. *TALKING.* It felt like a throwback to my childhood sleepover days, lying awake with my best friend, rambling. I made Cole walk me through different moments of our relationship from his perspective.

"When did you first think I was hot?"

"When did you first want to kiss me?"

"Why did you let me go after Blaze?!"

His answers?

"Right away."

"Right away."

"Because I wasn't sure where things were going with us. If Blaze was the guy you wanted, I wasn't going to brute-force him out of your life."

"Did you know he was involved with someone else?" I asked, studying his face for any tells.

"No, but I was . . . *hopeful.*"

Now, Cole leans down to kiss me and to shut down my idea of a quickie. "Tonight. You can come over to my place, and I'll wine and dine you."

"Ohhh, a coveted dorm invite?! Things *are* serious."

He looks at me kind of funny. "I don't live in a dorm."

"What?"

He laughs. "I have a two-bedroom villa on property."

"You're kidding me."

I don't know why this is so shocking to me. Why did I think Cole lived in a dorm like the rest of us poor schmucks? He's on the executive team. None of them live in the dorms. I guess I just wanted to imagine him that way, stuffed into an eight-by-ten room like the rest of us.

"But you use the cafeteria?" I ask, still trying to piece things together in my head.

"Because I don't have time to cook most days."

Oh.

"But you *do* have a kitchen?" I clarify.

"Yeah, a big one. New appliances and everything. I cook sometimes on the weekends."

I am flabbergasted. I can't stop. "How many bathrooms?"

"Two and a half."

"View?"

"The beach."

I smack his shoulder playfully. "Cole Clark! Stop it right now!"

He laughs. "You'll see it tonight. We can cook together if you want."

"I want!"

Cole helps me pack up my things while I hurry to get ready for work. I don't have to go downstairs right now. I checked, and I'm not supposed to be at my post for another hour, but I want to have as much time with Cole as possible before we get whisked away to opposite ends of the resort all day. He carries my duffel bag down for me, and we hold hands the entire way to my dorm. I keep expecting people on the path to stop and do a double take when they see us, but it's a big resort, and my little love story isn't all that relevant to most people. It's not like Cole and I were all that obvious with our antics over the last year. Short of Camila and Lara, I doubt anyone else even realizes how much attention we paid each other in the shadows.

Outside my dorm, I take out my keys and unlock my door. Then I fling the door open with a show-stopping "Ta-*da*! It's slightly more tidy than the last time you saw it."

Cole saw my room the night I was drunk, but it doesn't stop him from doing another curious perusal. I would do the same with him. I *will*, later.

"What's your favorite part?" I ask, anxious to pick his brain. I want to know everything there is to know about Cole Clark.

"The shrine of me you have tucked away in your closet."

I panic for a second, as if I actually *do* have a shrine in my closet and he's known about it this whole time!

Then he shakes his head and laughs. "The poster of the glacier," he says, pointing at the series of framed prints I keep over my bed, right beside my bulletin board.

"That's actually my mom's picture! She took it."

He eyes me skeptically.

I smile gleefully while I nod. "For real. My parents are marine biologists. They travel all over. For a while my mom dabbled in photography as well, just for some extra cash. She doesn't do it so much anymore, but yeah, that one is hers. She'll be happy to know you liked it. I'll tell her."

"They know about me?" He seems surprised by the idea.

I nod.

"Like they know about Blaze?" he continues with a slight edge to his tone.

Oh god. My cheeks redden. Why'd he have to go and bring that up?!

"I only ever had *one* conversation with them about Blaze, and the connection was spotty. My mom thought his name was Blake the whole time. Anyway, they . . . know that wasn't really going anywhere."

He doesn't hide his smile. "Oh, interesting. It's just . . . the way you went on about it seemed like they were practically planning the wedding."

"Yeah, yeah . . . listen, all's fair in love and war, right? It's not like you didn't use every weapon in your arsenal too. What about that time at the pool when you were flirting with Tamara right in front of me?"

My blood boils just thinking about it, but Cole frowns like he's having a hard time remembering what I'm talking about.

"The day you intimidated Blaze, Tamara strolled right up to flirt with you."

"If she was flirting with me, I didn't even realize." He shrugs. "She was just talking about work, if I'm recalling the right conversation. I don't know, I talk to a lot of employees every day."

"So it was barely a blip on your radar?" I step closer. "Am *I* just a blip on your radar?"

His eyes rake over me, and I swear dangerous thoughts are swirling behind his gaze.

"You're something else entirely."

He drags a hand through his hair and looks away, likely trying to cool himself off. I love that I have this effect on him.

"So you've told your parents about me?" he asks, circling us back to a neutral topic.

Oh god. This is embarrassing. "Yes . . ." He rears back, worried. "But not in the way you're thinking," I hurry to amend, reaching out to grab his forearms. "They think you're my friend."

"I *am* your friend," he reminds me.

"Yes, but well . . . they think you're *just* my friend, plain and simple. None of the other complicated enemy stuff. I didn't want to worry them with all the ways we tormented each other, and also, a part of me had hoped this whole time that maybe . . ." My voice lilts here, like I'm still too self-conscious to admit the truth. "I wasn't actually lying to them, you know? That eventually you and I *would* figure out how to happily coexist."

He likes this. "Well, you'll have to call and tell them the truth now, won't you?"

"What?" I ask lamely.

He grabs ahold of my waist and hauls me up against him, shaking me as he delivers a Jane Austen–esque monologue. "Turns out, Mother, I was blind to my own feelings! He was never my enemy! Not truly. And now I've found—*I've found I love him madly!*"

Okay, Matthew Macfadyen from 2005's *Pride and Prejudice*.

"Ha ha."

He leans down to kiss me, unbothered by my sarcasm. "I really have to run. I'm going to be late." He's already walking backward to the door. "Tonight, six thirty! Meet me in the lobby, and I'll walk you over to my house. It's a date."

A date.

Who would have thought?

Chapter Twenty-Three
COLE

I'm en route to my least favorite activity here at Siesta Playa: meeting with Todd. This hurricane has given me a nice little reprieve from him. We've been so busy putting out fires that he hasn't had a chance to pull me aside to continue executing his brilliantly idiotic plan of laying off valuable employees. His reasoning for the whole thing isn't even sound. He thinks he's going to save the resort a few bucks and our CEO's going to congratulate him for it? What happens when the guests start realizing that the service here took a nosedive? That all our best people—the ones who make their stay here worthwhile—are gone because of Todd's inability to see past his own thickheaded ideas?

It doesn't matter. I won't let Todd get to me. I'm in a good mood. Paige will do that to you, make you feel all warm and fuzzy inside. I'm walking like I'm in a bouncy house—lighter than air after last night and this morning.

I love her.

I pass a cleaning lady, and I almost grab her by the shoulders and spin her around to tell her.

"Did you hear? I love Paige!"

Surely those gardeners over there want to know.

"Guys! I'm in love and I don't care who knows it!"

The other reason I'm in a good mood? The Survival Preparedness convention wraps up today. The loons are leaving. Sayonara until next year! You'd think after this hellacious experience with the hurricane and power outages they'd rethink a return visit to Siesta Playa, but I know better. They'll be flocking here more than ever come next August. I shiver just thinking about it. Maybe I can convince Paige to take that week off with me. We'll book a trip somewhere, *anywhere*.

I turn down the executive hall, checking the time. Todd texted me this morning.

He texts me a lot, actually. It's always memes that were barely funny five years ago and therefore definitely not funny now. I don't even know where he finds these blurry JPEG relics from the past. A chain email?

I don't usually respond to his texts unless they're directly work related, but like death and taxes, they just keep on coming.

This morning's text was about this impromptu meeting. Despite walking Paige to her dorm, I'm still right on time. I knock once and then let myself into his office since his door's already open.

He sees me and nods. "Cole, good. Come on in, son. And shut that door behind you, will you?"

Being referred to as "son" by Todd is nausea inducing, but I do as he says, closing the door.

He's standing at his window, cracking open peanuts and trying to drop the empty skins into a trash can at his feet. *Trying* being the operative word. His aim is off; most of the shells wind up on the floor. When he sees me notice, he kicks the mess with his foot, trying to disperse it. Yup, that oughta do it.

"Take a seat. You want some peanuts?"

He shakes the two-gallon bag in my direction.

I pat my stomach. "Had a big breakfast. Thanks, though."

"Ah," he grumbles. "Trying to be careful with that dainty figure of yours?"

Dainty. Right. A tanker truck is dainty compared to Todd.

But I don't say this. Of course not. I merely nod because with Todd, it's best to say less. If I'm not careful, eventually I'll put my foot in my mouth one of these days. He'll figure out what I really think about him, and then the jig is up. I'd hate for that to happen when I can practically *smell* my freedom. Paige's too.

I'm officially onto him. Even with the hurricane, I've been working around the clock on this dilemma with Todd. Connie in accounting finally sent over the thick packet of expense reports I asked for a couple of weeks ago. I'd requested everything from the last year, hoping it would be enough. Turns out, it was.

I started running through them meticulously, day by day. Tracking the routine expenses of a resort as large as Siesta Playa is no easy feat. What I was searching for was akin to finding a needle in a haystack. Once I realized that I could rule out any expense reports that didn't include Todd's signature, my stack shrunk by a sizable amount. In the expense reports from March, I found my first discrepancy. It was a bill for $5,458.02 paid to Turtle Cove Equipment, LLC. The bill was signed off by Todd, and it stood out for two clear reasons. For one, on the expense report under "Description" it simply read: "Entertainment and Hospitality Department—supplies and equipment." On top of that, there were no receipts submitted with the report. None.

It should have immediately bounced back when he submitted it. Expense reports have to include itemized receipts—that way they can be easily tracked and verified. If this random LLC was providing us with, say, scuba equipment, there would have been a receipt to show for it.

I'd imagine the accounting department came back to Todd with these issues, but Todd likely used the power of his director title to push it through, no questions asked.

In May, again, Todd signed off on another bill from Turtle Cove Equipment, LLC, for close to $10,000 using the same generic description. In July, there was another bill for $35,000.

At first, I didn't outright assume these were inaccurate or fraudulent expense reports. We have a large entertainment and hospitality department that encompasses all the indoor and outdoor activities available for our guests. Sailboats, snorkel gear, yoga mats, bingo-night supplies—it all comes out of the E&H budget. All their equipment has to be maintained and routinely replaced, and that gets expensive.

But . . . then I remembered a string of annoying texts from Todd that came through in late July, where he was bragging about the shiny new Corvette he'd just purchased.

Cherry red. You likey?

The text included a picture of him posing in front of the car trying to do a cocky power stance with his legs spread wide and his arms folded over his massive chest. *Woof.*

It's not out of the question that a person in his position could afford a car like that, but he'd just purchased a boat the month before—I knew because he texted me about that as well—and Todd doesn't strike me as the type of guy to be *that* savvy with money. A new boat and a new car? Something wasn't adding up . . .

Now, Todd tosses another peanut into his mouth, and then he swipes his hands together to get rid of some of the peanut dust. When that doesn't work well enough, he wipes his palms on the back of his pants.

I merely sit, watching.

When he's satisfied, he points to me. "We did good over the last few days. You and me, we kept this place up and running when no one else could have. Mr. Durliat will be here tomorrow to assess the resort and get a progress report for any lingering damage. He'll no doubt commend us for our efforts over the last few days. It was my quick thinking that saved countless lives."

Todd's never had a quick thought in his life. I imagine his brain moves like molasses, same as his limbs. Another peanut gets tossed into his mouth. I'm surprised he has the dexterity to deshell them at all. I'd expect him to pound his meaty fist down onto them like a bear.

"Now, I know staff is back in place and we've resumed normal life," he continues. "However, I think we lucked out with some good damage from the storm. Those dorms that flooded, a few roof issues—in my opinion, it's enough to justify continued layoffs. We can play up the issues with the generators too. Mention a drop in upcoming stays because of fears about the weather . . . that sort of thing. I'm sure you and me can come up with good stuff."

First of all, the resort is well insured, so any damage caused by the storm will be covered, easily. The roof had a few shingles fly off that have already been replaced. The generators have been diagnosed and serviced. The flooded dorms are already getting repaired, starting today. In the end, any savings earned from laying off countless staff members will only go to line Todd's pockets, or should I say Turtle Cove, LLC's pockets. It doesn't matter. They're one and the same, and I know that now.

My silence irks him enough that he turns from the window and gives me his full attention. It's as if what he's about to say should really interest me.

"Now here's the thing, Cole. I'm prepared to promise you a share in the windfall. *Seven* percent of anything that comes my way." He winks like this should be enough to knock my socks off. "When I meet with Mr. Durliat tomorrow, I'd like you to be present. I'll hint at a possible promotion then as well . . . now, it won't come with a raise, per se, but there could be a title change, something more properly befitting my second-in-command around here."

I fear my general distaste for him is written across my face, but if it is, he doesn't see it.

Seven percent of his stolen money and a fancy new title.

Well gee golly, mister. Sign me up!

"I don't know what to say." Because truly, I don't know what to say that won't come out sounding condescending.

Todd holds up his hands and shakes his head like he's trying to look humble. "Now, don't go thanking me yet. We'll see how all this pans out. In the meantime, you know the drill." He zips his lips. "Let's keep things hush hush."

"Absolutely."

"Tomorrow. Eleven o'clock here in my office."

I stand and give him a mock salute, which he absolutely *eats* up. "Tomorrow, sir."

Then I walk out of his office knowing I need to hurry if I'm going to make it back to my office for a scheduled call with Joel Mira, Siesta Playa's CFO.

Enjoy your last twenty-four hours in power, Todd. Don't worry, I'll let you take your peanuts with you when you're escorted off the premises.

◆ ◆ ◆

Even with my hectic day, I haven't forgotten about Paige. She lives eternally on the periphery of my mind so that when I have a spare second or a moment to myself, she's the first thing I think of. As the workday draws to a close and it's almost time to meet her, I start to get nervous. Stupid, I know. What is there to worry about? I keep checking my watch every five seconds, and I'm shocked that more time hasn't lapsed. Surely it was 5:15 forty-five minutes ago.

"What time do you have?" I ask the receptionist.

"Five fifteen."

Damn.

I haven't seen Paige all day.

Between my meeting with Todd and my call with Joel, I also paid a visit to the accounting department on top of putting out all the usual daily fires in our resort.

The preppers are on their way out, begrudgingly dragging their bug-out bags and adventure gear behind them, bemoaning their reentry into normal society. I'm not ashamed to say I've enjoyed watching them go. Most of them are sporting some kind of bandage or wound wrap, and it looks as if our hotel amenities—warm showers and complimentary soap—were overlooked in favor of going au naturel, i.e., overgrown beards and visible stink lines. If you didn't know better, you'd think these guys just spent the better part of a week stranded on a deserted island instead of living in the lap of luxury.

Outside their group, many of the guests who chose to weather the storm with us are also departing today. We feel like we've gone above and beyond to accommodate everyone who stayed with us this week— fully comped stays, free food and beverages, credits toward future room reservations and amenities. Even still, I've been subjected to my fair share of complainers. Some people just can't be happy until you're on the floor crying in the fetal position.

I spot an older woman across the lobby. She's no stranger to me. She has crunchy highlighted curls, clippy-clappy sandals, and a charm bracelet so full it jinglejangles every time she gesticulates, which happens to be quite often. She's a hand talker. I know because I've dealt with her all week. Complaint after complaint, endless rounds of torturous apologies that I knew would never placate her. She wants me fired. Us *all* fired. Either that or blood.

What could we have done better in all this, you might be wondering? It's simple. Changed the weather.

"You know what?" she told me yesterday when she'd cornered me near a fiddle tree in the lobby. We didn't start there, of course. Our conversation began in the center of the lobby, and every minute or so, I'd take a subtle step back, trying to get away from her. Without meaning to, I'd cornered myself between her and the tree. One of the huge leaves was dangling down and tickling my head.

"You know who doesn't have hurricanes?! *Cabo*. I've never experienced *anything* like this in Cabo!"

Never mind that she was finishing a free coffee after eating a free breakfast during her free stay here. Her face was still red and flushed from her multiple comped treatments at the spa—none of it mattered. She was still threatening to sue us for "undue trauma" and her "future therapy bills." Would any of that hold up in a court of law? Absolutely not, but that's not the point. She was waving the litigious card as a means to an end. This here was a good old-fashioned shakedown. What other free shit could she grab on her way out the door? "Are those chairs bolted down? What about the fancy fish in the lobby tank? My niece would love that little Nemo-lookin' one."

Now, she's wheeling her luggage toward the door on her way out for good. She can barely keep track of all her stuff. The purse propped on top of her carry-on is overflowing with souvenirs from our gift shop. There's no room left for her neck pillow, so she has to wear it.

She looks over and spots me. Like a homing missile locked onto its target, she's about to pivot and pick up where we left off yesterday.

But alas, there's no time!

"Your airport shuttle is waiting for you right outside!" I say with a genuine smile, tacking on a wave. I'm exceedingly happy to deliver the news.

Don't let the turnstile hit you on the way out!

I only let out a sigh of relief when she's bump-bump-bumping in the back of the airport shuttle on her way back to torment the poor souls in her own life.

"Now what time do you have?" I ask the receptionist again.

"Five twenty-four."

Damn it.

By the time 6:30 rolls around, I'm so antsy, I can barely stand still.

I'm outside of the resort's lobby, waiting for Paige and rethinking everything. Earlier, I'd poked around the Siesta Playa gift shop, first considering a stuffed bear that was soft and cuddly, but it felt too juvenile. Then, I looked over a box of chocolates. A souvenir key chain. A Siesta Playa hoodie. I'd ended up putting it all back, and now I'm empty handed, which feels like the wrong choice.

Should I have picked up flowers or a corsage, maybe? What are you supposed to do in this situation? You know the kind where you're madly in love but it's also *just* the first date?

Worse still, Paige is late.

It's 6:34 and I'm sweating.

Then, up ahead on the gravel path, I see Paige dead-out sprinting. When she sees me, she immediately slows to a calm walk as if she's going to fool me.

"I *wasn't* running!" she shouts for my benefit.

"I saw you!"

"I thought there was a snake back there chasing me!"

She's close enough now that I can see she's breathing hard. "Listen, I was late, and I didn't want you to think I wasn't coming . . . also, there was a snake . . ."

She has no idea what she does to me. On the outside, I'm cool, calm, and collected, but it's a front. She has me twisted up inside, beside myself to have her.

She finally reaches me and stops right when she's nearly toe to toe with me. It's a dangerous move on her part, because I take her hand too easily. I'm still amazed that I'm allowed to just touch her like this without fear that she'll pull away and make some joke.

"Did you miss me today? I could lie and tell you I never thought of you once . . . ," she teases.

"Should I admit how nervous I've been?"

"Yes, tell me everything so I feel better. I could barely function all day because of you."

My gaze roves over her face, her flushed cheeks, her tentative expression.

On impulse, I bend down and kiss her, opting for a *Show, don't tell* approach.

Surely she understands now, as I tilt my head and deepen our kiss. We could make out here until my knees buckle, but we have an objective: dinner.

When I pull away, Paige looks dazed, like I've just shot her in the thigh with a mild tranquilizer.

"Are you hungry?"

"If I say no, can we just keep kissing?"

I smile and give her one more quick peck. "No."

She looks put out as she shakes her head. "Fine. Yes, I could eat. Also, I've been dying to see where you live. I told Camila and Lara about it, by the way."

"Oh yeah?" I take her hand, and we start down the path away from staff housing.

"Yeah . . . at lunch, they kind of pestered me for details about us."

"What'd you tell them?"

She looks up at me shyly, like she's a little hesitant to admit the truth. "All of it. You *know* . . . that we're a couple now. I mean, we *are* a couple, yes?" She starts talking faster. "You said that this morning so I was just repeating what you said—"

I can't help but smile. "Yes. We are."

The tension between her eyebrows eases, and her shoulders relax.

"They wanted every detail, but I just said we're taking things slow."

"Are we?"

Her eyes widen in horror. "God, I hope not. In fact, should we stop right here?" she asks, indicating a palm tree just off the path. "It's secluded enough."

I laugh. It's tempting . . .

I reluctantly tug us along. "Come on, I'm going to feed you first."

She groans. "Who can think about food at a time like this?!"

We round a bend in the path and continue on. It's not far now.

We're reaching the west end of the property. Out here, the forest grows dense as the path narrows. We brush past overgrown palms and elephant ears, plumerias and ferns. There are only two houses this way because most of the executives live on the east side of the resort's property. The houses there sit on a cliffside, which affords them slightly better views. I like it over here, though: it's more secluded, and I can walk right out onto the beach from my back porch. It's my own little slice of paradise.

We pass a cut-through road that leads to my neighbor's house. Marcus, the head chef at the Bistro, lives there with his wife. She keeps a garden, and when she harvests tomatoes and squash and peppers, she usually leaves some out for me on my porch.

Past their house, farther on, the path dead-ends in front of my house.

Here, the forest has been cleared a bit to allow for a small front lawn. I keep meaning to do something with it, but I haven't found the time.

I pause and turn to see Paige take it in.

The house itself is nothing to write home about. It's a white one-story bungalow with a screened-in front porch. It's weatherworn in some areas, but I repainted it myself last year, and that helped a lot. Still, it's not even half as nice as the houses where the other executives live. Todd's is a monstrosity.

My surfboard and kayak are tied to a small shed to the right. I didn't know how high the floodwaters would get this past week, and I didn't want to take any chances.

You can hear the waves splashing onto the shore behind the house. Most of the rooms have a view of the ocean, though the kitchen and main bedroom have the best vantage points.

I'm waiting for Paige to say something, but she's taking everything in with a detective's concentration.

"No one was living here before I moved in. I put a lot of work into it a few years ago. The inside is nicer—"

"I *love* it."

I can tell by her tone that she's being serious. I squeeze her hand and start to walk us up the well-worn path in the sandy grass.

"Did you get any flooding this week?" she asks.

"No. Fortunately. The house is built up enough that I was spared. But I lost power, so unfortunately, I had to toss out everything that was in my fridge. We'll see what we can cobble together. I thought I'd have time to go to the grocery store at some point . . ."

"We'll make do," Paige says with a reassuring smile.

We head up the stairs, and I pull open the screen door, wincing as the hinges squeal.

Paige doesn't notice, though. The defects don't seem to jump out at her. Maybe she doesn't see them at all.

As we walk through the front door, I explain the layout. There's a main corridor that runs the entire length of the house, leading from the front door to the back door. On the left-hand side, there's a living room divided from the kitchen by a large island. Off the hallway on the right is a bedroom that I'm currently using as a study. The main bedroom is at the far end of the house on the right.

She heads to the living room first. It's more modern in here. Wide-plank wood floors and an open-concept layout.

"I like that table."

She's pointing to the coffee table.

"Thanks, it came with the house, but I sanded it down and stained it with a lighter finish."

"And the chair?"

"Thrifted."

"I love the bright-blue fabric."

I rub the back of my neck, somewhat self-conscious. "I had it reupholstered. The lady who did it picked that fabric out for me. If you saw the way I grew up, the house, I mean . . . you'd understand why I didn't mind the color."

"Is your parents' house a bit boring?"

"*Boring* doesn't do it justice."

The kitchen is open and airy. There are no cabinets over the counters, just shelves with white plates and coffee mugs stacked in neat rows.

"Ah, *here's* the Cole I know," Paige teases, referring to the dishes. "Look at how perfect this all is."

"It doesn't have to be that way," I reply defensively.

She shifts a mug an inch to the right and waits for my reaction. I mostly keep my eyes from twitching, but then she laughs and moves it back.

"I don't mind it," she promises. "Better that than living with a total slob."

"Your dorm wasn't messy."

"No, I'm pretty clean, but I probably won't live up to your exacting standards."

"Maybe we'll rub off on each other . . ."

She looks back at me over her shoulder, studying me for a moment with a shadow of a smile across her lips. "Maybe . . ."

Then her gaze trails to the large window at the back of the kitchen, the place where I sit in the mornings to drink my first cup of coffee. The sunrise from that perch is unreal. Hopefully I'll get to show it to Paige.

"I can take you down to the beach if you want?"

She shakes her head.

"Want to see the front bedroom? The bathrooms?"

She shakes her head again and then turns back to face me.

"All right, I'll see what I have for dinner. I keep a few staples around."

Already, I'm heading toward the pantry, thinking of what I can cobble together—spaghetti, probably—but Paige shakes her head again.

I'm about to ask her what she wants, but then there's no need.

The answer is so obvious.

She walks toward me, trembling with nerves. Once she reaches me, her hand touches mine, and she laces our fingers together. Then slowly, gently, she rises up on her tiptoes to kiss me. I let her take the lead, her soft lips only barely touching mine as she works up the courage to lean in more. Our chests brush and I feel her shiver, and then her mouth parts mine and our tongues mingle. It's still so gentle it makes my chest ache with longing. It's like we've never kissed before, not just each other, but anyone. We're novices, scared and so preoccupied with every little movement.

She wants to impress me, *seduce me*, but there's nothing she has to do for that. I reach my hand up to cup the back of her head, tangling my fingers in her blonde hair. The strands are luscious and soft. My palm rubs against a sensitive spot at the base of her head, and she arches against me.

The fire burning low seems to suddenly flare. I back her up toward the kitchen island before I'm aware we're even moving. Her hips dig into it, and she moans. I lift her up, break our kiss for only a moment, reposition her head, and then kiss her again.

Everything we have to give is shared here, now.

I seem to be tearing at her, trying to burrow deeper, tongues lapping, lips clashing, teeth biting as we both plead for more.

Her arms wrap around my neck, and I hoist her up onto the counter. This new position works perfectly. My hips align with hers as I drag her right to the edge so that we can feel each other getting worked up.

Words are said and then forgotten.

More.

Cole.

Oh my god.

She's wearing these shorts—these little tiny shorts—and I hike them up with my hands, smoothing my palms up her thighs, underneath the bunched fabric. The tips of my fingers skim the edge of her panties, and she bucks her hips, rubbing against me harder, feeding off that delicious friction.

She doesn't know how good this feels. Just this. Clothes and all.

"Dinner," I say, trying, I think, one last time, to bring us back down to earth.

But neither of us registers it.

Paige's hands work ferociously fast unbuttoning my shirt with so little patience, I end up with claw marks down my chest. Fuck.

I kiss her harder, bite her bottom lip, listening to that responding whimper, and then my fingers slide deeper, over her panties, playing with her on top of the silk.

She wants it so badly, I can feel it in the way her legs squeeze my hips tighter, hear it in the little mewls, the gentle cries she doesn't bother to stifle.

Another heated kiss.

A begged whisper.

"Please."

And then my fingers brush her beneath her panties, finding her wet and hot.

A curse erupts out of me, a fiery warning of what's to come.

All my good-boy restraint? It's gone.

I unbutton Paige's shorts, and she helps me work them down her hips. Her panties stay on, but they're pushed aside. My fingers are at my waistband, undoing my belt, unbuttoning my pants, yanking that zipper down with hungry abandon.

I don't have a condom on me. Weirdly enough, I don't keep them in my kitchen.

I tell Paige, but she shakes her head, looking me square in the eyes, pleading. "I'm on birth control," she explains. "I'm . . . I haven't been with anyone in a long time."

Fucking hell.

"Same. *Same.*"

Then she reaches down and slides her hands into my boxer briefs, pumping me with her soft hand. Up and down, harder . . . tighter. My eyes flutter closed as she keeps going, increasing her pace, making me sweat.

Her strokes quicken. She adds a second hand. For a moment, I'm lost. Then, I knock her hands away quickly, anxiously. Too much more and I'm gone, I tell her. I lean in and kiss her again, asking her if she's certain. I can get a condom. I can cook her a goddamn spaghetti dinner. Four courses. Dessert. Whatever she wants.

But then our kiss turns hot again. This room feels like a furnace. I pull her right to the edge of the counter, line us up, and rub myself between her thighs, spreading her wetness around, making her shake with pleasure. When her eyes open and her glassy expression meets mine, I seat myself right where I belong and slowly start to press inside. Delicious inch by delicious inch, she surrounds me, squeezes me.

Her red lips tip open as I stretch her, and I growl like I'm possessed. *"Oh my . . ."*

She never finishes her sentence because I seat myself all the way to the hilt. Then she leans in and kisses me again, and I start to draw out, all the while rubbing her between her thighs with my thumb while I do it. Those soft circles against that sensitive skin undo her. She's absolutely laid bare for me as I stroke her slowly, then faster, picking up my pace until I feel her tighten around me, her stomach quivering, her eyes squeezed closed. A soundless cry falls from her lips, and I can't take it another second. I've wanted her for too long. Fantasized about this moment every damn day. I come in waves, rocking into her as pleasure racks through my body. I'm in another dimension. Off in a cloud-cuckoo-land.

"Cole?"

"Mmm . . ."

"Open your eyes."

"I can't."

She giggles and kisses my cheeks, one after another, until finally I pry my eyes open with a groan. She's all I see—flushed cheeks, blue eyes, shy smile.

I'm still in her, *a part of her.* It's the best I've ever felt. Whole, sated, loved . . .

Loved.

"I love you, Paige."

"That's good," she tells me with a light laugh. "Otherwise . . ." She grimaces. "I'd be in trouble."

"Say it back."

"It back."

"Paige."

"Love? You want me to say it?"

"Yes." I wrap my arms around her and pull her close until we're flush. My face is in her hair, smelling all the perfumed strands.

"I love you so much, Cole."

We eventually extricate ourselves from each other, albeit reluctantly.

"I could have done the rose-petals thing," I tell her. "Candles. Music."

"Next time?"

"Next time will probably be ten minutes from now," I point out. "We'll manage to make it to the floor instead of the counter."

She mulls this over. "True . . . Okay, next month, or the month after, when we finally have our wits about us again, we can do it nice and slow, with a curated playlist and everything."

"It's a plan." I kiss her forehead. "Are you hungry?"

"Not really. I kind of want to go for a swim."

"Then let's go for a swim."

She laughs wildly as I pull her off the counter and start carrying her to the back door. Our clothes aren't on properly; we're still sticky and wet.

"*Cole!*" Her protest is weak. I know she loves this.

We shed any remaining clothing as we walk along the sand toward the water. I'm not worried about us being seen. The beach curves between Marcus's house and mine, making it so we're on our own out here, just us and the fish.

Her bra's forgotten. Her panties too.

Paige is naked, traipsing into the ocean wearing an ear-to-ear smile. Already, I want her again, but it's more than that. I'm paralyzed. I can't take another step forward. She kicks the water and tells me to come on, but I can't even blink, let alone walk.

The sun is starting to set behind her, warm colors streaking across the sky. She's encased in it, pure sunshine backlit by all that golden light. She's the antithesis of everything I knew growing up. Vibrant and exciting. She's all the colors of Oz, and I'm dumbstruck Dorothy.

"Come in with me, silly," she says, bending down to splash me with water.

When I don't go in after her right away, she tips her head to the side, her expression gentling.

"It feels a little weird, doesn't it?" she broaches. "Finally being together, I mean."

I nod and start to walk toward her, but she doesn't let me reach her. She walks backward instead, drawing me deeper into the water until the waves splash up to my hips.

When I catch her, I hold my hand up like I'm flattening it against a pane of glass. She mimics me, pressing her hand to mine.

"You don't feel real," I admit.

She smiles wistfully. "I am."

I swallow, and she stares at my throat, at my Adam's apple as it bobs.

"It wasn't the same for me," I try to tell her. "I knew from the beginning. I knew I wanted to be with you."

Her emotions tangle inside her. Her eyebrows furrow in frustration. "You should have—"

I shake my head.

I know there's a million things I should have done, but we're here now. It took us this long. I want to apologize to us both, but then . . . does it matter? We survived the journey, and maybe this moment is all the sweeter because of it.

My fingers shift and lace through hers, and then I bend down to steal a kiss, then another.

Later, we lie in bed, utterly exhausted. The spaghetti was made and devoured; the chocolate ice cream was shared at the kitchen island. I had her on the bed after, my real dessert. Her legs spread and her hair fanned out around her. She fisted the sheets as I dropped my mouth between her legs and watched her unravel like a loose spool of thread. If I close my eyes, I can remember the details. Her toes curling as she came, the flush that covered her chest and neck, her smell, her *taste*.

I've never felt so defenseless. Loving her isn't getting easier, I'm realizing.

Having her hasn't eviscerated all my fears; it's heightened them.

Lying in bed, stroking her arm, I feel like my heart's completely abandoned me for her. She looks up at me with all the innocence of someone who doesn't realize this. To her, I'm just Cole.

"Promise me you won't break my heart," she says with a teasing tone, but I see the reality in her eyes. The truth lurking there.

The concept of breaking her heart is laughable. I think my body would self-sabotage in an effort to keep her happy and safe. But she can't comprehend that, so I just say, simply, "I promise."

My bedside clock is taunting me.

"We should get some sleep. We have a big day tomorrow."

She strokes my chest, focusing more of her attention there than on my words. "Oh?"

I nod reluctantly. "Todd has a meeting with Scott, and he'd like me to be there."

"Oh!" She sits up, suddenly interested. "Is this *it*?"

"This is it," I confirm.

"*Oh* . . . wow. Okay, so? What's the plan? Tell me everything."

Chapter
Twenty-Four
COLE

Todd's takedown has been a long time coming.

I've thought long and hard about how I want to go about it. Something quiet and tasteful could have sufficed, but I deserve a gotcha moment, preferably on camera. A slow pan of Todd's face as he realizes that he's royally fucked.

In lieu of a PowerPoint, I've opted for something tangible. A clear-front, bound presentation with a cover à la your sixth-grade book report. I made four copies. One is in the hands of Scott Durliat at this very moment.

Our CEO is the opposite of Todd in every way. Tall, trim, well dressed. He has salt-and-pepper hair, cut short and neat. There's a severity to his features that makes it feel like he means business. When he first arrived, I watched the valet crew skitter to their places, the receptionists stand tall, shoulders back, smiles on. He brushed past everyone on his way to the conference room where we now sit.

I'm positioned across from him, hands folded on the table.

He flips through pages of my report, reading slowly, digesting what I'm trying to spoon-feed him.

Everything is there: copies of the expense reports going back three years, as well as all the account transfers. I had the head of our accounting department contact our bank. You see, when you write a check to someone, they have to endorse the check when they go to cash or deposit it. This signature goes onto the back of the check, in zone one. The institution that receives the check also has to mark the item before it's processed back to the originating financial institution. That mark goes in zone two. The originating institution (i.e., our bank) received electronic images of the front and back of every processed check. Every single one of them was endorsed with Todd's signature.

He really is stupid. Embezzling money from your company is reckless. Signing the fraudulent checks with your full legal name before you deposit them? Now that's just . . . bafflingly dumb.

I can see the rage setting in for Scott—$86,924's worth of rage.

He's like me, exacting and ill tempered. Though maybe I'll be less ill tempered moving forward now that I'll no longer have to deal with Todd *and* I'll have Paige in my bed every night. *Paige.*

"He also verbally promised me a share of the windfall if I stayed quiet and worked alongside him on this," I tack on. That part didn't fit well within my organized presentation. Besides, I thought it was best delivered face to face anyway.

"That fucking bastard," Scott hisses under his breath, refocusing my attention on the task at hand.

He slaps the report closed and tosses it onto the conference table. It slides across until I stop it with my hand.

For a moment, his sharp gaze locks on me, and the heat is still there. I'm the messenger about to be killed.

"Has the accounting team seen this yet?" he asks.

"I reviewed it with Joel but no one else. He helped me hunt through the expense reports so we could total up everything, and he also reached out to our bank concerning Todd's checks. I wanted to be absolutely certain. Joel was going to reach out to you first thing, but I told him I was already meeting with you today. Should we get him on the phone?"

He nods, and I stand to reach for the conference phone on the table. It's a quick call.

Joel is as mad as Scott.

They go through the reports together while I sit quietly. Joel confirms my findings. The dominoes fall into place, and I have a hell of a time keeping the smile off my face.

A surge of power has me buzzing as the clock ticks down. Karmic retribution is just so . . . *satisfying.*

Todd is due to join us any minute. He'll be surprised to find Scott and I are already here. After all, the three of us weren't due to meet until 11:00 a.m. Never mind that Scott and I have been here for over an hour.

The call ends, and Scott's gaze flits back to me. He's only now remembering I'm in the room.

"To be clear, you'll be replacing Todd. Active immediately. Work out compensation with HR. Figure out what you want. Obviously, we're not in a position to negotiate here. I don't want this getting out. You'll sign an NDA. Do you understand?"

Replace Todd?

What? No! I couldn't possibly . . .

"Done," I say, confident and succinct.

I can already picture *Cole Clark, Director of Operations* on my email signature.

Mwhahah.

"Also, sir, there's one more thing I'd like to discuss before Todd gets here . . ."

Epilogue
PAIGE

The day Todd is fired will go down in infamy. We all hurried over to witness his removal from the hotel. It was . . . loud, among other things.

His booming voice carried throughout the resort almost from the very beginning.

From down the executive hall, we were treated to several outbursts, including but not limited to:

"You're firing me?!"

"Fuck you and *fuck you*!"

"You're replacing me with this kid?! He's a total idiot!"

There was no going gently into retirement for Todd. His reaction was on par with being wrongfully arrested and convicted of a crime he didn't commit. And to be clear, in the beginning, he *wasn't* being arrested (that came later). The two security guards should have been enough on their own. They were supposed to escort Todd to his office so he could collect his personal items. Then things took a turn when Todd tried to carry out cash that he was apparently stowing in one of his desk drawers. The money was in a nondescript duffel bag that screamed *illegal*, though he claimed it was just his gym clothes. Never mind that Todd hasn't seen the inside of a gym since '87.

"This is my property!" he shouted as a security guard tried to take it from him. "I'M CALLING THE FUCKING COPS!"

No need there. The police were already on their way just as Todd had moved the spectacle from the executive hallway out into the main lobby. Mad that he wasn't leaving with his bag of stolen money, he tried to make up for it by stealing stationery and pens from reception on his way out. One of the computer monitors got wrenched free as well, but that didn't last long. Security got that back immediately.

Sensing his opportunities starting to dwindle as the sirens drew closer outside, Todd settled for breaking the fourth wall. We were no longer audience members at the Greatest Play I've Ever Seen; we were participants. He started shouting at us all at the top of his lungs. Spinning in a wide circle, his finger wagging, spittle flinging everywhere. "YOU'RE ALL WRONG! *I WAS THE BEST THING THAT HAPPENED TO THIS PLACE!*"

Then he ducked out of the reach of one bumbling security guard and made it over to the sitting area, where he pushed a guest down in an attempt to get away. With nothing left to lose, he started throwing the stolen Siesta Playa pencils and pens behind him like he was dropping banana peels in *Mario Kart*.

Guests continued to flock to the scene, filled with the same morbid curiosity as the rest of us.

I was manning the excursion desk, so I *had* to be there.

Cole was across the lobby, standing beside our CEO.

For everyone else, Cole kept his expression stoic and sincere. But when our eyes locked, the barest hint of a smile sneaked out. I already knew we would be breaking down this entire scene later over a shared bottle of wine.

"What was your favorite part?" I'd ask him, topping off his glass.

Cole would puff out a breath, overwhelmed with options. "What was there *not* to love? Oh, maybe when he tried to jump over the back of the couch but failed miserably?"

"That's when the police finally got him, right?"

It was a day that will live in infamy at Siesta Playa. The dragon was vanquished once and for all by none other than our very own in-house knight. News about Cole's role in Todd's exit spread like wildfire through the resort (which was partially my fault because I spilled the beans to Lara and Camila, and neither of them knows how to keep a secret). Immediately thereafter, anyone who was on the fence about Cole immediately switched course and acted as if they were always on his side from the start.

"Cole Clark? Yeah, I always liked that guy."

"Cole? Best director we've ever had here. Super-cool guy too."

"Cole wears slacks and a sweater on Wednesdays, so I wear slacks and a sweater on Wednesdays."

Of course, I get the benefit of liking Cole before it was cool to like Cole.

He's my boyfriend now. My *official* boyfriend. I know it sounds braggy, especially when you see his abs, but it's only because I am, in fact, bragging.

Our slow and torturous start has the benefit of launching us into a no-holds-barred frenzy of a relationship where at any moment of the day, if the timing and situation are right, we're gonna be making out. My lips are perpetually red. My hand has permanently conformed to the shape of Cole's ass. I have every dark corner of this hotel cataloged in my head: which ones have enough space for Cole to haul me up against the wall, and which ones will afford us a *tiny* bit of privacy, but not enough to get really carried away.

This is our running tally:

Number of guests who've accidentally caught us kissing: 4. (To be fair, they were all part of one family. The mom gasped and covered her children's eyes, but it's not like they could really see anything . . .)

Number of times HR has had to call us in for a debrief on Siesta Playa's relationship policies: 1.

Number of times I've been late for work because Cole has kept me up too late the night before: 2.

There were a few weeks right in the beginning where we tried the good old-fashioned dating strategy of swapping where we stay each night: a night at his place, then a night at mine. Outside that, we'd meet for lunch and dinner—frantic for more time together—and then, when we were nearing the one-month mark, Cole suggested that I inform HR that I want to move out of my dorm.

It happened one Sunday morning when we were on the pebble path walking from the cafeteria to my dorm. We both woke up late craving the crispy bacon and syrup-covered pancakes the staff cafeteria makes on the weekends. It was worth the schlep from Cole's place to the cafeteria because we got to eat with Lara and Camila, and afterward, once our bodies were more syrup than blood, we decided to stop off at my dorm so I could grab a change of clothes. Our hands were interlaced as we strolled on the path with no real plan in mind for the rest of our day.

"We could go down to the beach?" I offered.

"I kind of want to hike."

"Oh, that could be fun!"

Then *BAM*.

"What if you moved out of your dorm?"

I glanced over at him with big round eyes.

"I'll be homeless then," I said, dumb as a rock.

Cole smiled a crooked little smile. "You'll be moving in with me . . ."

I'm not sure if he meant for me to move in that day, but I did. We turned right around on that pebble path and headed back to my dorm so we could pack it up. I don't have all that much, actually. I've always been a lady of few items. My clothes fit into a big duffel. My miscellaneous junk filled a few boxes. Then Cole borrowed one of the resort's golf carts and we hauled everything to his place in two easy trips.

I became the second toothbrush in his bathroom, the soft pink pillow on his otherwise blue-and-white bed, the misshapen ceramic mug on his kitchen shelves.

He was the one to suggest that we hang my mom's series of photos over the couch in the living room, and we FaceTimed my parents to show them the setup once we were done.

"I love it!" my mom exclaimed. Then she asked more seriously, "So it's officially official?"

"I know it's fast . . . ," I started, worried my parents were going to warn me away from acting rashly. Moving in with someone is a big step; I understand that.

I expected a lot of things: a reproachful frown, a drawn-out warning about taking things slow, possibly even a horribly belated birds-and-bees speech. *Sweetie, sometimes when a man loves a woman . . . they touch . . . intimately.*

My mom did the exact opposite. She guffawed. "Are you kidding?! If I had to listen to you talk about Cole, *complain* about Cole, *wax poetic* about Cole for one more minute, I was going to lose it. For the last six months it's all you brought up."

Oh dear god.

"It was endless, truly. I thought we were going to have to come there and sort it out ourselves—"

I clamored for my phone.

"Sorry! Mom?!" I made sure to speak very loudly over her. "Mom?! *Weird.* You're cutting out!"

"Paige?" she asked, coming through crystal clear.

Then, oops, my finger pressed the red button to end the call.

I didn't move. I squeezed my phone in the palm of my hand as I willed the color to drain from my cheeks. No such luck. After a beat or two of awkward silence—without much choice—I slowly lifted my face toward Cole. The torture was one sided. He was smiling sinfully at me. He'd never been happier in his life. He'd never let me live this down, I knew it.

"So . . . just how much did you talk about me to your mom?"

I winced and closed my eyes before assuring him that it was "a normal, infinitesimal amount. Hardly at all."

"Oh? Hmm." He didn't buy it. He pointed to my phone. "Should we call them back to verify?"

Panicked over the idea, I chucked my phone, and it skittered to a stop on the floor clear across the room. The screen probably cracked, but what did I care?

Cole only gloated more, and I was forced to take matters into my own hands. I pivoted and turned to face him, scooting closer. Already, his breath hitched. Then I climbed up and over him until I was sitting on his lap with my hands delicately placed on his shoulders.

Immediately, his hands found my waist and he tightened his grip, ensuring I wasn't going anywhere.

"Sure . . . ," I said, starting to unbutton his shirt, because yes, Cole still wears button-downs, even on Sundays. It's his MO, and I'm not breaking him of the habit. Why would I? *I like it.* "We could call my parents back if you want?"

I sounded like a seductress, and it was working. Already Cole's eyelids were growing heavy with desire. Once the first few buttons were undone, I bent down to kiss along his neck and collarbone, taking my time and appreciating every sculpted inch of him. He's gloriously tan. Those Sicilian grandparents of his were getting a letter of thanks first thing in the morning.

I traced my finger down the center of his chest, watching his lungs constrict and expand. I loved knowing I was the reason he was breathing so hard. All his precious control was starting to slip . . .

"*Or* we could enjoy our first night as roommates," I suggested innocently.

"You're more than my roommate," he said, his tone full of fire. He slid his hands into my shirt and started to lift it up and over my head. It was too easy. He had me down to my bra in an instant.

"Oh, right. More than roommates . . . Friends, then?" I quipped, knowing it would rankle him. We are most definitely past that point, but I still can't help but tease him about it.

His gaze sharpened on mine, and he hoisted his hips just enough that I tipped forward, flat against his chest. My girlish yelp only served to satisfy him as he reached up to unclasp my bra. The soft material slipped off my bare skin, and I shivered in his arms.

"You want to be my friend?" he asked huskily, his mouth flush against my ear. "Be my friend, Paige. Grind down on me."

Mama MIA.

That's the thing about Cole, his dirty little secret. He might be a buttoned-up director of operations during the day, but at night, in the bedroom, Mr. Spreadsheets and Numbers takes *no* prisoners.

He looked me up and down with pure possession, trailing his eyes with his hands so he could unbutton my shorts and work them off my hips. I complied, trying to hide my desperation, but he saw it all the same; he heard it in the way I sighed with relief when we were skin to skin, flushed and sweaty. Warmth radiated from where we touched, and tingles skittered across my body.

He took me there on the couch, with my head thrown back and my hands propped behind me on his knees. It was a precarious position, and I'd have been scared I'd tumble back onto the floor if not for Cole's tight grip on my waist. He thrust up into me, seating himself to the hilt, and once there, he groaned and closed his eyes like he couldn't help it. It was too good. It might've been too much as he fought to regain his composure. When he opened his eyes again, his lips twisted up into a salacious smile.

"*You are such a good friend,*" he said as he started to rock his hips, and his teasing praise made me feel hotter than ever.

He hit a spot that undid me, and my lips parted as I sucked in a sharp breath. All the while, he kept right on talking. "The *best* friend."

I became a passive participant, pliant in his arms as he hoisted me up and down using his grip on my waist. When he was deeper than ever, a weak cry spilled out of me.

Cole can be tender and sweet, but right then, he left the softness at the door.

He picked up the pace, faster, and my grip tightened on his knees. I was forced to close my eyes. It was all too much and I came too fast, too soon. His fingers bit into my waist as he felt me ride it out on him, and the delicious curses that wrung from his mouth sent me tail-spinning even harder.

I came out of it in a frenzy, almost angry at the way he made me feel. I blinked my eyes open, leaned forward, and kissed him hard as he continued, so close behind me it was only seconds before I felt him jerk and thrust, moan, and then go perfectly still. Our wild breathing was the only sound in the room.

Then I sort of chuckled.

He laughed.

I turned my cheek, and he kissed me, checking in. "You okay?"

"Barely."

It's a wonder we still have time for life outside of our relationship, but I make a point not to cut myself off from the rest of the world. At least not completely.

The next night, I took Cole with me to a bonfire Oscar and Théo were setting up. That's right. I finally invited Cole to a bonfire. Big steps here, people. I halfway assumed he was going to don his most practical suit and tie and head down to the beach in penny loafers. The whole thing was going to be so awkward, I knew it. I was in the bathroom, finishing putting on my bikini and cover-up, and when I walked out, Cole was in gray board shorts and a T-shirt fitted enough that it wasn't too loose or too tight, i.e., perfection. A gasp sputtered out of me.

"What are you wearing?"

He frowned and looked down, running a hand over his stomach. "My shirt?" he asked, clearly confused. "Is there a stain or something?"

So it turns out I was wrong about Cole. His wardrobe is far more diverse than I long assumed. And his people skills? Not half-bad either. He wasn't the biggest social butterfly there ever was at the bonfire, but it's because he's reserved, not stuck up. He's the quieter one out of the two of us, the yin to my yang, but he still chatted with Oscar and Théo, and when they were having trouble with the fire, he stepped up to help them when it was clear no one else really wanted to volunteer for the task. Afterward, with sparks fanning up into the darkening sky, we sat in a circle, all spread out on our lounge chairs, towels, and blankets. It was a smaller group than usual. Just the guys, Lara, Camila, and me. Everyone passed around the small cooler filled with cold, mismatched beers and seltzers. My contribution was snacks: the all-important marshmallows and a few bags of chips. Later, when we were filled with all the white sugary fluff we could handle, I tugged a bag of sour Skittles out of my pocket and secretly waved them at Cole like I was his dealer trying to entice him.

"Now you're speaking my language," he said, practically yanking them out of my hand.

I pulled them out of reach just before he succeeded.

"*Ah ah ah,*" I tsked. "Not so fast. I bought these with my hard-earned money."

He smiled, falling into character and cutting to the chase. "What do you want?"

My eyebrow quirked. "What are you *offering?*"

His gaze raked down my body like he wasn't the least bit perturbed by the fact that we were in public.

"Cole Clark," I hissed under my breath, warning him. "You're looking at me like you're about to—"

"What?" he said, leaning in, his eyes intently focused on my lips. "About to what? *Say it.*"

"Eat. Me. Alive."

His gaze sparked like it was a brilliant idea.

Suddenly sweaty at the prospect of just how far he'd take this in front of our friends, I tossed him the Skittles. It felt like I was trying to escape an angry bull by distracting him with something red and shiny. It worked for a little while. Right up until the end of the night, when the sky was a million stars and the bonfire had burned down to glowing embers. The conversation was lazy and quiet, but no less good.

Cole looked over to me and nodded his head toward the path, asking a silent question.

We gave our farewells but insisted that no one get up on our account.

"Should we do this again soon?" Théo called out as we walked away.

"Soon!" we promised.

"Ready to go home?" Cole asked me when we were walking along the pebble path.

His home. *Our home.*

I smiled. "Let's go."

Weeks passed, and though Cole is concretely part of our weird, eclectic group now, my favorite nights aren't when we're out on the town with friends; it's when he and I are building a life together, the steadfast, solid kind—the one that a teenager would find dead boring but that I find absolutely lovely. We've decided to take up cooking. We're working our way through a cookbook by Chloe Ricci—it's filled with easy summer meals and pastry desserts. We're not too precious about it, so our finished products barely even resemble the glossy pictures in the book, but they taste amazing, so who even cares?

Believe it or not, we even cooked dinner for Serge and Blaze the other night. It was a double date. And more than that, it was fun!

On our days off, Cole and I explore the island together—hiking, biking, kayaking, snorkeling. We love it all. He's even helped me come up with some new and exciting excursion ideas, including creative ways to make them slightly less injury inducing, so it's a win-win for everyone.

This morning, we have an all-staff meeting at the crack of dawn in the Turtle Cove Ballroom. Cole is leading it, and I'm so proud of him, I'm front row center. I was the first person here (mostly because I walked here with him), but I still would have been early otherwise. If it were appropriate, I'd be wearing a T-shirt with his name on it and holding up a little witty sign like I'm a fangirl at his concert. In case it's not completely obvious, I'm smitten. In love, deeply, obnoxiously, hopelessly. Lara and Camila joke that my relationship with Cole makes them want to throw up, and I get it! *I* make me want to throw up, too, but I just can't stop smiling!

Lara and Camila suddenly look at me, and I try to relax my face, but I can't.

I expect another eye roll, an audible gag, but they're smiling too.

"*Girl*," Lara hisses, her eyes widening with excitement.

What? What'd I miss?

This has been a long meeting—there's a lot of ground to cover during these things because we don't have them very often—and my caffeine isn't cutting it this morning.

Cole worked late last night preparing for today. By the time he got home, I was already in bed, asleep. He woke me up by stringing a line of kisses up my stomach, starting at my navel as he pushed my night-shirt *slowly* up as he went. It was that delicious half-asleep, half-awake sensation that had me absolutely crazed for him by the time I came to and realized he was crawling on top of me while unbuttoning his shirt.

The moonlight was streaming in through the drapes on either side of our bed, the cool light highlighting his sharp cheekbones and piercing eyes. He slid into me slowly while he watched my reaction, feeding off my soft moans. I pulled him down to me and kissed him, and he whispered against my lips.

"I missed you today."

And so, yeah, your girl is *h-a-p-p-y*.

But also highly distractible.

"What's going on?"

I feel like the entire ballroom is looking at me, and upon further inspection, they totally are, even Cole.

"Paige, would you mind coming up onstage?" he asks me, his tone brimming with barely restrained excitement.

Oh god.

This feels ominous, and my first thought is that Cole is about to propose. Which is absurd. We haven't even been dating all that long, *and* we've talked about it. I've told him that I would rather my future fiancé—we both agree it's him—pop the question to me somewhere private, just the two of us. I don't want it to be a spectacle. Oh my god, if he proposes to me during a staff meeting, I'll kill him. I'll kill him—resuscitate him—and then kill him again.

I know that's not what's about to happen, but still, I feel woozy as I get to my feet.

Why on earth is he calling me up onstage?

It's dead silent in the ballroom as I ascend the stairs.

"Woo! Go, Paige," Lara calls out, trying to help cut the tension, but it's not enough.

Camila follows this up with a resounding whistle.

I scurry up the last few steps as fast as I can, hoping to get this over with swiftly.

"What is this?" I hiss at Cole as I reach him.

His smile widens. "A promotion."

I stutter to a stop.

Then he turns to address the audience. "Over the last few months, we've conducted a random survey to get a baseline for what our guests value most here at Siesta Playa"—he turns back to me—"and your excursions ranked as one of the top resort activities . . . right after our beloved buffets."

The crowd laughs.

Meanwhile, I'm close to tears. I have to look away and collect myself. It's one thing to love what I do and to give it my all day in and day out, strategizing how best to lead a rowdy group through a sailing trip or being my most chipper self during a hike even when I'm not feeling up to it. It's another thing to actually be recognized for it. I always hear the complainers and the squeaky wheels. The guests who hate every minute of the torture I subject them to shout the loudest and therefore stick in my mind the most. Sure, every now and then someone will make a point to stop and tell me they had a great day or they enjoyed a particular activity. But I had no idea I was a fan favorite around here.

There are other employees who work excursions who've been here longer than I have, but none that care about the job like I do. For Camila and Lara, this job is a means to an end. They enjoy having a carefree island life; they aren't looking to move up in the company.

"A promotion has been long overdue," Cole tells me.

"In front of everyone, though . . . ?" I whisper, giving the massive audience the side-eye, like, *Hello! You can see them, too, right?*

Cole shrugs off my concern. "Everyone will find out eventually. This way we all get to celebrate with you."

I hate him.

That is . . . until he tells me my new title. Right into the microphone, nice and loud, he knights me "Paige Young, director of excursions within the entertainment and hospitality department at Siesta Playa, a subsidiary of . . ." Yada yada, you get it.

Oh *wow*. I can quite literally feel my head expanding like a hot air balloon with this surge of new power. My heels come off the stage a little.

I'll never let Cole live this down. Tonight, at dinner, he will have to refer to me as *Director* Paige Young if he wants me to pass the salt, or maybe even the *esteemed* Paige Young. Are only lawyers allowed to use *esquire*? Because that could be a seriously cool title too . . .

I'm so lost in my thoughts that it takes me a moment to realize the crowd is clapping for me, and not just in that half-assed way where they think if they do it, it'll make this whole thing end faster. *Okay, the girl got a promotion. Whoop-de-do.*

They're actually happy for me!

When I look out at the sea of smiling faces, my eyes well up with unshed tears. There's Dr. Missick right up front, giving me two enthusiastic thumbs up. Desiree and Maddox are going crazy right behind him, thankfully fully clothed today. Serge and Blaze sit a few rows back, and I see Blaze mouth "Good job, Paula!" And for a microsecond I'm concerned that the poor guy just cannot get it together enough to remember my actual name. Then he winks and redeems himself.

Camila and Lara, Oscar, Théo—they all cheer the loudest.

Just when I think the crowd might band together and do a proper wave or give a resounding *Go, Paige! Go!*, the clapping trickles down and people mostly get bored again, like, *What now? Am I getting a promotion?*

"Will there be refreshments in the lobby? A custom cake in the shape of my head?"

Cole's expression sobers. "No. Meeting adjourned. Back to work."

There're only weak protests as everyone shuffles out.

Cole turns his microphone off and nestles it back in the stand before turning to face me with a sheepish smile.

"Do you hate me?" he asks, tilting his head in that adorable way.

With that face, if I was harboring any anger, it would have already dissolved.

I narrow my eyes. "Only a little. I would have appreciated a heads-up."

"But that would have ruined the surprise."

"Hmm . . . surprise, huh? *Well*, give me the details. Does my promotion come with a raise?" I waggle my eyebrows at the possibility.

He keeps his smile in check when he replies. He's the boss man right now, and I'd be lying if I said I didn't love it a little. "Yes, I've suggested one with HR. You'll work out the kinks with Beverly. Also, the excursion team will get a sizable budget increase."

What! Under Todd, our budget was laughably small. There was no way to keep all our equipment up to date, and all our complaints fell on deaf ears. When we worked up the courage to bring it up with him, Todd would inevitably shoo us out of his office with a brush-off equivalent to *Here's five dollars . . . don't spend it all at once, kid.*

"*Oh my god!* We can upgrade our yoga mats and paddle boards. Oh! *Oh*, we can get better snorkeling gear!"

Cole's smiling, watching me flail around. I can't wait to tell everyone. They'll be so excited. We'll have to catalog and inventory our current gear and then create a system to figure out what we need to replace first. My heart skips a beat I'm so excited.

Oh dear.

Maybe I'm more like Cole than I thought. This much excitement over work?!

"We'll celebrate tonight," Cole tells me, his gaze holding a dangerous promise.

My stomach flutters, and I step closer. I can't touch him, even though I'm dying to. We're still up onstage, and while most everyone has already trickled out, it's still not appropriate. We'll have to save it for later.

Speaking of . . .

"I know just the way to celebrate. You should do a *real* excursion with me! Y'know . . . goat yoga, hot-coal walk, late-night forest trek. Your choice." I wink.

He fights to hold back an eye roll. "As tempting as it sounds to exercise with hooved animals, I was thinking of something a little more private . . ." His leisurely gaze eats me up from head to toe. "Maybe like a personal, behind-the-scenes tour of your . . ." He leans in close and finishes his sentence by whispering a word into my ear.

"COLE!"

I playfully shove him back. My cheeks are on *fire*.

He doesn't even look slightly contrite. Mostly just smoking hot. Ugh. The injustice of it all!

I recover from shock and decide to turn the tables a little. "Well, just so you know . . . that excursion can be a bit strenuous—are you *sure* you're up for it? I wouldn't want to be the cause of any more injuries."

Cole's whiteboard in the break room has officially been retired. I'd hate to have to bring it back out of storage.

"I think I'll manage," he says confidently, grasping my hand firmly so he can start to lead me toward the stairs.

"All right, well, before every excursion I like to make sure my guests are prepared physically," I tell him. "There are no injuries I should know about?"

"None whatsoever," he replies seriously.

"And equipment wise? What are you packing?" I look pointedly down at his crotch to emphasize my double entendre.

He barks out a laugh, and then—even though we're still in plain sight of everyone—he leans down and presses a swoon-worthy kiss to my lips.

"What in the world am I going to do with you?" he asks as he pulls back.

I smile innocently up at him. "Oh . . . I don't know. Love me for a lifetime?" I respond lightly.

His mischievous gaze says, *All right, Paige. Game on.*

Don't miss another full-length standalone romantic comedy from *USA Today* bestselling author R.S. Grey

Read on for an excerpt from *Not So Nice Guy*

Chapter One
SAMANTHA

This morning, we're having sex inside the army barracks again. It's hot and heavy. The enemy is advancing—we might not make it out alive. Explosions rumble in the sky and in my pants. I'm sweating. Ian started out wearing camo fatigues, but I ripped them off with my teeth. That's how I know I'm dreaming—my mouth isn't that skillful. In real life, I'd chip a tooth on his zipper.

My alarm clock fires another warning shot. My waking mind shouts, *Get up or you're going to be late!* I burrow deeper under my covers, and my subconscious wins out.

Dream Ian tosses me over his shoulder like he's trying to earn a Medal of Honor, and then we crash against a metal bunk bed. Another indication that this is a dream is the fact that the fleshy part of my butt hits the corner of the bunk, yet it doesn't hurt. He grinds into me, and the frame rattles. I scrape my fingers down his back.

"We're going to get caught, soldier," I moan.

His mouth covers mine, and he reminds me, "This is a war zone—we can be as loud as we want."

A staccato burst of machine-gun fire erupts just outside. Heavy boots begin stomping toward the locked door.

"Quick, we'll have to barricade it!" I implore. "But how? There's nothing useful in here, just that standard-issue leather whip and my knee-high combat boots!"

He hauls me up against the door, and we lock eyes. The wordless solution suddenly becomes clear: we'll have to use our own writhing bodies as a sexy blockade.

"Okay, every time they kick the door, I'm going to thrust, got it? On the count of three: one, two—"

Just as my dream gets to the good part, my phone starts blaring "Islands in the Stream" by Kenny Rogers and Dolly Parton. Cool '80s country pop serenades me at max volume. There are synthesizers. I groan and jerk my eyes open. Ian changed my ringtone again. He does it to me every few weeks. The song before was another silly throwback tune by two old kooks.

I reach out for my phone and bring it beneath the covers with me.

"Yeah, yeah," I answer. "I'm already showered and heading out the door."

"You're still in bed."

Ian's deep, husky voice saying the word *bed* does funny things to my stomach.

Dream Ian is blending with Real Life Ian. One is a hunky lieutenant with arms of steel.

The other is my best friend, whose arms are made of a metal I've never had the pleasure of feeling.

"Dolly Parton this time? Really?" I ask.

"She's an American treasure, just like you."

"How do you even come up with these songs?"

"I keep a running list on my phone. Why are you breathing so hard? It sounds like you're over there fogging up a mirror."

Oh god. I sit up and shake off the remnants of my dream.

"I fell asleep to reruns of *M*A*S*H* again."

"You know they've continued making television shows since then."

"Yes, well, I've yet to find a man who titillates me like Hawkeye."

"You know Alan Alda is in his eighties, right?"

"He's probably still got it."

"Whatever you say, Hot Lips."

I groan. Just like with Major Houlihan, that nickname annoys me . . . kind of.

I sweep the blankets aside and force my feet to the ground. "How long do I have?"

"First bell rings in thirty minutes."

"Looks like I'll have to skip that ten-mile morning run I was planning."

He laughs. "Mm-hmm."

I start rummaging through my closet, looking for a clean dress and cardigan. Our school's employee-wardrobe requirements force me to dress like the female version of Mr. Rogers. Today, my sundress is cherry red and my cardigan is pale pink, appropriate for the first day of February.

"Any chance you filled up an extra thermos with coffee before you left the house?" I ask, hopeful.

"I'll leave it on your desk."

My heart flutters with appreciation.

"You know what, I was wrong," I tease, affecting a swoony lovesick tone. "There is a man who titillates me more than Hawkeye, and his name is Ian Flet—"

He groans and hangs up.

Oak Hill High School is a five-minute bike ride from my apartment. It's also a five-minute bike ride from Ian's house. We could make the morning commute together, but we have drastically different morning rituals. I like to roll the dice and push the limits on my alarm clock. It thrills me to sleep until the very last second. Ian likes to wake up with the milkman. He belongs to a gym, and he uses that membership every morning. His body-fat percentage hovers in the low teens. I belong to the same gym, and my membership card is tucked behind a beloved

Dunkin' Donuts rewards card. It leers out at me each time I make a midday strawberry frosted run.

Those barbaric contraptions at the gym intimidate me. I once sprained my wrist trying to change the amount of weight resistance on a rowing machine. And have you seen all the different strap, rope, and handle attachments for the cable machine? Half of them look like sex toys for horses.

Instead of subjecting myself to the gym, I prefer my daily bike rides. Besides, there's really no fighting my physiology at this point. I'm a twenty-seven-year-old woman still riding the wave of pretend fitness that comes naturally with youth and the food budget of a teacher. The only #gains in my life come from binge-watching Chip and Joanna Gaines on *Fixer Upper*.

Ian says I'm too hard on myself, but in the mirror I see knobby knees and barely filled B cups. On good days, I'm five foot three. I think I can shop at babyGap.

When I make it to school (ten minutes before the first bell), I find a granola bar next to the thermos of coffee on my desk. In my haste to get to school on time, I forgot to grab something for breakfast. I've become predictable enough that Ian has stowed snacks in and around my desk. I can pull open any drawer and find something—nuts, seeds, peanut butter crackers. There's even a Clif Bar duct-taped under my chair. My arsenal is more for his own good than mine. I'm the hangriest person you've ever met.

When my blood sugar drops, I turn into the destructive Jean Grey.

I scarf down the granola bar and sip my coffee, firing off a quick text to thank him before students start filing into my classroom for first period.

SAM: TY for breakfast. Coffee is LIT.

IAN: It's the new blend you bought last week. Are your students teaching you new words again?

SAM: I heard it during carpool duty yesterday. I'm not sure when to use it yet. Will report back.

"Good morning, Missus Abrams!" my first student singsongs.

It's Nicholas, the editor-in-chief for the *Oak Hill Gazette*. He's the kind of kid who wears sweater-vests to school. He takes my journalism class very seriously—even more seriously than he takes his crush on me, which is saying something.

I level him with a reproving look. "Nicholas, for the last time, it's Miss Abrams. You know I'm not married."

He grins extra wide, and his braces twinkle in the light. He's had them do the rubber band colors in alternating blue and black for school pride. "I know. I just like hearing you say it." The kid is relentless. "And may I just say, the shade of your dress is very becoming. The red nearly matches your hair. With style like that, you'll be a missus in no time."

"No, you may not say that. Just sit down."

Other students are starting to file into my class now. Nicholas takes his seat, front and center, and I avoid eye contact with him as much as possible once I begin my lesson.

Ian and I have drastically different jobs at Oak Hill High.

He's the AP Chem II teacher. He has a master's degree and worked in industry after college. While in grad school, he helped develop a tongue strip that soothes burns from things like hot coffee and scalding pizza. Seems stupid—*SNL* even spoofed it—but it got a lot of interest in the science world, and his experience makes the students look up to him. He's the cool teacher who rolls his shirtsleeves to his elbows and blows shit up in the name of science.

I'm just the journalism teacher and the staff coordinator for the *Oak Hill Gazette*, a weekly newspaper that is read by exactly five people: me, Ian, Nicholas, Nicholas's mom, and our principal, Mr. Pruitt. Everyone assumes I fall into the "If you can't do, teach" category, but I actually like my job. Teaching is fun, and I'm not cut out for the real world. Hard-hitting journalists don't make very many friends. They jump into the action, push, prod, and expose important stories to the world. In college, my professors chastised me for only churning out puff pieces. I took it as a compliment. Who doesn't like puffy things?

As it is, I'm proud of the *Gazette* and the students who help run it.

We start each week with an "all-staff meeting," as if we're a real, functioning newspaper. Students pitch their ideas for proposed stories or fill me in on the progress of ongoing work. Most everyone takes it seriously, except for the few kids who sought out journalism for an easy A—which, off the record, it is. Ian says I'm a pushover.

I'm talking to one of those students who falls into that second category now. I don't think she's turned in one assignment since we got back from Christmas break. "Phoebe, have you thought of a story for next week's newspaper?"

"Oh, uhh . . . yeah." She pops her gum. I want to steal it out of her mouth and stick it in her hair. "I think I'm going to ask around to see if the janitors are, like, banging after hours or something."

"You leave poor Mr. Franklin alone. C'mon, what else you got?"

"Okay, how's this . . . 'School Lunches: Healthy or Unhealthy'?"

Inwardly, I claw at my eyes. This type of exposé has been done so many times that our school's head lunch lady and I have worked out a system. I keep students out of her kitchen, and in return, I get all the free Tater Tots I want.

"There's no story there. The food isn't healthy. We all know that. Something else."

There are a few snickers. Phoebe's cheeks glow red, and her eyes narrow on me. She's annoyed I've called her out in front of the entire class. "Okay, fine." Her tone takes a sassy and cruel edge like only a teenage girl's can. "How about I do something more salacious? Maybe a piece about illicit love between teachers?"

I'm so bored, I yawn. Rumors about Ian and me are old news. Everyone assumes that because we're best friends, we must be dating. It couldn't be further from the truth. I want to tell them, *Yeah, I WISH,* but I know for a fact I'm not Ian's type. Here are four times this has been made clear to me:

- He once told me he's never imagined himself with a redhead because his mom has reddish hair. HELLO, MOST GUYS HAVE MOMMY ISSUES! LET ME BE YOUR MOMMY ISSUE!
- He's only ever dated tall broody model types with wingspans twice as long as mine. They're like female pterodactyls.
- We're both massive LOTR fans, and guess what—SAM IS THE BEST FRIEND, NOT THE LOVE INTEREST.
- Oh, and then of course there was that one time I forced myself to dress up as slutty Hermione (his weakness) for Halloween and tried to seduce him. He told me I looked more like frizzy-haired Hermione from the early years and less like postpubescent Yule Ball Hermione. Cue quiet meltdown.

◆ ◆ ◆

Ian and I became friends three and a half years ago, close to 1,300 days, if some loser out there were keeping count. Upon accepting teaching positions at Oak Hill, we were placed in the same orientation group. There were fifteen new hires in total, and Ian immediately caught my eye. I can remember the first time I saw him, recalling specific, random details more than anything: how big his hands looked holding our orientation handbook, how tan he was from summer vacation, the fact that he towered over the rest of us. My first thought was that he should have been incredibly intimidating, what with the sharp blue eyes and short, slightly wavy brown hair. But he cut away the pretense when he aimed a smile at me as our eyes locked over the crowd of new teachers. It was so disarming and easygoing, but most importantly, it was seriously sexy. My heart sputtered in my chest. He was the boy next door who'd grown into a man with a chiseled jaw and solid arms.

He was wearing a black T-shirt I focused on as he made his way toward me through the crowd.

"You're a Jake Bugg fan?" he asked. "Me too."

I responded with a poorly executed "Huh?"

His Crest smile widened a little farther, and he pointed down at my shirt. Oh, right. I was wearing a Jake Bugg concert T-shirt. We struck up polite conversation about his last US tour, and I kept my drool in my mouth the entire time. When it was time to get started, he asked if I wanted to sit with him.

For a week straight we endured instructional videos about sexual harassment and workplace protocol together. While choppy VHS tapes from the '90s played on a rolled-in TV stand, Ian and I passed cheeky notes back and forth. Eventually, we just pushed our desks together and kept our voices barely above whispers as we got to know each other. We had so much to talk and joke about. Our words spilled out in rapid fire like we were scared the other person would go up in a poof and disappear at any moment.

We didn't pay attention through the entire orientation, but the joke was on us.

They gave us a test at the end of the week, and we both failed. Apparently, it was an Oak Hill first. The test is ridiculously easy if you paid the least bit of attention. We had to retake the orientation class, and our friendship was cemented through the shared embarrassment and shame.

At the end of the second week, we celebrated our passing scores with drinks—Ian's idea. I tried not to read too much into it. After all, we were both inviting plus-ones .

That's when I met the girl he was dating at the time: a gazelle-like dermatologist. At the bar, she regaled us all with interesting stories from the exam room.

"Yeah, people don't realize how many different types of moles there are."

She gave me unsolicited advice, such as "Due to your fair skin, you really ought to be seeing someone for a skin check twice a year." She, by the way, didn't have a visible pore or freckle on her. When we both stood to use the bathroom midway through the evening, my inadequacies multiplied. Our size difference was obscene. I could have fit in her pocket. To anyone watching, I looked like the preteen she was babysitting for the night.

The only silver lining was that I had her check out the smattering of freckles on my shoulders while we were waiting for the stalls to open up. All clear.

At the time, I was dating someone too. Jerry was an investment banker I'd met through a friend of a friend. This outing was only our third date, and I had no plans to continue seeing him, especially after he droned on and on about Greek life back at UPenn.

"Yeah, I was fraternity president my junior and senior year. HOO-RAH."

Then he proceeded to holler his fraternity chant for the entire bar to hear. I think he thought it was funny, but I didn't feel like I was in on the joke. I wanted to press a red button and exit through the roof. Ian's eyes locked with mine over the table, and it felt like he knew exactly what I was thinking. He could tell how uncomfortable I was, how much the situation made me squirm. We both proceeded to fight back laughter. My face turned red with exertion. He had to bite his lip. In the end, I caved first and had to excuse myself to go to the bathroom again so I could crack up in private.

Ian's date later told him she was concerned I had an overactive bladder.

By the time lunch rolls around at school, I'm ready for a break. My journalism classes are interspersed with on-level senior English classes. It's not my favorite part of the job, but it's the only way Principal Pruitt can justify keeping me on full time. The students in these classes are already checked out, blaming their late homework and poor quiz scores on senioritis. I type the illness into WebMD to prove it isn't a real thing. They don't look up from their cell phones long enough to listen. Most of them wouldn't be able to pick me out of a lineup.

Last week, one kid thought I was a student and asked for my Snapchat.

Ian doesn't have this problem. His classes are filled with overachieving nerds, the kids who've already been accepted to Ivy League schools but still feel the need to take twenty-seven AP classes. Most of them intimidate me, but they treat Ian like he's their Obi-Wan.

"Tell us more about the tongue strip, Mr. Fletcher!"

"Bill Nye's got nothin' on you, Mr. Fletcher!"

"I wrote about you in my college admissions essay, Mr. Fletcher. I had to pick the one person who's inspired me to pursue learning the most!"

I sit down for lunch in the teachers' lounge and puff out a breath of air, trying to move the few strands of hair from my forehead. They are evidence that I've tugged at my ponytail in distress too many times this morning.

Ian slides into his designated seat across from me, and his positive energy clogs the air between us. It could also be his delicious bodywash.

"Let's see it," he says.

"It's not my best haul."

I've got a cheese stick, pretzels, grapes, and a peanut butter and jelly sandwich.

He has a multilayer turkey sandwich with avocado and alfalfa sprouts, sliced watermelon, and almonds.

Without a word, we start the exchange. I take half his turkey sandwich. He takes half my PB&J. My cheese stick gets divided in two. I let him keep his nasty almonds—they aren't even salted.

"Let me have some of your pretzels," he says, reaching over.

I slam my hand down on the bag, effectively cracking most of them in half. Worth it.

"You know the rules."

His dark brow arches. "I have chocolate chip cookies from one of my students back in my classroom. His mom baked them as a thank-you for writing him a rec letter."

In the blink of an eye, my threatening scowl gentles to a smile. My dimples pop for added effect. "Why didn't you say so?"

I turn my bag of broken pretzels in his direction.

Even though the teachers' lounge is packed, no one sits at our table. They know better. We're not rude; it's just hard for other people to keep up with us. Our conversations involve a lot of shorthand, code, and inside jokes.

"All-staff go well?"

I try for my best local-news-anchor tone. "Ian, is the food in our cafeteria healthy?"

He groans in commiseration.

"Yeah, then the same student tried to threaten to expose our relationship."

"You mean the one that doesn't exist?"

"Exactly."

"All right. All right!" Mrs. Loring—the drama teacher—shouts near the fridge, cutting through the noise in the lounge. "Guess what today is . . ."

"The first of the month!" someone shouts enthusiastically. "Confiscation Station!"

For the next few seconds, there's an overwhelming amount of applause and chatter.

Confetti might as well be raining down from the ceiling.

"Okay. OKAY! Settle down," Mrs. Loring shouts excitedly. "Does anyone have late entries?"

Ian stands and withdraws a crumpled note from his pocket.

People clap like he's a hometown hero returning from war.

"Snatched it up during first period," he brags.

A few female teachers act as if they're going into cardiac arrest as they watch him cross the room. Mrs. Loring holds out her mason jar, and he drops it inside.

He reclaims his seat across from me, and suddenly, it's time for the Reading.

On top of the fridge in the teachers' lounge sits a medium-size mason jar, into which we drop notes we've seized from students during class. The moon waxes and wanes, and that jar fills up. On the first of every month, Mrs. Loring interrupts our lunch for a dramatic reading.

It might sound cruel, but don't worry, we keep the notes anonymous. No one knows the source except the confiscator. As a result, Principal Pruitt doesn't really care about our ritual. It's good for our morale. Think of it as team bonding.

Mrs. Loring swirls her hand into the bowl like a kid searching for candy on Halloween, and then she comes up with a neatly folded note.

I turn to Ian, giddy. Our gazes lock. Last year I sat in while he did an experiment with his students. He burned different elements to show that they each produced a different color of flame. Calcium burned orange; sodium burned yellow. The students were amazed, but then so was I, because when he burned copper, it produced a dark, vivid blue flame—the exact color of Ian's eyes. I've kept a little bowl of shiny pennies on my nightstand ever since.

Mrs. Loring clears her throat and begins. She's the best person for the job. There is no half-assing on her part. She's a classically trained actor, and when she reads the seized missives, she affects different accents and performs with a convincing earnestness. If I could, I'd bring my parents in for an evening showing.

"Student #1: Hey, did you see that [name redacted] sat by me during first period?

"Student #2: YES! I think he likes you.

"Student #1: We're just friends. He's not into me like that.

"Student #2: C'MON! YOU JUST NEED TO GO FOR IT! Next time you hug, push your boobs up against him. That's my secret weapon."

A smattering of snorts interrupts the reading before Mrs. Loring restores order.

"Student #1: Let's say that actually works—what if it changes everything? What if it messes up the friendship?

"Student #2: Who cares? We're about to graduate. You need to getchasome.

"Student #1: Okay, sleazeball. I, for one, actually think it's possible to have guy friends without banging them all.

"Student #2: You're delusional. It's only a matter of time before best friends of opposite sex morph into LOVERS."

The bolded final word, read with overblown dramatics, produces uproarious laughter. But at our table, there is conspicuous silence. Crickets. The note parallels my life too closely. I fidget in my chair. Heat crawls up my spine. I've broken out in hives.

Maybe I'm having an allergic reaction to Ian's turkey sandwich. In fact, I wish I were—anaphylactic shock sounds wonderful compared to this. It feels like someone just transcribed the thoughts and words of the little angel and devil on my shoulders.

I hate this game.

I hate that Ian is trying to get me to meet his blue-flame gaze, probably trying to make some friendly joke.

When lunch is over, I'll stand and make a break for it. I'll decline his invitation to accompany him back to his classroom for cookies, and when we part ways, I'll try hard to keep my tone and my gaze calm. He'll never know anything was wrong.

I've had to tread lightly for the last 1,300 days. Ian and I have a relationship that depends greatly on my ability to compartmentalize my feelings for him at the start of every school day and then slowly uncork the bottle at night. The pressure builds and builds all day.

It's why my dreams are filthy.

It's why I haven't dated anyone else in ages.

This whole tightrope walk is getting harder and harder, but there's no alternative.

For 1,300 days, I've been best friends with Ian Fletcher, and for 1,300 days, I've convinced myself I'm not in love with him. I just really, really like pennies.

About the Author

USA Today bestselling author R.S. Grey is Rachel, a die-hard Bravo fan, avid reader, and dessert addict. After graduating from the University of Texas, she was on track to pursue a career in medicine, but a friend noticed her love of writing and challenged her to write a book. While working as a medical assistant, she spent all her evenings and weekends writing, and in 2014 she self-published her first novel, *Behind His Lens*, through Kindle Direct Publishing.

Now writing full-time, Rachel has published over thirty novels, including seven #1 bestselling romantic comedies. Her sports romance *Scoring Wilder* achieved the *USA Today* Bestselling Booklist. *Not So Nice Guy* was the #1 bestselling romantic comedy on Amazon, and *Hotshot Doc* ranked in the Top 10 Paid in Kindle Store.

With a knack for witty banter and hilarious pop-culture references, Rachel aims to make her readers laugh out loud. She lives in Houston with her husband and two daughters. Find out more at https://rsgrey.com, and follow her on Instagram @authorrsgrey.